WORTH THE WAIT . . .

Cori held the door open for Brad to enter. She followed him inside and turned to make sure the door was completely closed. Then she turned to face Brad and was immediately pinned against the door by his masculine presence. He reached for her, taking her face in his hands. Before she could draw a breath, his full, firm lips were pressed against hers, triggering all the electricity of a mega-watt lightning bolt. Her eyes widened in surprise. She wanted to protest, but Brad's tongue, warm and insistent, traced a pattern on her closed lips, urging them to open. Cori gave herself over to the warmth spreading from the center of her soul and radiating out to all parts of her body until even her fingertips felt the heat. Her eyes closed, and slowly, sensuously, her mouth parted, welcoming the probing warmth of his tongue.

Finally the kiss ended, leaving Cori dizzy and off balance. Slowly, she opened her eyes and looked at him with questions clearly etched in their brown depths.

"I probably should apologize for that," Brad said huskily, his breathing just returning to normal, "but I can't. I have been waiting to do that for so long. I was afraid I would explode if I didn't kiss you . . . and soon."

"And was it worth the wait?" Cori asked.

"It was beyond my wildest dreams."

LOOK FOR THESE ARABESQUE ROMANCES

CHERISH

Crystal Wilson Harris

Pinnacle Books
Kensington Publishing Corp.
http://www.arabesquebooks.com

For all those who have gone before, especially Aunt Pat and Granddaddy. You're never very far from my heart.

PINNACLE BOOKS are published by

Kensington Publishing Corp.
850 Third Avenue
New York, NY 10022

Pinnacle and the P logo Reg. U.S. Pat. & TM Off.

First Printing: April, 1998
10 9 8 7 6 5 4 3 2 1

Printed in the United States of America

ACKNOWLEDGMENTS

Many thanks to Sharon, my traveling buddy and spiritual guide; to Monte and all the racing fans who shared with me their love of the sport; to Bernadette for helping me see a better way; and, as always, to my loving and supportive family for sticking by me during the crazy times.

Chapter 1

"What have you done now, Mikey?" Corinthia Justice heaved an exasperated sigh. She had a bad feeling about this.

"Aw Cori, don't be that way." Michael Foster looked earnestly at his sister. "This is the opportunity of a lifetime!"

"You know what, Mikey? You have had enough 'opportunities' to fill a thousand lifetimes—and none of them have turned out to be worth the time of day." Corinthia turned a stern eye to her younger brother. "Remember the earthworm farm, the door-to-door home security sales, that crazy pyramid marketing thing? Why on earth would this 'opportunity of a lifetime' be any different?"

"Just hear me out, Cori. You'll see—this is the real thing."

Cori shook her head wearily. These schemes of her brother's were starting to take their toll on her. At thirty-four, Corinthia Justice had experienced more than her share of stress and heartache. They'd moved to Charlotte from Chicago in hopes of starting over, planning to leave the bad memories behind. And now, after only three months in their new home, Michael was at it again.

Cori settled back in the restaurant's padded booth, pushed back an unruly lock of thick, chestnut hair that had escaped from her ponytail, and braced herself for Michael latest plan.

"You know how we've been talking about ways to get more people in the restaurant?" Michael's face was alive with excitement.

Cori eyed him warily. "Yes . . . but as I recall we decided to concentrate on updating the menu and let the food speak for itself. Foster's has a wonderful reputation in this town."

Michael snorted at that. "Foster's has a wonderful reputation among the old guard in this town—and they just are not going out to eat very much anymore. Hell, most of them are dying off!"

"Michael!"

"Well, Cori, you know it's true. Our grandparents retired and gave us this restaurant to run because they were getting too old, and that's the same reason why their customers have stopped coming in." Michael gestured expansively around the elegant room. "Look. It's mid-afternoon and this place is nearly empty."

Cori, too, looked around the dining room, her gaze taking in the beautiful oak and brass interior of the family business. "Mikey, it's not uncommon for a restaurant to experience downtime after the lunch rush. Dinner isn't for a couple of hours yet. I'm sure we can lure more customers in with good food—not with one of your opportunities."

She focused her appraising look back on her brother. Michael's classic features were of a smooth, caramel color. His tall, slender frame could have belonged to a basketball player, but Michael had never developed much of an interest in the sport, choosing to expend his efforts on money-making rather than game playing. At twenty-nine, Michael was only five years younger than Cori, but at times the difference seemed more like a million light-years. She thought, for at least the millionth time, *What a waste.*

"Michael, you are so smart, and your mind is so quick. Why don't you use those powers for good every once in a while? Or better yet, just focus your creative energies on something more worthwhile—like one of those Charlotte belles who has been trying to catch your eye ever since we got off the plane."

"Don't go there, Cori. And stop trying to change the subject. Once you hear what I've done, you'll be so excited," Michael bubbled.

"Well, out with it."

"I stumbled across an incredible advertising opportunity. You know how popular auto racing is here?" He hurried on without giving her a chance to respond. "Well, I heard about this driver who needed a sponsor, so I signed us up. We'll get to put our name and logo all over the car, and it'll be seen by the thousands of people who go to these races. And when our car wins, we'll get all kinds of publicity."

Cori stared at Michael, waiting for the punch line of what had to be a joke. The stunned silence stretched uncomfortably between them. Slowly, the truth of Michael's words reached Cori.

"I can't believe you did that." Cori's doe brown eyes brimmed with tears. "What were you thinking? You know how I feel. . . ." Her voice broke. "Mikey, you know. . . ."

A flash of guilt shot through Michael, momentarily eclipsing his excitement. "Cori, it's been five years." His soft voice was full of compassion. "You've got to let it go."

The pain that was an integral part of her now was evident in her eyes. "It's not that easy, Mikey—five years or five hundred years."

"Just let me explain. There's a local racer who has the potential to be a big money winner. All he needs are sponsors. That's where we come in." Michael's enthusiasm resurfaced. "I signed Foster's up to be his major sponsor. That way, we not only get great advertising, we also get a percentage of his winnings."

So many questions filled Cori's brain that it was difficult to sort them out. Anxiety about what Michael was saying crowded out the pain-filled memories.

"Signed Foster's up? What exactly does that mean?"

"We'll be the primary sponsor for the race car. Our colors and logo will be all over the car, the driver, and the uniforms for the pit crew. Just think of how much exposure we'll get!"

"How much?"

"Have you ever seen the crowds that go to those races? There will be thousands of new customers who'll see our name!"

"I meant, how much money?"

"Think of it as an investment in our future."

"How much?"

"And don't forget, it's not just advertising exposure. We'll also get a cut of the winnings. That can be put right back into the restaurant to pay for some of those upgrades you want to do."

"HOW MUCH MONEY, MIKEY?!"

Michael turned away from the reproach he saw in her face. "Twenty thousand," he mumbled.

"Twenty thousand," she repeated incredulously. "Dollars? American dollars?" She shook her head in disbelief. "You've got to be kidding, right? I mean, this is some kind of joke."

"We don't have to pay it all out at once," Michael said lamely. "It's basically just a commitment to support the race team."

"To the tune of twenty thousand dollars!" Cori shouted angrily. "Mikey, how could you do this? We don't have that kind of money."

"I've got that all figured out. See, it takes about two thousand dollars to run each race, to pay the crew and maintenance on the car and all." Michael spoke with confidence. "So we only need to actually put up enough to cover the first three or four races. After that, the winnings and the increased profits from the restaurant will sustain the car."

"Oh, I get it now. We only need to put out between six and eight thousand dollars up front." Cori's voice was thick with sarcasm. "Why didn't you say so before?"

"Actually . . ." Michael said, hemming for a moment, "the truth is I've already paid for two races. I just need you to agree to keep going after that." He braced himself for the explosion he was sure was coming.

She sat, staring at him in amazement, for a few moments. Finally, she pushed her way out of the padded booth and crossed the room to the bar, Michael close on her heels. Stepping behind the bar, Cori filled a highball glass with ice.

"Cori," Michael's eyes widened, "don't."

"Relax, Mikey," Cori said impatiently. She unscrewed the cap of a bottle of flavored sparkling water. "What I drink is not what we need to focus on right now. Suppose you tell me where you came up with four thousand dollars." She spoke with a calmness she did not feel.

Michael looked away, fiddling idly with a nearby stack of cocktail napkins. "I got it from Gram and Poppy. I told them it was for the restaurant."

Cori slammed the empty bottle down on the bar. "You lied to our grandparents?"

"It wasn't a lie, Cori!" Michael protested. "It *was* for the restaurant. We're going to make a bundle of money behind this. Just you wait and see."

"Forget it, Mikey," Cori said flatly. "You're just going to have to get that money back, and there's no way I'm going along with this. Foster's cannot afford this stupid scheme of yours."

"I can't. It's too late." Michael turned a pleading look on his sister. "Just give it a chance, Cori. I am so sure about this. There are tens of thousands of people at those races. But don't take my word for it," he cajoled, "the driver and the crew chief are coming by later to meet you. They can tell you all about it."

"You know what, Mikey?" Cori glared at him. "They aren't going to tell me jack, because I'm not interested. You had no right to commit us to something so extravagant without talking to me first. And there's nothing this speed demon of yours can say that will change that." Corinthia came out from behind the bar and stalked to her office. The plush carpeting muffled her angry stomps, but nothing could silence the reverberations from the slamming of her office door.

Michael released a heavy sigh. *Well, that went well,* he thought sarcastically. He walked behind the bar and poured himself something considerably stronger than flavored water. He checked his watch and realized there was very little time before the driver and crew chief were expected to arrive. After taking a deep draw from his drink, Michael muttered, "Get ready for round two."

Cori practically flung her body into her office chair. "What on earth was that boy thinking? How could he? A race car, of all things!" Slowly, the anger and exasperation aimed at her brother seeped away, only to be replaced with much more painful feelings. Her eyes drifted to the antique pewter picture frame sitting on the corner of her desk. She reached for the frame and pulled it closer, although every detail of the photograph was burned in her memory.

The tall man squatted down on his haunches to gather a small girl into his arms. The little girl, ponytail tied with bright purple ribbons, wrapped her arms around the man's neck while nuzzling her cheek next to his. Both cocoa brown faces were lit with brilliant, identical smiles.

Cori felt the familiar welling begin behind her lashes. *God, I miss them so much.* Gently, she replaced the frame in its spot. She leaned back in the plush chair and closed her

eyes. Almost instantly, the film that replayed daily inside
her head began. . . .

It was the end of a glorious sunny day, the kind that
has made Chicago summers famous. Surrounded by
the people she loved most in the world, Cori leaned
back in the car seat, content. She was glad the ride
home wouldn't take too long; Brianna needed a bath
before bed. Cori twisted to look at the backseat. Brianna was sleeping peacefully, thoroughly worn out
by the activities of the day. Cori smiled, struck again
by the beauty of the child.
The jazz Tony favored was playing on the radio,
filling the car with soft, soothing music. Cori couldn't
remember a time when she'd felt happier or more
at peace. She reached for Tony's hand. He turned
his attention from the road to smile at her. Only for
a second. . . .

Cori jerked herself out of her reverie, consciously pushing the tormenting memory away. *I need to figure out how
to get Foster's out of this corner Mikey's painted us into.* Grateful
for the diversion, Cord steepled her hands under her chin
and leaned back to consider her options.

Chapter 2

It was times like these that Brad felt the closest thing to pure joy he ever experienced. The beautiful North Carolina scenery was reduced to a color-filled blur. The sounds of rushing air swirled around him. And the sheer power of the race car vibrated through him. He could feel it in the steering wheel he gripped; the power surged up from the accelerator he pressed relentlessly to the floorboard. Power caressed his heavily muscled thighs, throbbed in his chest, and rattled through his teeth.

During these practice laps, when there was no jockeying for position, no strategies to consider, no crash debris to avoid, Brad could push the car and himself to the limit. With one eye on the tachometer, Brad shifted gears and pressed the accelerator pedal even further into the floor. The stock car roared in response. As he approached turn number two, he knew he should ease off the gas. That sharp, steep curve called more for finesse than power. But Brad, full of the joy of speed, decided to punch it. The car fishtailed slightly, but Brad quickly brought it under control.

"Whoa, Cowboy!" The voice boomed in Brad's ear. "Pushin' that puppy a little hard today, aren't you?"

"C'mon Vern," Brad yelled into the headset's microphone, "don't be such a baby!"

"Just bring her in. Your practice time is up." Vern clicked off the stopwatch he held.

Reluctantly, Brad pulled the car into the pit area. As he unhooked the protective netting from the window and climbed out of the car, his pit crew began the routine maintenance and safety checks. Vern approached, holding the stopwatch out for Brad's inspection.

"Not bad, Cowboy. Even with that reckless move in turn two." Vern shook his head disapprovingly at the younger man. "Cars don't grow on trees, Boy. You crack that one up during practice and you'll be shit-out-of-luck come race day."

Brad pulled off his helmet and peeled the driving gloves off his hands. "Relax, Old Man. There's no way I'm gonna wreck—during practice or any other time." Brad flashed a cocky smile.

Brad Marshall was six feet of pure, radiant confidence. In a sport with precious few African-Americans, Brad's muscular, ebony presence was especially noteworthy. When he wasn't in his car, he was in a gym, working on the upper body strength and leg muscles that helped him keep control of his race car. He kept his head shaved gleamingly bald so as not to interfere with the crash helmet he had to wear. What hair he didn't have on his scalp was compensated for by the thick mustache and goatee he kept meticulously trimmed. His clear eyes, which could change from brown to nearly black depending on his mood, proud African nose, and rich, full lips melded to create a face that had figured in many a female fantasy.

Brad tucked his helmet and gloves under his arm and walked with Vern toward the garage. "So how come you ended practice so soon today?"

Vern shook his head impatiently. "We're supposed to

go to that restaurant and meet with the new sponsors this afternoon. Remember?"

"Oh yeah," Brad nodded. "I forgot. Why do we have to do this? I thought that Foster guy already signed on."

"Yes, he did, but only for two races. To get any commitment beyond that he needs the approval of his business partner. We're supposed to go and make a pitch."

Brad made a face. "Man, this is the part I hate the most. These dog and pony shows where we go begging for our supper. It's just not fair—I'm a race car driver, not a salesman!"

Vern chuckled slightly. "Boy, the only way you can be a driver is to *be* a salesman. What do you think all that advertising on the car is all about? Selling a product. And the driver is the chief salesman."

Vern Ramsey was a racing veteran. In his younger years he'd been a driver, but now, at fifty-nine, Vern used his skills as crew chief, a job that was part coach, part mechanic, part mother hen. Although Vern was a full head shorter and had a much slighter build than Brad, the driver deferred to his crew chief about almost everything. Practically the only area the men butted heads over revolved around sponsorship issues.

Vern checked his watch. "You'd better hurry. You need to get cleaned up so we can head over to the restaurant." He pulled open the door to the garage's locker room.

"Cleaned up?" Brad looked down at his practice gear, today a gray fleece North Carolina A & T sweatshirt and jeans. "Why can't I go like this?"

Vern studied him carefully. "Come sit down. We need to talk." Vern walked into the tiny office in the garage. He cleared a stack of papers from a chair and pulled it out for Brad, then perched himself on the edge of the desk, arms crossed in front of his chest.

Warily, feeling himself soon to be on the receiving end of a blistering lecture, Brad settled in the metal chair.

"Vern, look, it's not that big a deal. I'll shower and change if that's what you want."

"It's not about what I want, Boy. It's about you. Do you want to make it in this business?" Vern leaned in toward Brad. " 'Cause to have a prayer of making a name for yourself in racing, you have got to be competitive. And I'm not talking about your driving. You are one of the boldest, most instinctive drivers I've ever seen. The way you push that car is damn near poetry."

"That ought to be enough," Brad interrupted. "I get paid to win races, not suck up to sponsors. As long as I'm doing my job—"

"Don't be a fool, Brad!" Vern exploded. "Sucking up to sponsors **IS** your job! You think that car can get repaired and that crew can get paid just on your pretty face? It doesn't make a bit of difference how good a driver you are if you can't afford to put a car in the race. And the last time I checked, you didn't have no rich uncle footing your bills."

"It's just not right." Brad sulked. "I bet the big boys up in NASCAR don't go around with their hands out."

"Boy, if you ever get to The Show, you'll see how wrong you are about that. But the bottom line is you won't ever be asked to participate in a NASCAR race until you establish yourself at these smaller races. And you won't ever get established at these smaller races without a sponsor to keep your car running." Vern leaned back and pulled off his baseball cap. He rubbed his hands wearily over his short, graying hair as if trying to slough off stress. "So what's it gonna be? 'Cause believe you me, I will happily walk away from this racing life. If you're not gonna do your part, I'm not gonna keep hanging around."

Brad slouched in the chair and stretched his long legs in front of him. He covered his eyes with his hand and sat for a moment, deep in thought. "You're talking about more than just me changing my clothes, aren't you Vern?"

Vern didn't answer; he kept a steady, expectant gaze fixed on his driver.

"You mean a whole change of attitude, huh? Think I need to see sponsor schmoozing as an opportunity, not a hassle, right?"

"What do you think?" Vern asked, impatience dripping from the words. "You know the old saying: 'If you do a dance, you gotta pay the band.' For you, 'if you want to keep dancin', you gotta keep payin'.'"

Brad heaved a heavy sigh that was part frustration, part acceptance. "Okay, Old Man, you win. What do we know about these new sponsors?"

If Vern felt any relief, he did not show it. "The only one I've met is Michael Foster, and I don't know much about him. He and his business partner just recently moved to Charlotte from up north somewhere—Chicago, I think— and they run a restaurant in town. Foster came to us, real excited about sponsoring a car."

"Well, if this Foster is so damn excited, why did he only sign on for two races? And why do we have to meet with his partner?" Brad was both confused and annoyed.

"That's the part I don't know." Vern shrugged. "But whatever the reason, we've got to get their support. We need to be able to finish out the season on top if we want to get invited to the show."

Brad nodded shortly. "Guess I'd better hurry." He rose from the chair and headed toward the locker room. "Wouldn't want to keep my new best friends waiting."

In the garage's shower stall, Brad hurried through his bathing, hoping his anxiety would swirl down the drain along with the soap. Despite his petulant attitude with Vern, it was not pride that caused his reluctance to meet the new sponsors. He knew, as well if not better than Vern, how important this sponsor was. If they couldn't find someone to replace the sponsor who just quit—*Check that,* he thought, *'decided not to renew the contract'*—he'd have to sit out the rest of the season. So mainly, Brad was just plain worried. It unnerved him to have so much of his future taken out of his control.

Control was why he'd started racing, and control was why he was so good at it. On the track, Brad was the master. He felt there wasn't anything he couldn't do in a race car. He routinely finished in the top five, usually in the top three—that's when he was able to compete. Lately, he'd had to sit out a few races for lack of money. It doubly frustrated Brad to have to work so hard to get sponsors. It didn't seem as if the white drivers had this much trouble. Although nobody said anything overtly, Brad always felt as if he were an intruder. That just pushed him harder. He had been in position to win the track championship when his last sponsor pulled out. Brad would always believe that the sponsor, a small sporting goods store owner, had been pressured about putting his advertising dollars on the back of a black driver.

This time will be different, he tried to convince himself. *This sponsor will stay with me, and I will make them buckets of money!* He quickly finished his shower and jumped into his clothes.

Shortly, carefully decked out in a fresh pair of black jeans and a loose-fitting, mustard colored shirt, Brad joined Vern in the garage office.

"Well, can I go now?" Brad held his arms out from his sides for inspection.

"I suppose you're fit to go out in public," Vern said gruffly. "Look, Brad, I know how much you hate this, but you've just got to keep your eyes on the prize."

"I know, I know." Brad grabbed a black baseball hat from a nearby hook. "Let's just get it over with." He put the hat low on his forehead and headed for the door.

The two men walked along a blacktop path to the parking area. Just as they approached Brad's Blazer, a woman emerged from a nearby car.

"Hey, Cowboy," she greeted Brad in a husky voice, "forget about our date?"

"Lisa! How could I forget about you?" Brad flashed her a brilliant smile.

"Yeah, sure. And you were just on your way over, right?" Lisa folded her arms in front of her chest.

"Well, first I've got this business meeting, but then—"

"Brad!" Lisa's tone was full of exasperation. "We were supposed to meet for lunch—hours ago."

Vaguely, Brad recalled a mention of lunch, but for the life of him he could not remember committing to a specific time or day.

"I'm sorry, Doll," Brad hedged. "This meeting came up at the last minute, and I couldn't get out of it."

"And before that?" Lisa demanded petulantly.

Instantly, Brad's attitude changed from conciliatory to indignant. "Before that, I was practicing. And I am absolutely positive I did not agree to meet with you during my practice time." He scowled slightly at her.

Realizing she had pushed too far, Lisa backed down. "It's just that I was looking forward to spending some time with you, Sugar. I'm just disappointed, that's all." She walked over to him and rubbed his arm. "Will I see you later?"

Brad looked at the hand that rested on his bicep and then into the coffee-colored face that gazed at him so beseechingly. "I'll call you after my meeting and we'll see what develops."

"You do that, Sugar." Lisa slowly slid her hand down his arm. "I'll be waiting." She turned and strolled back to her car. With studied sultriness, she eased into the seat. After blowing a kiss Brad's way, she started the car and pulled away.

"Nice to see you too, Lisa," Vern said sarcastically.

"Aw, don't mind her," Brad shrugged, "she's got a one-track mind."

"Yeah, just like all track groupies, and I can see what track it's on. I don't suppose she has any idea she's just the 'Flavor of the Month'."

"Careful, Old Man," Brad joked lightly, "you done commenced to meddlin'."

Vern shook his head. "I swear, if you put the same energy into courting sponsors that you do into these track groupies, we'd have more money than God."

Brad laughed, "Come on. Let's go sing for our supper."

The pair climbed in the truck and headed for Foster's.

Chapter 3

Michael tapped a swizzle stick nervously against his high-ball glass. His anxious gaze alternated between his watch and the restaurant's front door. Even though Brad and Vern were not late, Michael desperately wanted a few moments alone with them before Cori came out of her office. He was positive that together the three of them could convince her to go along with the plan.

Brad double-checked the address before pulling the Blazer into Foster's parking lot. He had seen the ornate script sign out front, but he simply could not believe this elegant restaurant was interested in the racing game. Foster's was housed on the street level of a large, antebellum country home in the exclusive Dilworth section of town. The house was bordered by an expansive verandah that wrapped around the front and the sides. A few cafe tables were scattered around the verandah, for guests who wanted to eat in the fresh air of late spring Charlotte. The main entrance of the restaurant was flanked by several pairs of French doors, each set decorated with panels of white sheer fabric. Brad turned to Vern as they stood in the parking lot assessing the building.

"You're sure this is the right place?" Brad asked.

"Positive . . . a cut above the sporting goods and auto parts store sponsors we've had in the past, huh?" Vern straightened his shirt and squared his shoulders. "C'mon, we don't want to be late."

Brad pulled the ball cap off his head and opened the heavy doors. The men stepped into the restaurant. The interior was a perfect complement to the restaurant's impressive exterior. The French doors allowed great streams of sunlight to pour into the room. Oak paneling, tables, and columns, combined with brass light fixtures and accents, lent the dining room a rich, sumptuous air.

The floor was covered with lushly patterned carpeting which was predominately burgundy colored.

Trying not to gawk, Brad and Vern approached the hostess stand. They stood patiently, waiting for someone to notice their arrival. From his station at the bar across the room, Michael spotted them almost immediately. He rushed over to greet them.

"Hello! Vern Ramsey, right?" Michael held out his hand. "I've been waiting for you."

"I hope we're not late, Mr. Foster." Vern shook the extended hand.

"No, no, not at all. And call me Michael. I guess I'm just excited about this deal." Michael turned to face Brad. "And you must be the driver, Brad Marshall. It is truly a pleasure to meet you."

Brad smiled and returned the enthusiastic handshake. "It's very nice to meet you too, Michael. Great place you've got here."

"Thanks. Actually, my grandparents built this place. I'm hoping to take it into the next generation." Michael's grin spread across his face. "Please, come have a seat." He led the men to a secluded booth near the back of the dining room.

"So, where is your business partner?" Brad asked after they'd been seated. "I'm anxious to meet him."

"Him?" Michael laughed lightly. "No, not 'him.' My business partner is my sister, and I've got to be honest with you—she's not as enthusiastic about this sponsorship deal as I am."

Brad and Vern exchanged a look. "What exactly do you mean, Michael?" Vern asked cautiously.

"Cori . . . well, Cori is not convinced that auto racing is the best venue to advertise the restaurant," Michael conceded. "She is very, uh, leery of the amount of financial commitment a full sponsorship requires."

"So what are you saying—that we can't count on your support?" Brad demanded, more sharply than he had intended.

"No, no, no." Michael put his hands out to calm the driver, "I'm in, for sure. It's just that we're all going to have to work on convincing my sister. I'm sure if you two could just explain the benefits to her, she'll agree with me."

"And we have to have her okay before Foster's can underwrite any additional races, is that right?" Vern asked.

Michael looked down sheepishly. "That's about the size of it. Without Cori, there is no deal."

Brad felt his earlier frustration resurfacing with a vengeance. "So when do we get to meet this decision maker?"

Vern shot Brad a withering look. He turned his attention back to Michael. "Yes, where is your sister?"

"She's in her office." *Still fuming, no doubt,* he thought. "I'll go get her now. I just wanted to make sure you were forewarned." Michael left the table and went in search of Cori.

Brad exploded as soon as Michael was out of earshot. "Oh, that's just wonderful! My whole future is in the hands of some Yankee restaurant owner."

"You need to settle down," Vern said sternly. "Your whole future is in *your* hands. Foster said his sister could be convinced. It's up to you to do it. And, Boy, you'd better can the attitude."

Brad leaned back against the padded booth and crossed his arms in front of his chest. He couldn't believe this was happening. Based on Michael Foster's description, this sponsorship was anything but a sure thing. Brad could feel Vern's disapproving stare, but at that moment he couldn't have cared less. *So close,* Brad thought, *so damn close. I've got to make this work. I need this to work!*

Michael knocked lightly on the oak door. In her office, Cori took a deep breath before answering. "Come on in, Mikey."

Michael entered tentatively and stood with his hand on the doorknob. "They're here, Cori. Are you going to come out and meet them?"

" 'Them?' You mean Speed Racer and his trusty side-kick?" Cori made no effort to hide her disdain.

"Cori, that's not fair. These men are professionals. They deserve at least that much respect." Michael looked at his sister, appealing.

"Whether or not they are professionals is hardly the issue." Cori's eyes blazed. "We cannot afford this little scheme of yours, Mikey. And you had no right to put Foster's in this position!"

"Who said you were the only one who knows what's right for Foster's?" Angrily, Michael jumped on the defensive. "The restaurant is half my responsibility too, you know. Gram and Poppy turned it over to both of us."

"And haven't you already shown yourself worthy of their trust." Cori's words were thick with sarcasm. "Scamming four thousand dollars from them."

"It wasn't a scam! That money was an investment in the future of this restaurant." Michael released the knob and took a seat on the edge of the cream-colored chaise lounge against the wall. "Look, Cori, I know what this is all about, and you have every right to be skeptical. I *do* have a history of crazy schemes and bad decisions."

Fuming, Cori didn't answer.

"But," Michael continued, "I believe with every fiber of my being that this racing sponsorship is going to be a huge success for Foster's. I didn't just make this commitment on the spur of the moment. I checked around and did some research. Brad Marshall is the only black driver on the local circuit. Because of that fact alone, he attracts a lot of attention. But that's not all—he's really good, Cori. He wins his races most of the time."

"If he's so good and so popular, why does he need us?" Cori demanded.

Michael shrugged. "I don't know . . . it's a 'good ol' boy' kind of sport, he's a lone black man . . . you do the math. All I know for sure is Brad Marshall deserves the support of the black business community. If we don't help him, who will?"

Cori sat silently for a moment, letting Michael's argument sink in. Slowly, her eyes drifted to the pewter picture frame. Her vision clouded as she thought about the image from her past. Finally, she turned to face her brother.

"Of all things, a race car, Mikey? You know. . . ." Her voice trailed away.

Michael walked over to her desk and gathered her hands in his. "What I know is that you won't ever get on with your life if you don't let it go. We came to Charlotte to start over. Brad Marshall and his race car could represent a new beginning for both of us. It's my chance to prove to you that I can do something right. And it's your chance to put your demons to rest."

Cori looked deeply into the eyes of the handsome young man she had always regarded as a flighty ne'er-do-well. She saw a sincerity and a compassion in him that had never been there before. She could tell how important this sponsorship deal was to him.

After a long, tense moment, Cori finally nodded. "Okay, Mikey. I'll meet your Brad Marshall. And since you've already paid for the first two races, I won't do anything to try and stop it."

Michael whooped with joy and leaned over to hug his sister.

"Wait a minute." Cori put her hands up in front of her. "I'm going to reserve judgment on any further commitment until after I see how these first two races go. Agreed?"

Michael completed the hug he started. "Agreed!"

Cori gave herself over to the bear hug. "A race car driver," she muttered. "Why couldn't you have found a needy jockey or something?"

Laughing, Michael released her and walked toward the door. "Let's go meet our driver."

"You go ahead. I need a minute to freshen up." Cori walked with Michael to the door. "Don't look at me like that—I'll be right there."

Michael's face betrayed his impatience. "We'll be at table number thirty-four. Hurry up," he admonished as he walked out the door.

After retrieving her purse from a desk drawer, Cori went over to the small mirror mounted on the back of the door. Quickly, she pulled her ponytail holder off and combed her chestnut hair. Pulling it back, she decided a chignon would be more professional, so she wrapped the thick hair into a bun. She rummaged around in her purse until she found a tube of wine-colored lipstick. Leaning in close to the mirror to apply a light layer of color to her lips, she was struck—again—by the circles under her eyes. She couldn't remember a time when her eyes weren't ringed with deep sadness. Shaking off the melancholy before it could grab hold of her, Cori reached for a black blazer hanging on a hook near the door. She slipped into the jacket, straightened the collar and lapels, and decided she was ready. After a deep breath, Cori stepped out of the safety of her office.

* * *

When Brad saw Michael Foster approaching the table alone, his heart sank. *He wasn't able to convince her,* Brad thought. *The whole thing is off!*

Michael pulled out a chair and sat at the end of the table. "My sister will be joining us shortly," he announced somewhat triumphantly.

A smile spread across Brad's ebony features. "Excellent," he purred. "Absolutely excellent."

Just then, Cori approached. She scanned the area, looking for her brother. Her eyes locked with the ebony depths of the eyes of a stranger. For an electric moment, the whole room fell away, and the only thing that existed was the commanding, exquisite presence of a bald mystery man. Cori shivered slightly as some unnamed and long forgotten emotion shot through her.

Brad felt the smile freeze on his face. Suddenly, unexpectedly, he felt an almost magnetic pull tugging at him from across the room. The eyes from which this unseen force originated seemed to look not just at him, but through him—clear to his soul. Coherent thought deserted him as he stared at the elegant, caramel-colored woman walking toward the booth.

Michael and Vern both noticed the abrupt change in Brad. Michael turned to see what had so captivated the driver's attention.

"Cori." Michael stood to welcome his sister. "Come and join us. We've been waiting for you."

Automatically, Vern and Brad stood as Cori settled into a chair. *Cori?* Brad's mind clicked into gear. *This is Michael's sister?*

Cori's movements were mechanical as she struggled to collect her wits. For some reason, it just would not register that the intriguing mystery man and the race car driver she was so prepared to dislike were one and the same. She didn't know what she expected a driver to look like, but this sculpted ebony Adonis was not it.

She found her voice. "Gentlemen, please sit down. Mr. Marshall, I presume? Michael has told me so much about you."

Brad could only manage to nod dumbly; his voice had not quite caught up with him yet.

Sensing Brad's distress, Vern came to his rescue. "I'm Vern Ramsey, Brad's crew chief. We're real happy to have Foster's as a sponsor."

Cori turned her attention to Vern. "It's a pleasure to meet you, Mr. Ramsey. Fortunately, my brother is so convinced this sponsorship will be a good investment for Foster's that he's happy enough for both of us."

Her words felt like a slap across the face to Brad. "That sounds like you don't agree, Miss Foster." He fought to conceal the anger he felt.

Cori's vision blurred momentarily as the smiling faces of her lost family flashed before her. Suddenly, despite her promise to Michael, Cori could hold her tongue no longer.

"My name is Justice—Mrs. Corinthia Justice—and no, I don't agree." Cori's eyes blazed with an emotion that had nothing to do with racing or Foster's or Brad Marshall. "I can think of a million things the restaurant needs a lot more than having our name painted on the side of a speeding car!"

"I'm sorry you feel that way, Miss Fos . . . I mean, Mrs. Justice." Brad ground out the response between clenched teeth. "I only hope you'll give us the opportunity to prove you wrong."

Cori sat silently, not trusting herself to say anything further. The tension at the table was palpable.

Vern cleared his throat. "I can understand your hesitation, Mrs. Justice, but I really think you're in for a pleasant surprise. Brad here is one of the finest drivers on the circuit. He'll do you proud."

Cori turned to face the crew chief. "Mr. Ramsey, this is not a question of Mr. Marshall's driving abilities. I am concerned about the effectiveness of the advertising. Foster's is a family business. We simply do not have any money to waste on unproven schemes."

"Unproven?!" Brad spat the word. "How can you say race advertising is unproven? Have you ever been to a race or seen the crowds there? You don't have any idea what you're talking about."

Brad and Cori locked eyes again, but this time there was no question where the electricity came from—anger. Michael and Vern exchanged a look.

"Cori, you promised to give it a chance," Michael pleaded.

"Mrs. Justice, would you at least consider coming to this Saturday's race?" Vern asked. "That way you can see for yourself how effective your investment can be. I can send tickets over for you and Mr. Justice."

Cori recoiled as if she'd been struck. She pushed away from the table and got up abruptly. "That won't be necessary," she stammered. She practically ran away, back to her office.

Stunned, Brad and Vern could only watch her departure in slack-jawed confusion.

"What was that all about?" Brad demanded.

Michael shook his head sadly. "My sister has a few things on her mind."

"But what did we do? What did we say?" Concern was etched on Vern's features.

An uneasy silence fell over the men as Michael struggled over how to answer. Ever protective of his sister, Michael chose each word with infinite care.

"It's not your fault. There's no way you could have known." Michael took a deep breath. "There is no Mr. Justice. Cori is a widow."

The silence deepened as Brad and Vern processed that information.

"But she insisted on being called 'Mrs.' Justice. . . ." Vern's voice trailed off uncertainly.

"I know," Michael nodded, "and it worries me." He stood to go to his sister. "Gentlemen, please excuse me. I will see you at the race Saturday."

Brad and Vern watched Michael's retreating back. "Well," Brad said, his voice heavy with sarcasm, "that went well."

Chapter 4

Brad sprang out of bed, a half hour ahead of his alarm, energized by what the day would bring. He twisted open the blinds, letting brilliant sunlight stream into the room. "Looks like a winning day." He smiled. Brad strode confidently into the bathroom to begin his race day rituals.

Short minutes later he stood in front of the mirror, his head covered with fragrant shaving foam. Slowly, methodically, Brad ran a straight-edged razor over his head, revealing clear lanes of smooth scalp. Once his head was freshly shorn, Brad rubbed on a soothing moisturizing lotion. That task completed, Brad shed the tank shirt and boxer shorts he'd slept in and stepped into the shower. He adjusted the showerhead so that the water offered a pulsating massage. Standing with his back to the water flow, Brad allowed the water to beat down on his thick shoulder and neck muscles. While the water flowed over him, he visualized the track, steering through each turn in his mind, plotting his winning strategy.

Satisfied, Brad quickly lathered up and completed his shower. He wrapped a towel around his waist, turned on his stereo, and slid a Prince CD into the player. Shortly, the hard-driving notes of "Little Red Corvette" boomed through Brad's condo.

His race day rituals continued as he moved to the kitchen. Through the years he had learned the importance of eating before the race. He reached for a blender and filled the container with a banana, vanilla yogurt, orange juice, and a high protein supplement. While the mixture blended, Brad toasted half of a bagel. In short order, he sat down to consume his "power breakfast."

Just then, the phone rang, jarring his concentration.

"Yes?" he barked into the receiver.

"Mornin', Sugar. You don't have to bite my head off. I just called to wish you luck." Lisa's voice drifted from the phone.

Brad swallowed the heavy sigh he felt. "Lisa, you know I don't like to be disturbed before the race."

"Well, sorrrrry!" Lisa pouted. "I didn't know I was such a disturbance."

"I just need to focus on race day. Totally focus." Brad's tone was stern.

Lisa giggled at that. "So I disrupt your focus, eh? I'll take that as a compliment."

"Take it anyway you like," Brad snapped. "I'm going now."

"Sure thing, Sugar. See you at the track." Lisa hung up before Brad could respond.

Brad slowly replaced the receiver. *Track groupies.* He chuckled as Vern's description came to his mind. Shaking his head, Brad turned his thoughts back to the race. He visualized the track again, picturing himself in the car tearing through the turns. Abruptly, the vision stopped.

Suddenly, he realized that since this was the first race with Foster's sponsoring, the car would be painted to the restaurant's specifications. *What color is the car?* he wondered. *For that matter, what color is my driving jumpsuit?*

Thoughts of Foster's evoked the memory of the team's newest benefactor and his sister. Especially his sister.

Mrs. Corinthia Justice . . . wonder if she'll come to the race?

Shrugging, Brad returned to his rituals.

"Come on, Cori. It'll be fun!" Michael trailed his sister around the kitchen at Foster's.

"Forget it, Mikey. I couldn't be less interested." Cori's eyes never left the inventory sheet clipped to the board in her hands. "I've got far too much work to do to be off at the races."

Michael put his hand squarely in the middle of her clipboard, forcing her attention to him. "Too much work? Is that the only reason?" His eyes bored into hers.

"What other reason could there be?" she asked innocently.

"Didn't your momma ever teach you not to answer a question with another question?"

"Didn't yours?" she shot back.

For a moment, two pairs of similar brown eyes locked in battle. Then they dissolved into laughter.

"This is silly, Cori. We don't need to fight about this." He tilted his head to one side and regarded her carefully. "But aren't you even a little curious?"

Cori's laughter quieted as she considered his question. She had to admit she was the tiniest bit interested. Her mind conjured up the masculine image of Brad Marshall. She remembered the fire in his eyes when he thought she threatened the sponsorship. Although she'd only crossed paths with the driver once, she could not forget the encounter.

Cori abruptly shook her head in an effort to clear her thoughts. Watching her, Michael took the head shake as refusal. He shrugged his shoulders.

"Okay . . . I'm not going to beg you to come. You're

missing out on a lot of excitement, though." Michael turned and walked out of the kitchen.

The muscles in Cori's legs tensed slightly, as if she were going to follow him, but then she caught herself. *I can't,* she thought, *not now . . . maybe not ever.*

Brad parked his Blazer in the driver's lot at Carolco Speedway, one of the many tracks that dotted the landscape around North Carolina. The race wasn't due to begin for another three hours, but he wanted plenty of time to get ready. He made his way to the garage area, looking for his team. The garage was a hive of activity; the pit crews of all the race teams were already at work, putting the final touches on their cars' engines.

He made his way through the garage, nodding greetings to other drivers and crew members. They were really one big community—this racing brotherhood. During the season they were together most every weekend, if not at Carolco then at one of the other tracks within a 200 mile radius. These teams all traveled together like one big racing circus, from track to track, pitting their skills against one another, vying for the weekly purse. And they all shared the same dream, all drove toward the same pot of gold at the end of the rainbow—NASCAR.

"Hey, Marshall!" The call stopped Brad's stroll through the garage. "I see you're back."

"Can't get anything past you, Roberts." Brad extended his hand. The men shook warmly.

"Guess you got another sponsor, huh?"

"Yep, guess so. Just in time to run your tail off the track." Brad laughed.

"In your dreams!" Cliff Roberts puffed out his chest. "I don't care how many sponsors you get, that raggedy ol' Chevy of yours will never beat my Ford."

"Roberts, I could drive a riding lawn mower around the track and still beat your slow butt." A confident grin lit Brad's ebony face.

"I guess we'll just see about that." Cliff nodded. "Good to have you back."

"Thanks, Man. Good to be back." Brad continued his search for his team.

Vern waved to attract Brad's attention. "Over here, Cowboy. Got somebody I want you to meet."

Curious, Brad headed in Vern's direction. As he approached, his pit crew was lined up shoulder to shoulder, hiding something behind them.

"Brad Marshall, I'd like you to meet car number thirty-four, the Foster's Restaurant Chevrolet." Vern motioned for the crew to step aside.

Brad's eyes grew wide as he got his first good look at his car. The Chevy had been painted to match the restaurant's interior—a deep, rich burgundy with metallic gold racing stripes along the side. The 34 and a script-lettered Foster's Restaurant were also painted in the same metallic gold. On the trunk of the car, the restaurant's name and address were painted in bold block letters. And on the driver's side door under the window opening, in much smaller script, his name was painted in gold: *Brad Marshall—The Ebony Warrior.*

"She's beautiful," Brad breathed. "That paint job is spectacular. But aren't we getting a little ahead of ourselves? Foster's has only committed for two races so far."

Vern shrugged. "That's what I thought, too, but Michael Foster insisted. He's convinced once his sister sees the car, she'll be sold. Oh, and there's one more thing." Vern turned to one of the younger crew members. "D.J.?"

D.J. pulled his hands out from behind his back and held out a burgundy driving jumpsuit. Brad stepped forward and held the jumpsuit up to take a good look at it. The rich burgundy color was a perfect match to the car's paint job. His name was sewn in gold thread over the left breast pocket. On the back, enclosed in a golden oval, was the Foster's Restaurant name in script type.

"Well, looks like we're all set." Brad smiled ruefully,

"Sure hope Foster's right about his sister, or else somebody's wasted a lot of money."

"Don't worry about that now," Vern advised. "Now you need to go get ready to race."

Brad nodded and took his jumpsuit to the locker room to dress. The uniform fit him like a glove. He headed back out to the garage. His crew greeted him with a round of teasing whistles and catcalls.

"Well, aren't you the pretty boy?" Vern commented. "I think burgundy is your color. Brad accepted their ribbing in stride; he was just glad to be back in the game.

Finally, it was time to line up for the start of the race. He climbed into the car and snapped the seat belts into place. He put on his helmet and adjusted the chin strap. Then he turned the key. The engine roared to life around him. A slow smile spread across his face. *I'm home,* he thought. Shifting into first gear, he eased the car away from the pit wall and followed the procession of other cars lining up for the start of the race. Because of his late entry in this contest, Brad's starting spot was near the back of the pack. *Not for long.* He grinned. He revved the engine slightly, nodding his satisfaction at the sound of its response. Once the cars were in place, the drivers powered down their engines to wait for the starter's signal. Pit crews scrambled around the cars, checking last minute details.

"Ready, Cowboy?" Vern's voice boomed in his ear.

"More than I've ever been," Brad said confidently into the helmet's headset. "I feel lucky today!"

"Luck don't have nothing to do with it, Boy. You just drive that car like I taught you."

Brad just shook his head and grinned. "Whatever you say, Boss."

A voice crackled over the track loudspeaker. "Gentlemen, start your engines!"

A thunderous roar rose from the track as the engines

of twenty-five stock cars sprang to life. The clamor was sweet music to Brad's ears. Adrenaline coursed through his veins—this moment, this time right before the cars shot off the start, was a moment he treasured. His hands flexed and released on the leather grip of the steering wheel. His right foot, which was currently pressing the brake to the floor, literally itched to punch the accelerator. The pace car began its lap around the track. The racing field followed, moving at the leisurely pace which was customary for this first show lap. Brad twisted the steering wheel from side to side, causing the car to weave slightly across the track, testing the feel of the car. "Perfect," he purred.

Finally, the pace car pulled out of the way and the starter waved the green flag. The race was on! Brad punched the accelerator; the speedometer sprang to life. The needle moved past 90, then 100, then 110. Within seconds, Brad was pushing the Foster's-sponsored Chevrolet through the turns at 130 mph. He easily passed the two cars immediately in front of him, taking the inside lane at turn one. Confidence growing, Brad pressed the accelerator further, crowding a red car in front of him. A few moments later, the red car's driver eased off enough for Brad to pass him on the outside.

"Pace yourself, Boy!" Vern coached. "You just started— got another ninety-eight laps to go!"

"Just had to get around those snails, Vern. Relax." Brad adjusted his speed to match the group of cars he was trailing. He systematically passed the cars ahead of him, weaving in and out of traffic so fluidly it looked as if the other cars were parked.

Midway through the race, he'd settled in at the number five slot.

"Come on in for a pit stop." Vern's command crackled through the helmet's headset.

"Not yet," Brad protested. "I need to move up a few spots first."

"Bring 'er in, Cowboy," Vern insisted. "You need new tires. Trust me, you'll have plenty of time to catch up."

Brad reluctantly deferred to his crew chief's expertise. As soon as he pulled in to Pit Road, the crew swarmed around the car like ants on honey. Vern spoke to Brad through the window netting.

"You're running good out there, Cowboy. Watch out for the number fifteen car. He's been on your tail all afternoon."

Brad nodded shortly. "Number fifteen'd better watch out for me!"

Within seconds, the crew finished their servicing and Brad sped back onto the track. The race was winding down; there were twenty laps left to go. After his pit stop, Brad reentered the race in seventh position. He floored the accelerator and almost immediately worked his way up to fifth.

"Why did you pull me off, Vern? I lost a lot of time on the leaders!" Brad's anger was clear through the headset radio.

"Patience, Cowboy," Vern responded calmly. "I know what I'm doing."

Just as Brad was about to complain again, the leading cars all went in for their scheduled pit stops. By pulling Brad in for his pit stop a few laps early, Vern had positioned him to be ready to take advantage of the leaders' pit schedules. Their departures cleared the way for Brad to sail into the lead.

Five laps left found Brad battling the number fifteen car to hold on to the lead. He had the pedal pressed all the way to the floor; the car had no more power to give. Finesse was what he needed to win the race. Brad stayed low and inside on the turns, forcing the fifteen car to the outside lane to attempt to pass. As his competitor closed in on the outside, Brad eased his car up on the track, so near the number fifteen that the cars were almost touching.

No fear, no fear. The words repeated over and over again in Brad's head. It was like some high-speed game of chicken, both drivers waiting to see who would blink first.

Finally, the driver of number fifteen eased up on the gas. The gap widened slightly between the cars. Brad turned his attention to the finish line. He zoomed under the checkered flag just milliseconds ahead of the second place number fifteen.

"All right!" Vern's cheer was deafening in Brad's ear.

Brad drove to Victory Lane and climbed out of the car. He grabbed Vern and wrapped him in a bear hug. "If I ever question you again, just slap me, okay?"

Vern's grizzled brown face split into a wide, toothy grin. "Whatever you say, Cowboy, whatever you say."

Michael burst into Cori's office door, excitement sparkling in his eyes. Surprised, she looked up from the linen supply order form she'd been working on.

"We won, Cori!" Michael rushed over to scoop his sister in a hug. "Our car won!"

Michael's enthusiasm, however, was not contagious. "So Speed Racer pulled it off, huh?" She gently extricated herself from her brother's embrace. "That's really nice, Mikey."

" 'Nice?' Girl, are you crazy?" Michael looked at his sister incredulously. "It's fantastic! Our car won! That means everybody at the track saw our car in Victory Lane. Everybody heard Brad Marshall thank his new sponsors—us! Oh Cori, it was a beautiful thing . . . you should have seen it!"

Cori shook her head, refusing to be drawn into Michael's excitement. "Wasn't that sweet of Mr. Marshall to acknowledge us?" she said sarcastically. "What I'm anxious to see is if that damned car makes one bit of difference to the bottom line. Because if 'everybody at the track' doesn't show up here for lunch or dinner, then this sponsorship will be just one big waste of money—money we don't have, I might add." She fixed a stern eye on her brother.

"Aw c'mon, Cori, lighten up! We won! That's got to count for something."

"Okay," Cori conceded, "maybe it does. You said we won, so there must have been some prize money involved. What was the restaurant's cut? You can use it to start paying Gram and Poppy back." She looked expectantly at him.

Michael turned away from her steady gaze, fidgeting with the pencil cup on her desk. "Actually, it's not quite that simple."

Cori shook her head slowly. "Do I need to sit down for this explanation?"

"Don't make a big deal out of this, Cori. Because Marshall's race team had been operating with a deficit when we signed up, the contract stipulated that the initial winnings would go to the team."

For one astounded moment, Cori just looked at him. Then suddenly, unexpectedly, she burst into laughter. "Mikey, this sponsorship package just keeps getting better and better. I can't even get mad anymore, it's just so incredibly stupid! What other provisions did you stipulate to? Did you agree to sign over the deed to the restaurant? Or to rent the waiters out to work in the pits?"

Michael was trapped between anger and defensiveness. "That's not fair, Cori! There are no other provisions."

Wiping away tears of laughter, Cori nodded. "Looks like we'll be claiming a big loss on our taxes this year. Thank God you only signed us up for two races."

"You don't know that it's going to be a loss," Michael asserted. "If he wins the next race, the restaurant does get a cut. They just needed this first prize purse to get out of the hole. And we still have to make a decision about sponsoring the rest of the season," he reminded her.

"Oh, I think that decision's already been made," she said dryly.

"You said you'd give it a fair chance. You can't make any decision yet. There hasn't been enough time." Michael sounded slightly panicked.

"We'll just see, Mikey. We'll just see."

Chapter 5

The morning sunlight streamed into Brad's bedroom, searing away the last vestiges of sleep. He rolled over, hiding from the sun, but it was too late. The damage was already done; he was awake. Reluctantly, he tossed the blanket aside and sat up on the side of the bed. Stretching, he was surprised to discover the muscles across his shoulders were a little stiff and sore. Then, it all came rushing back to him.

I won! The memory exploded into his consciousness. *I won yesterday!* Brad got off the bed and strode into the bathroom, a huge smile plastered on his face. He remembered last night's victory celebration. He and the crew had partied until the wee hours of the morning, exhilarated about being back on top. Brad reached for his wallet on a nearby nightstand and pulled out the prize money check.

"I just wanted to make sure it really happened," he murmured.

Convinced, he hurried through his morning routine, anxious to get to the garage and check on the condition of his race car. With his aggressive driving style, Brad had come in contact with a couple of other cars during the race—contact he described as "kissing" and Vern classified "ramming."

By the time he got to the garage Vern was already there, just as Brad knew he would be, with only his legs showing from under the car.

"Hey, Old Man!" Brad cheerfully greeted his crew chief. "How's it feel to be on the winning team?"

Vern rolled out from under the car. "Sleepin' in this morning, Cowboy?"

"Just savoring the thrill of victory." Brad squatted down on his haunches. "How's my girl this morning?" He patted the side of the car. "She really felt good yesterday."

"Think you'd treat her with a little more respect," Vern grumbled. "You keep rammin' into other cars, and I'm not gonna be able to patch her up anymore."

Chastised, Brad chuckled. "But we won, didn't we? I told you if we could just get back on the track, we'd start winning again. Man, it felt good to be back in Victory Lane. And first thing tomorrow morning, I'm going to cash that prize money check and pay the team."

"Yeah, well, enjoy it while it lasts," Vern said ominously as he stood up.

"What's that supposed to mean?"

"You seem to have forgotten that Foster's has only signed on for one more race," Vern pointed out. "While you're 'savoring the thrill of victory' you ought to be protecting yourself from the 'agony of defeat'. Michael Foster's sister did not seem interested in continuing to sponsor you."

Brad waved his hand dismissively. "That was before we won. She'll come around now."

"Wouldn't be too sure of that if I were you." Vern reached for an oil filter wrench. "She's gonna need some convincin'." He walked around to the front of the car and popped open the hood.

"Relax, Old Man. Convincing women is one of my specialties," Brad said cockily.

"This one is not like the track groupies you're used to dealing with." Vern's voice was stern. "That pretty face of yours ain't goin' do you much good with her."

"Tell you what, Vern. You take care of the car, and let me take care of the sponsors." Brad feigned innocence. "Isn't that what you've been telling me to do all along?"

"Uh huh." Vern sounded skeptical. "I'm warning you Brad, the rules are different with this one. Mark my words."

"C'mon, the rules can't be but so different. I mean after all, she is a woman, isn't she?" Brad checked his watch. "It's almost noon. Foster's is probably open for Sunday brunch. Why don't I just go on over to the restaurant now and talk to her?" Brad flashed a confident smile and strode out to his truck.

Shaking his head, Vern turned his attentions to the car's engine.

All the way over to Foster's, Brad planned what he was going to say. He was confident now that he'd won the race, Michael Foster's sister would see the sponsorship plan in a whole new light.

Remember her name is Justice, not Foster, Brad made a mental note. *Mrs. Corinthia Justice.* For a moment, the image of Cori, tall and caramel-colored, appeared before him. The one feature that had lodged itself enduringly in his memory was her sad, piercing eyes. He thought about that now, wondering what had so ringed her eyes with sadness. He remembered Michael saying Cori was a widow, and assumed that was part of it, but the depths of sadness indicated that it was not only the loss of her husband that put the shadows in her eyes.

After a moment, he shook his head. *I'm not trying to get into Corinthia Justice's business.* The thought made him chuckle, thinking about the purpose of this visit. *Well, maybe I am, after all, but just the restaurant business, not her personal business.*

Foster's was open for brunch, just as Brad suspected. After parking the Blazer in the restaurant's lot, Brad headed inside.

"One for brunch, Sir?" The hostess near the door smiled up at him.

"Actually, I'd like to see Mrs. Justice," Brad said. "Could you tell her Brad Marshall is here, please?"

The waitress shook her head apologetically. "I'm sorry, Sir. Mrs. Justice is not here right now."

Disappointed, Brad asked, "Do you expect her soon?"

"She usually gets in from church a little after one."

Church? The question erupted in his mind. Determined to speak with Cori today, Brad decided to wait. "Well in that case, one for brunch it is."

"Right this way, Sir." The hostess led Brad to a small cafe table next to one of the French doors that faced the front of the restaurant. "You'll be able to see Mrs. Justice when she arrives," the hostess said helpfully. She handed him a menu and returned to her stand.

Brad looked around the restaurant, admiring the elegant interior. He couldn't help thinking it strange that a classy restaurant like this one would be interested in stock car racing. Realizing that Corinthia Justice probably had that same thought, Brad's resolve to convince her strengthened.

Putting aside those concerns for the moment, Brad scanned the menu. When the waiter arrived, Brad ordered a smoked salmon omelet with rye toast, fresh fruit, and coffee.

Before long, his food arrived. The delicious smells wafting from his plate reminded Brad that he hadn't eaten all day. He attacked the meal with relish, savoring the perfectly prepared omelet. His appreciation for Foster's deepened with every bite.

When he looked around for his waiter, Brad was startled to see Cori standing near the door talking to the hostess. So intent was he on his meal that he had missed seeing

Cori approach the restaurant. As he watched, the hostess
pointed in his direction. Cori turned to follow the pointing
finger, and within seconds two pairs of eyes locked in a
surprised stare.

Cori murmured her thanks to the hostess and slowly
crossed the restaurant, approaching Brad's table.

Wiping his mouth and hands quickly, Brad stood to meet
her. He noted with appreciation the fine cut of the stylish,
peach-colored coatdress she wore. Crowning her head was
a matching, peach pillbox hat with white netting pulled
down in front of her eyes.

"I understand you were waiting for me, Mr . . . um,
Marshall, isn't it?" Cori feigned forgetfulness.

"Yes, Mrs. Justice, I was. I was hoping we could talk
about the sponsorship." Brad extended his hand.

Arms folded protectively in front of her body, Cori
regarded the outstretched hand for a moment. Finally,
after an uncomfortably long moment, Cori briefly shook
it.

"It's Sunday, Mr. Marshall. I make it a policy never to
do business on Sundays," Cori said flatly. "I'm sorry you
came all the way to the restaurant." She nodded at his
nearly cleaned plate. "I hope the meal at least made it
worth the trip for you."

Brad stood fuming, a muscle twitching reflexively at
his temple. "If I could just have a few moments of your
time—"

"Does racing cars cause one to lose his hearing?" Cori
asked pointedly. "I said I do not discuss business on Sundays. You may come back another day if you'd like. But
please feel free to stay and finish your meal." Cori made
a move to leave.

"I think I'm finished here," Brad said in controlled fury.
He reached for his wallet, tossed a bill on the table, and

strode out of restaurant with as much dignity as he could muster.

Well, that was unnecessary, Cori thought as she watched him leave. She wasn't sure if "unnecessary" referred to his actions or hers. *I'm not usually so short with people. What is it about that man that irritates me so?* Shrugging her shoulders, Cori turned to go to her office.

"Excuse me, Miss." The hail came from one of the tables as she walked near. "Wasn't that Brad Marshall the race car driver?"

Cori nodded, surprised. "You know him?"

"Well, not exactly know him," the man said, "but I sure know *of* him. He's one of the best local drivers around. That win he got yesterday was real exciting."

"You saw him win yesterday?"

"Yeah, sure." He gestured to his companion. "That's why we're here today. Saw the name on the car and decided to check the place out."

"Oh, I see," Cori said slowly. "Thank you for coming in. Enjoy your meal." She walked away from the table, processing the conversation. *Maybe I really do need to give this sponsorship a chance.*

Chapter 6

Cori awoke Monday morning to the tempting smells of perking coffee, frying bacon, and baking muffins. Smiling, she stretched the morning kinks out of her neck and shoulders. *Gram hasn't quite gotten the hang of "retirement" yet,* she thought. She hurriedly scrubbed her face and pulled her chestnut hair back into a ponytail. Wrapped in a thick chenille robe, Cori went downstairs to join her grandparents for breakfast.

"Good morning, Gram." Cori planted a kiss on her grandmother's cheek. "Still up cooking at the break of dawn, I see."

"It's hardly the break of dawn, Corinthia," Gram said with mock severity. "It's after seven."

"Leave the woman alone, Cori," her grandfather said, winking between bites, "somebody's got to fix breakfast."

Cori shook her head and chuckled. William and Mabel Foster were two of the constants in her life. Even when everything around her was in upheaval, her grandparents were steady, secure, and loving. William and Mabel were her father's parents, and in many ways she was closer to her Gram and Poppy than she was to her own parents. Perhaps the buffer of a generation had allowed a closeness to develop between grandparents and granddaughter that just wasn't possible between parents and daughter. William and Mabel had been instrumental in Cori's decision to move to Charlotte.

"You're just wasting away up there in Chicago. There's nothing there for you anymore," William Foster had reasoned.

"We need you here. Come to Charlotte and take over the restaurant," Mabel had pleaded. "Come to Charlotte and start your life again."

Mabel and William had made it extremely easy for Cori to decide. They offered her a job, a home, and a support system to help her keep the demons at bay. In the end, when Cori took stock of her life in Chicago, she realized they were right; Chicago held nothing but painful memories. So with an impulsiveness that was completely out of character for her, Cori gave her employer her notice on a Monday, packed, and was in Charlotte by that Saturday. And she had never regretted her decision.

She smiled now, sitting down at the table with two people she knew loved her unconditionally.

"Mikey come down yet?" Cori asked.

Mabel set a plate of bacon and eggs in front of Cori. "Child, you know it's too early for that brother of yours to be up and about."

"Oh, I see," Cori said dryly. "Mikey out all night again?"

"Now, Cori, you leave that boy alone," William admonished. "He's a young man getting to know a new town. Ain't nothing wrong with him staying out late."

"At least he's getting out," Mabel said pointedly as she removed muffins from the oven.

Cori rolled her eyes slightly. "Are you trying to make a point, Gram?"

"You have been in Charlotte for three months now, Corinthia, and you haven't been anywhere but the house, the restaurant, and church." Mabel shook her index finger at her granddaughter. "That's no kind of way for a beautiful young woman like yourself to live."

William, who was busily stirring sugar into his second cup of coffee, nodded but said nothing.

"Don't worry about me, Gram," Cori said lightly. "Mikey gets out enough for both of us."

Mabel made a *tsking* sound in her throat and shook her head. William regarded his granddaughter closely, noting the changes he'd seen in her these past three months. The sallow tone of her skin when she'd arrived had given way to a warm, healthy, caramel glow. The arms, legs, and hips that had seemed painfully thin and undernourished were filling out, curves appearing in all the right places. Even her hair was flourishing, growing longer and thicker, and shining as if it were lit from within. The one thing that had not yet yielded to the healing powers of Charlotte were her eyes. Even when she smiled, which was more and more often, her eyes held a deep sorrow. Knowing what had put the shadows in her eyes, William understood, but it saddened him nevertheless.

"Leave the girl alone, Mabel. She'll go out when she's ready." William smiled at his beloved granddaughter. "The last thing she needs is to be pressured."

Mabel glared at her husband. "No, Will, the last thing she needs is to be coddled. Cori's a big girl now."

"Hey, hey!" Cori interrupted. "Quit talking about me as if I'm not sitting right here, guys. You two need to stop worrying about me. I'm fine—I've just been concentrating on learning the business, so I haven't had time to gallivant all over town."

"So how are things down at Foster's?" William asked.

Cori shrugged her shoulders. "Everything seems to be going fine, I guess."

Mabel turned away from the bacon she was tending. "You don't sound too sure of yourself."

"It's this race car sponsorship Mikey's gotten us into.

I'm not too sure about that. What do you two think about it?''

"Well, it's not something I would have done—" William began.

Cori pounced on his words. "See! I knew it. It's a stupid, expensive plan."

"Let me finish, Corinthia," William said sternly. "It's not something I would have done, but I think it's an exciting, innovative idea. I was a little skeptical at first, but after we talked with Michael I think it seems like a good investment. That's why we gave him the money."

"But Poppy, racing is such a stupid, dangerous sport . . . grown men driving as fast as they can in a circle. How can something that . . . that . . . *destructive* be any good for Foster's reputation?"

"That doesn't sound like a business reason, Cori," Mabel said gently. "That sounds much more personal." She studied her granddaughter carefully.

"Keep an open mind," William counseled. "And make sure any choices you make for the restaurant are sound business decisions. You've got to keep your personal feelings out of it."

Cori's thoughts swirled around the foolishly dangerous sport and the strikingly handsome driver. "I'll try to keep my personal feelings out of it," she muttered, "but that's easier said than done."

A short time later, Cori had dressed and headed to the restaurant. Although they did not open to the public until 11:00, Cori liked to get there by 9:30 to gear up for the day. The restaurant was close enough to her grandparents' home for her to walk to work—a fact that was a selling point in her decision to move to Charlotte in the first place. The less time she had to spend in cars, the better.

She was usually the first one to arrive, so she was surprised when she approached the parking lot to see a black

Chevy Blazer already parked there. As she walked nearer, the door of the Blazer opened. Fumbling with her brief-case, she watched, curious, as a tall, lean figure emerged from the truck. As the man approached her, recognition dawned.

"Hello, Mrs. Justice. I've been waiting for you." Brad smiled.

"Mr. Marshall. I didn't expect to see you again so soon. How can I help you?" Cori's tone was frosty.

Her demeanor grated on him. "I just wanted to talk to you. I get the feeling you don't like me. Is it something I said or did?"

His voice was so plaintive that Cori felt a stab of guilt. She put her briefcase down on the asphalt and crossed her arms in front of her chest, taking a moment to consider her answer.

"No, Mr. Marshall," she said finally. "There is nothing you've done. I guess I'm still a little angry about the way this whole sponsorship deal went down. It just seemed a little underhanded to me."

Brad's face clouded up, and he opened his mouth to protest.

"Not on your part," she quickly added. "I'm sure your intentions were honest and forthright. It's just . . ." She paused, searching for the right words. " . . . just that I've been through this with my brother before. He makes these rash decisions and leaves me to pick up the pieces. I thought Charlotte would be a new beginning, but it's start-ing to feel like same old stuff, brand new town."

"Well, I'm probably not the most neutral person on the topic," Brad conceded, "but I think your brother is trying to do the right thing. Stock car racing is an excellent way to advertise your business."

Cori smiled in spite of herself. "You wouldn't be a little bit biased, now would you, Mr. Marshall?"

Brad laughed in return. "Look, Mrs. Justice, you ought to at least see what you've paid your money for. Won't you please go to the track with me and let me show you around?"

His expression was so earnest, so sincere, that Cori felt her resistance weakening.

"I really don't think that's such a good idea, Mr. Marshall," she said finally.

Brad heaved an exasperated sigh. "Let me tell you what I think. I think somehow we have gotten off on the wrong foot, and I think this 'Mr. Marshall' 'Mrs. Justice' routine is not helping at all." He moved closer to her. "So here's the deal from now on—I'm Brad, and you're Corinthia." He made a mock formal bow. "Now then, Corinthia," he said, putting a dramatic emphasis on the name, "I will only take a couple hours of your time at the track, and it might just change your mind about this situation."

Cori resisted the urge to back away from Brad's masculine closeness. "Mr. Marshall . . ."

Brad gave her a warning look.

"Okay, Brad," she corrected. "Even if I agreed to go on this little field trip you've suggested, I couldn't possibly go now. We'll be opening soon, and then it will be time for the lunch rush, and I need to be here for that."

Brad nodded his understanding. "Fine, Corinthia. How about I pick you up at two? You'll have a wonderful time." His voice lowered invitingly. "I promise." He cocked his head jauntily to the side, waiting confidently for the positive response he was sure was forthcoming.

Cori looked at him impatiently. She allowed the silence between them to stretch until it was bordering on uncomfortable.

"That roguish charm of yours might work at the track," she said finally, "but I am not the one."

Stunned, Brad could only stare.

"Now then, I will go with you to the track, not to have a 'wonderful time' but because I'm a businesswoman looking after my investment. You may pick me up at two-thirty." Cori picked up her briefcase and started toward the restaurant. "Oh, and by the way, my friends call me Cori." She flashed a brilliant smile at him before continuing her purposeful stride to the back door.

Her departure broke the frozen astonishment that had wrapped around Brad. Abruptly, a rich, full laugh gurgled up from his throat. And he could hear Vern's voice as clearly as if the crew chief were standing next to him.

Mark my words, Boy, the rules are different now.

Brad could only laugh and nod his agreement.

Chapter 7

At promptly two-thirty, Brad returned to Foster's. He stopped at the hostess stand. Before he could state his business, the hostess said, "You're here to see Mrs. Justice—right?"

Brad was caught off guard. "Uh . . . yes . . . how did you know?"

"Oh," the girl said flirtatiously, "I remember you from yesterday."

Brad smiled, nodded, and leaned in to whisper conspiratorially, "Well, let's hope today goes a little better."

Cori emerged from the kitchen just in time to see the hostess giggling up at Brad. Cori shook her head. *I'll bet he's used to women fawning all over him, just like that.* She lifted her chin and squared her shoulders. *Well, it's not that kind of party here.*

Cori approached the hostess stand, making little effort to control the disdain she was certain was displayed on her face. "Thank you, Jasmine," she addressed the still giggling hostess, "I can take it from here." Jasmine nodded, and after a secret wink at Brad she left the pair alone.

"You certainly seemed to have entertained Jasmine," Cori observed dryly.

"She's a nice girl," Brad responded easily, "she was just wishing me luck."

"Luck with what?"

Brad unleashed a mega-watt smile that seemed almost luminous in contrast to his ebony complexion. "Luck with the boss lady, of course. I hear she's a tough sell."

"And don't you forget it." Cori tried, but could not hold her stern look. In spite of her best intentions, Cori smiled in return.

"There, now," Brad teased, "that didn't hurt a bit, did it?"

"Can we just go on this little outing of yours? I don't have all day."

"Whatever you say, Boss Lady." With a playfully dramatic flourish, Brad swept the door open for her.

Cori, more determined than ever to not fall victim to Brad Marshall's charms, mustered a businesslike air as she walked past him into the afternoon sunlight. As they approached his Blazer, Brad hurried a few steps ahead to open the passenger side door.

"Quite the gentleman, aren't you?" Cori commented as she settled in the seat. "Or quite the salesman. You wouldn't be trying to butter me up, now would you?"

"My mama taught me to treat ladies with respect. I guess it's a Southern thing—you Northerners just wouldn't understand." Brad closed her door and walked to his side of the truck, his jaw tightly clenched.

When he climbed in next to her, Cori immediately went on the defensive. "What do you mean, 'Northerners wouldn't understand'? There are lots of men in the North who open doors for ladies."

"I just assumed no one had ever done that for you, since you seemed so surprised."

"Surprised is not the word I would use," Cori said flatly. " 'Suspicious' is more like it."

Brad turned to face her. "Suspicious of what?"

"I can't help but wonder what you're after, Mr. Marshall."

"Oh, Lord. We haven't gone back to the 'Mr. Marshall' routine, have we?" Brad shook his head. "Look, Cori, I have no hidden agenda. You know what I'm after—your support of my race team. But I didn't open your door because I'm trying to win you over. I opened your door because I'm a nice guy." He smiled at her. "If you relax, you might find that out for yourself."

"In other words, give you a break," Cori replied.

"That would be a good place to start."

Brad turned to start the engine. Unexpectedly, Cori felt fingers of panic begin to close in on her. She stiffened in the seat and unconsciously clutched the door. Brad noticed her anxiety.

"Are you okay?" he asked, concern etched on his face.

Cori nodded. "You don't drive this thing like a race car, do you?"

"Oh no, not at all. I have a healthy respect for speed . . . I've seen what it can do. I leave my racing for the track. Promise." He reached over for her seat belt. "Buckle up," he commanded softly.

Cori felt strangely soothed by the solid feel of Brad's arm as he reached across her and pulled the lap and shoulder harness into place. She willed herself to relax.

What is that all about? he wondered. "Ready to go?" Brad looked at her questioningly.

"Yes." Cori nodded. "Yes, let's go." *And get this over with,* she thought.

Brad eased the truck out of the parking lot, driving more cautiously than usual. He had no idea what was bothering Cori, but instinctly he knew she needed assurance that her safety was not at risk.

"Are we going to the Speedway?" Cori asked, searching for a distraction.

"I wish." Brad laughed shortly. "Naw, the Speedway is

for the big time—NASCAR. My garage is on the outskirts of town. I've made arrangements to take my practice time this afternoon, so that you can see how your car performs.''

"To be completely honest, Brad, I know next to nothing about cars. I won't be able to tell much about its performance.''

"Don't worry," he said as he maneuvered through traffic, "I'll teach you all you need to know.''

The pair was silent as the unintended double meaning of Brad's words swirled around them. Finally, after an impossibly long moment, Brad cleared his throat, breaking the silence.

"How did you know about the Speedway?" he asked. "Have you been out there?"

"Heavens, no." Cori chuckled. "Before I decided to move here, my grandparents sent me all kinds of brochures and tourist information about Charlotte. The Charlotte Motor Speedway—that's the name, right?—was featured in almost all the literature about the town. Apparently, no visit to Charlotte is complete without a trip out to the track.''

Brad smiled and nodded. "So they say. So have you seen any of the attractions of our fair city?"

"Actually, no I haven't. The restaurant takes up almost my every waking moment.''

"That's no way for a young woman to live. There's more to life than work.''

Cori smiled. "Now you sound like my grandparents. They're always after me to go out more.''

"Well, maybe they're right. All work and no play makes Cori a dull girl," Brad teased.

"That's strange advice coming from you," Cori countered. "Seems to me that every time I've seen you, you've been working.''

"Is that what you think I'm doing—working?"

"Aren't you? Aren't you working to get my support?"

Brad considered his answer for a moment. "I guess I

can understand how you'd see it that way, but I don't consider it work at all. To me, my work *is* play, because I love what I do."

"And what—exactly—is it that you do, Brad?"

"I push cars harder and faster than anyone thinks they can go—to the edge of the envelope and back. When I'm in a race I exist in another dimension, a place where the only things that matter are speed and power and winning. Anything else I do—no check that, *everything* else I do— is geared toward keeping me in that car and keeping that car on the track. Because as long as I can stay on the track, I can win. Racing is not something I do . . . racing is something I am."

Cori nodded, impressed by his passion. *I don't think I've ever felt that way about anything,* she mused.

They rode in silence for a few minutes more. Then Brad pulled off the main road and drove toward what looked to Cori like just a big open field. As they drew closer, she could see a worn metal entrance gate next to a sign that read Carolco Raceway. They didn't enter that gate, as she expected. Instead, Brad drove around to a side entrance and parked next to a garage building. He hopped out and opened Cori's door. This time, she just smiled and accepted the courtesy. As she stepped out of the truck, she got her first good look at the track.

It was a paved asphalt oval, about a quarter mile in diameter. Grandstands had been erected alongside both straightaways. In the center of the oval was an area with a checkered flag pattern painted on the asphalt. The lettering proclaimed Victory Lane.

"It's much nicer than I expected," Cori said.

"What did you expect?"

"I don't know . . . dirt track, maybe, with just a few bleachers for spectators."

Brad laughed. "Can't run these cars on dirt. It'll ruin the engines. And a few bleachers wouldn't begin to hold the number of fans who come out for these races."

Cori nodded. "Guess I've got a lot to learn."

Brad pointed in the direction of the garage door. "Our car's in there. Come on, let me show her to you."

Our car? Cori smiled at the reference.

Brad led the way into the garage. Then, with the dramatic flourish she was beginning to recognize, he presented the car.

"Mrs. Corinthia Justice, I'd like you to meet the Foster's Restaurant Chevrolet."

Again, Cori found her expectations shattered. She was struck by the beauty of the burgundy and gold car. Stepping forward, she slowly ran her hand along the hood, fingering the bold lettering of the restaurant's name.

"It's the same color as the restaurant," she said wonderingly. "I didn't realize that. And the address is on here, too."

"Well, of course," Brad said. "How else could we expect someone to find the restaurant?"

"But I don't understand. With you speeding around the track at warp two, how can anybody see the name or the address?"

A confident smile lit Brad's face. "They see it when the car is parked in Victory Lane."

"Oh." Cori walked around the car and peered in the driver's side. She noticed there was no passenger seat, and the car had been stripped of all but the most essential parts. *The sport may be called "stock car" racing,* she thought, *but this is no showroom model Chevy.*

"This doesn't look real comfortable," she said.

"She's not really built for comfort." Brad laughed. "We want to get every second of speed we can out of her, so plush upholstery is the first thing to go."

Cori looked at him sharply. "You're laughing at me."

"No, not at all." Brad grinned at her. "But you're right: you do have a lot to learn."

Cori felt her reserve soften slightly. "You're the expert, so teach."

Brad shook his head. "I'd rather show." He looked around the garage. "Let me find Vern. He'll take you down to the track so you can watch me practice. Wait right here."

Cori watched as Brad left in search of his crew chief. In spite of herself, she noted how his well-worn jeans hugged his thighs and backside. Her eyes traveled upward and she experienced a split second loss of rational thought as she admired the broad expanse of his shoulders and the muscled firmness of his biceps. Brad Marshall was the antithesis of everything she thought she liked in men: He was too tall, too dark, too muscled, too bald. At least, that's what she kept telling herself.

He's not at all like Tony. The thought blazed across her mind. Instantly, she felt guilty. Somehow, admiring Brad was equivalent to betraying Tony.

"Afternoon, Mrs. Justice. Glad you could make it out today." Vern's greeting startled her; she was so engrossed in her thoughts that she hadn't seen him approach.

"Hello, Vern. Your driver here can be very persuasive." Cori nodded at Brad. "And by the way, my friends call me Cori."

Vern broke into a toothy grin. "Then Cori it is. Come with me, Cori, and let's watch the cowboy do his thing."

Vern led Cori out to the track. For so large a facility, Carolco seemed unnaturally quiet to her. Vern and Cori walked over to an area next to the inside wall of the oval track.

"During a race, this area is called Pit Road," Vern informed her. "This is where the drivers pull in for gas and tires and sometimes repairs."

"Repairs?"

"Yup. Sometimes racing is a contact sport," Vern said sagely.

"I knew there were accidents, but I assumed if a car was in an accident, it was out of the race." Cori looked confused. "Why would you need to do repairs in the pits?"

"Not every accident is bad enough to put the car out. In fact, an accident that bad is really kind of rare." Vern nodded over at the Foster's car. "At this level of the game, these drivers don't have a lot of backup cars, so they really protect the ones they have. Out of the race for these guys could mean out for the season."

Cori quietly processed the information. "So is that why my sponsorship is so important? So he can have a couple of backup cars for when he crashes that one?"

Vern studied her closely. "I don't know what you think of Brad, but you should know he is one of the best drivers I've ever seen. He's not the type of man who would recklessly ruin a car, even if he did have one or two in reserve. Your sponsorship is important for a lot of reasons: so can keep the car in top running shape, so we can keep the car in races, and so the team can get paid. It's not just about Brad."

The simple dignity of Vern's words shamed Cori. She realized she was being difficult, and she was slowly coming to realize that these two men were professionals, and didn't deserve her potshots.

"I'm sorry, Vern. I . . . I didn't know."

Vern brushed away the apology. "This is a learning experience for all of us."

Before Cori had a chance to ask for an explanation, the Foster's car roared onto the track. As she watched, Brad sped around the track, kicking up clouds of dust in his wake. The car became a burgundy blur as Brad circled around again, this time seeming to move even faster. Cori's emotions wavered between fascination and fear. The very idea of moving that fast filled her with horror, but she had to admit Brad kept the car perfectly under control.

Brad passed Pit Road again, this time with enough speed for Cori and Vern to feel the pull of the air as he whooshed past. Cori felt the beginnings of alarm building in her chest. She struggled to push it away, knowing that the panic would envelop her if she didn't fight.

Brad screeched to a halt in front of his small audience. The glare of the sun reflecting off the stock car momentarily blinded Cori. That flash of light swept away the present and landed Cori squarely in the past. She felt cold fingers of panic again, and this time she couldn't stop them from closing in around her soul. The squeal of Brad's tires evoked the memory of twisting metal and exploding glass. Suddenly, she was no longer at a racetrack in North Carolina but on the side of a highway in Chicago. Suddenly, the roar in her ears came not from a speeding race car but from a speeding ambulance. The color drained from her face as Cori, unaware, gripped the fence in front of her. She was sweating and shivering all at the same time.

Cori took several deep breaths, trying to rein in the pain before it consumed her. She shook her head vigorously in an effort to clear her mind, but the memories were so visceral, so vivid, she found it hard to let them go.

Vern, unaware of Cori's distress, left her side to show Brad the stopwatch. Brad climbed out of the car and checked his time.

"Not bad, huh?" Brad said enthusiastically.

Vern nodded. "How'd she feel today?"

"A little loose through the turns, but nothing I couldn't handle." Brad nodded toward Cori. "What did *she* say?"

"Not much," Vern said slowly, "better go talk to her."

Brad stepped around Vern and approached Cori. He took one look at her ashen face and haunted eyes and knew immediately something was wrong.

"What is it?" His deep voice rang with concern. This was the second time today Cori had seemed spooked.

"Nothing," Cori answered shortly.

"You sure?" Brad asked, unconvinced.

"Yes. Everything's fine." Cori managed a halfhearted smile.

Brad decided to change the subject, "Well, what did you think of your car?"

"It was very nice," Cori muttered.

"Nice? That's all—'nice'?" Brad rolled his eyes.
"C'mon, Cori. It's so much more than just 'nice.' Maybe
you should take the car for a lap around the track. You
know, learn a little more about her, maybe come to appreciate her more."

Cori recoiled as if he'd slapped her. She unconsciously
took a few steps back from the fence—and the car.

Cori's refusal was a disjointed jumble of panic-stricken
words. "I . . . I . . . I couldn't—no—I can't . . ."

"It's all right, Cori. Relax. You don't have to drive the
car if you don't want to." Brad's confusion and concern
were multiplying with every passing second. Obviously
something was wrong, but he had not a clue as to what it
might be. Somehow he sensed it had very little to do with
him. "We can just go to the garage. I wanted you to meet
the pit crew—they're supposed to be here around four."

"N . . . no," Cori whispered. "Please, take me back to
Foster's."

"But we just got here," Brad protested.

"Please, Brad, please take me back to the restaurant.
I've seen all I need to here."

Her voice was so plaintive, her eyes so haunted and
forlorn, that Brad could do nothing but grant her request.
"Sure, Cori, we can go back to Foster's. Just give me a
minute to get the car squared away." Brad turned to Vern,
who had been watching the whole exchange.

"Just go, Cowboy," Vern said. "I'll take care of the car.
You take care of Cori."

Brad nodded gratefully and turned to Cori. "Come on.
Let's go back to Foster's."

Cori murmured her thanks and followed Brad to his
Blazer. Woodenly, she climbed into the truck. Instead of
waiting for Brad's help, she immediately snapped both the
lap and shoulder belts in place. She leaned her head back
against the seat and closed her eyes, trying to block the
visions that assailed her.

Settling into the driver's seat, Brad stole a glance at his

motionless passenger. *What is it?* he wondered. *Why is she so upset? What can I do to help?* They were questions with no answers. After a moment, he started the truck and pointed it in the direction of Foster's.

She was silent all the way back to town. As desperately as she wanted to forget the whole experience at the track, she couldn't. She was shaken by how vividly the memories of five years before were imprinted on her mind. She was grateful that Brad respected her need for silence. *I couldn't handle any conversation right now,* she thought.

Shortly, they arrived at the restaurant. Brad turned in his seat and looked at her expectantly. Cori held her head down, trying to find something to say, something that would explain her behavior, but she couldn't. She willed herself to meet his eyes.

"I'm so sorry," was all she could manage to say.

Before Brad could respond, she unfastened the seat belts and bolted from the truck, overcome by the need to be alone . . . in her office . . . with her memories.

Brad watched as she all but ran toward the restaurant. He hurried after her.

Inside Foster's, Michael was at a table near the door, idly stirring a drink. He'd heard about Cori's outing from Jasmine the hostess, and was anxiously awaiting her return.

Michael looked up from his drink just in time to see Cori rush through the restaurant. He rose to call out to her, but she disappeared into her office before he could get the words out. Puzzled, Michael started in the direction of Cori's office. Before he had taken more than a couple of steps, Brad entered the restaurant, his face a mask of confusion and concern. As he looked around, searching for Cori, his eyes lit on Michael.

Maybe he knows what's going on. Brad changed directions and stalked over to Michael's table.

"Hey, Brad." Michael warmly extended his hand. "How'd it go?"

The two men shook hands. "I'm not sure how it went,

Michael. One minute we seemed to be getting along great, and the next minute she freaked out."

" 'Freaked out'? What does that mean?"

"I mean, when I talked to her before my practice lap she was fine, but when I got out of the car afterward she was spaced out. She wouldn't talk. She could barely look at me." Brad's eyes bored into Michael's. "What's up with that?"

"You say she changed after the practice lap?" Michael asked thoughtfully.

"Yeah, Man. It was kinda scary. Something spooked her bad."

"Damn," Michael muttered under his breath. "Look, don't worry about Cori. I'll take care of her." Michael started in the direction of his sister's office.

"Wait a minute!" Brad called. "What's going on here? You have to tell me something."

But Michael didn't answer. Remembering how his sister had dulled her pain before, all his attentions were focused on being by her side.

Brad watched as yet another member of the Foster family disappeared through the office door. Bewildered, Brad stood rooted in that spot for several long moments, waiting to see if either Michael or Cori would emerge from the office. After neither of them did, Brad finally decided that leaving was his only option.

Guess I'll go out to the garage and make sure Vern got the car back okay. He was making an effort to put the events of this day behind him, but that was a task easier said than done. He found himself fuming all the way to the garage. Cori's strange behavior and Michael's even stranger reaction had planted a puzzle in his mind—a puzzle that demanded a solution. So far, nothing Brad could think up seemed a valid explanation.

When he pulled up in front of the garage Vern came out to meet him.

"So what happened? Is Cori all right?"

Brad shook his head slowly. "I don't really know what happened. I also don't know if Cori is all right. She didn't say a word all the way back to town, and as soon as we got to Foster's she practically ran to her office." Brad's voice was thick with frustration. "I spoke to her brother, and either he didn't know what was wrong with her—which I doubt—or he wasn't talking. I'm telling you, Vern, something strange is going on with that woman."

Vern studied his protégé, whom he knew better than Brad knew himself. *Something is going on, all right,* Vern thought, *and it's not just with Cori.*

"Well, you have to try again," Vern said matter-of-factly.

"What?" Brad looked stunned. "Why would I do that? Obviously something about racing scares her to death. Why would I try again?"

"If racing scares her, then you'll have to try something else," Vern persisted. "You can't just give up. This is too important."

Although neither man said anything, they both knew Vern was not talking about the sponsorship. After a silent moment, Brad nodded.

Chapter 8

Tuesday morning found Brad with extra time on his hands. Normally, he ran his practice laps on Tuesdays, but in order to show Cori around he'd switched days. The extra time loomed especially large today because he'd had a restless, uneasy sleep the night before. He hadn't been able to shake the image of Cori, her haunted eyes impossibly huge in her ashen face.

I hope she's all right, he thought yet again. *What could it have been? Did I do something? I just wanted to introduce her to racing—I never meant to upset her.* The thoughts had battered at him, keeping him from sleep, and were now keeping him from enjoying this time off. He prowled restlessly through his apartment, too agitated to spend more than a few minutes at any activity. He needed to do something, but for the life of him he couldn't figure out what.

The shrill ring of his phone demanded his attention. "Hello?"

"Congratulations, Brad! Mom and Dad told me you won last weekend." The cheerful voice belonged to his older sister, Julie.

"Yes, I did. Not that any of you saw it, though," Brad complained. "How come you weren't at the race?"

"Aw, Brad, be fair," Julie protested. "We didn't know you were back on the track. The last I heard, you'd lost your sponsor and had to bow out."

"Oh," Brad muttered. "Guess I forgot to tell you all about that."

"Guess you did," Julie agreed. "I have to admit I was a little surprised to hear you got a new sponsor. I thought maybe you'd just sit out the rest of the season."

"Why would you think a thing like that?"

"Quite honestly, Brad, you're getting a little long in the tooth to keep speeding around in circles," Julie said gently. "Maybe it's time to start thinking about life after racing."

"Who you calling 'long in the tooth'? Remember, you're two years older than me," Brad laughed.

"Hey, I didn't say you were old, period—just too old for racing. It's time to find a real job."

Brad rolled his eyes in exasperation. "Not you, too. You're starting to sound like Dwayne."

"Our baby brother just wants what's best for you." Julie was quick to jump to Dwayne's defense.

"No, Dwayne just wants me to be exactly like him—wearing a suit and tie to work behind a desk, making calls all day and driving a Volvo home at five. I swear, for such a kid, Dwayne's really boring."

"Dwayne's a successful young up-and-comer. And he's thirty now—not quite a kid anymore."

"Whatever," Brad snapped impatiently. "Why are you raggin' on me today? I thought you supported my racing."

Julie sighed. "Oh, Brad, you know I'm in your corner—no matter what you do. I love you. And I don't mean to rag on you. It's just that I'm worried about you getting hurt."

"In a crash?" Brad laughed shortly. "Don't be ridiculous, Julie. I'm too good for that."

"No . . . not in a crash—although you need to quit acting

like it couldn't happen," Julie admonished. "No, I meant hurt if your dreams don't come true. I know how much you want to drive for a NASCAR team, but Honey, it just doesn't look like it's going to happen."

"Where did that come from?" Brad was thoroughly confused.

"Well, Brad, you've been driving for ten years, and you haven't gotten an invitation yet," Julie pointed out. "And now you've started having sponsor trouble. Maybe it's time . . ."

"You don't know what you're talking about," Brad said flatly. "I *was* having sponsor trouble . . . but that problem is almost solved."

"Explain."

Quickly, Brad told Julie about the Foster's sponsorship, and the situation with Michael and Cori.

"Is she pretty?" Julie asked slyly.

"Wha—?" Brad was caught off guard by the question.

"This Cori Justice, is she pretty?"

"I suppose so. But what does that have to do with anything?" Brad demanded.

"I just figured you'd have unleashed that Marshall charm by now. Especially if she's a pretty girl."

Remembering when he'd thought the same thing and been put squarely in his place, Brad heaved a frustrated sigh. "Believe me Julie, as Vern says, the rules are different with this one."

"That's very intriguing, Little Bro." Julie perked up considerably. "What's going on with you and this new sponsor?"

"Nothing much," Brad grumbled. "Not that I haven't tried. Yesterday, I took her out to the track to watch practice. I figured she'd be interested in seeing what her sponsorship was supporting."

"Is that all you figured she'd be interested in seeing?"

Brad ignored the question. "But once I finished my practice laps, she was acting really strange."

"Strange, how?"

"I don't know, Julie. I'm still trying to sort it out for myself." Brad paused, considering. "But something scared her out there. I've never seen anyone get so spooked before. And she wouldn't talk about it afterward. I don't think she said ten words after that. I'm telling you, Julie, it was weird!"

Listening carefully, Julie heard something in her brother's voice, some level of concern and involvement that he might not even be aware of yet. "Well, you have to try again," Julie said finally.

Brad chuckled. "That's the same thing Vern said."

"We're both right. You can't just leave things like this. You need to see her, today, and make sure everything is okay. The 'something' that scared her might have been you—have you considered that? If so, you need to show her what a nice guy you are."

"Why on earth would she be scared of me?" Brad protested. "That doesn't make sense."

"Well, she's upset about something, and it's up to you to find out what," Julie said authoritatively. "Spend some time with her, let her get to know you. Off of the racetrack."

"You certainly are busy running my life this morning," Brad observed dryly. "How **do** you find the time?"

"It's a dirty job, but somebody's got to do it," Julie teased. "And don't think I don't realize you just changed the subject. Today, Brad. See her today."

"I guess it is important for the sponsorship," Brad allowed.

I'd guess it's important for more than that, Julie thought. "Good luck, Honey. Let me know what happens."

Brad mumbled something that could have been agreement and hung up the phone. Replaying the conversation in his mind, he realized that two of the people he respected most in the world, his sister and his crew chief, had given him the same advice. *"You have to try again."* The words rang in his ears. *But how?* he wondered. He pondered the situation for a few minutes, and then an idea came to him. "Perfect," he purred.

"Are you sure you're all right? Maybe you should stay home today." Michael poured a second cup of coffee into his sister's mug.

"I'm fine," Cori assured him. "Thanks for not saying anything to Gram and Poppy."

"They're worried about you enough already. I didn't see any reason to lay this on them, too." Michael settled into a dinette chair across the table from his sister. Mabel and William Foster had already gone for their customary morning stroll through the neighborhood, leaving Cori and Michael alone. "So what happened yesterday? You never really did say."

Cori studied the depths of her coffee mug, considering. "I don't honestly know, Mikey. Something about that race car, the noise or the vibrations or something, reminded me of the accident. It was positively terrifying." She took a deep swallow of coffee. "And it wasn't just the memory itself that was so frightening, but the fact that it was so vivid. I swear, Mikey, it was like living through it all over again." Cori's eyes grew distant. "And then, as if that weren't enough, all I could think of all the way back to the restaurant was pouring myself a drink. I just kept thinking if I could get a drink, everything would be all right." She reached across the table and grasped her brother's hand. "Thank you for being there, Mikey. I don't know what I would have done without you."

"You know I'll always be there for you, Cori." He squeezed her hand. "Look, Cori, I realize I keep saying this to you, but you're going to have to learn to let it go. Tony and Brianna will always be with you, but you've got to stop letting their memory control you."

The mention of her lost husband and daughter caused

Cori to flinch involuntarily. "I know . . . I know. It's just not that easy."

"If sponsoring this race car is going to upset you this much, we'll just let it go. It's not worth it," Michael said protectively. "You haven't had a drink in over two years. I'm not going to let this stupid sponsorship cause you to slip up. Brad Marshall will just have to get another ride."

"No, no. I'll be okay. It's true I haven't had a drink in over two years, but that doesn't mean I haven't wanted one. I just take it one day at a time." Cori shook her finger at her brother. "We can't make a business decision based on emotions, remember? I'm not going to hold yesterday against Brad Marshall, and don't you, either. He had no idea what was going on."

"Does that mean you want to continue the sponsorship?" Michael was stunned.

"Let's just say the jury is still out on that one." Cori stood up and put her coffee mug in the sink. "Come on, partner. We need to get moving—we've got a business to run."

Brad picked his time carefully. Too early, and he would catch her at the start of the lunch rush. Too late, and he ran the risk of missing her altogether. At 1:45, Brad walked into the restaurant. He figured the lunch crowd would have thinned, giving Cori a few minutes to spend with him. Jasmine the hostess seated him at a table near the verandah doors and left to find Cori.

Jasmine found Cori in the kitchen. "Mrs. Justice, there's someone here to see you."

"Who is it, Jasmine? I don't have time for any suppliers today."

"It's not a supplier," Jasmine said slowly. "Table seventeen." Jasmine hurried out of the kitchen before Cori could question her further. Puzzled, Cori watched the girl disappear through the swinging doors. *What was that about?*

she wondered. With a shrug, Cori grabbed a towel from a nearby counter and began wiping her hands. She emerged from the kitchen and started in the direction of table seventeen.

Brad, who had been intently watching the kitchen door, rose when he saw her approach. Cori's step faltered a bit when she realized who the mystery guest was. Her breath caught in her throat at the sight of Brad, his bald head gleaming, casually dressed in Levi's, a bright purple, polo-style shirt, and athletic shoes.

Good Lord, that man is fine! The thought burst into her mind. That thought was quickly crowded out by another: *What is he doing here?* Cori slowed her step the slightest bit, trying to use the last few seconds before she reached his table to collect her wits.

"Hello, Brad." She greeted him with a smile. "This is a surprise."

"I know. Please forgive me for coming by unannounced, but I had to see you today." Brad returned the welcoming smile. "If for nothing else, then to make sure you're okay."

Cori lowered her lashes and looked away. "I'm sorry about yesterday. You must be terribly confused. Believe me when I tell you it had nothing to do with you or your car."

"Then what was it, Cori?" Brad asked gently. He bent and twisted slightly in order to meet her eyes. "I want to help if I can."

Cori met his eyes and was momentarily lost in their sensitive brown depths. She took a deep breath before responding.

"I can't . . . please understand . . . I just can't talk about it."

Sensing her distress, Brad decided to not to push. "Tell you what—let's forget about it, for now at least. I have a plan, something that will put Foster's and racing and *whatever* completely out of your mind."

Intrigued, Cori looked up at him. "So what's the plan?"

"Well, I know you're fairly new to Charlotte, and I know that you haven't taken any time to get to know our fair city—apart from reading the tourist brochures—so I thought I'd take you on a tour." Brad's radiant smile was inviting. "There's so much more to Charlotte than Dilworth."

"Dilworth?"

"See, now that's just sad," Brad teased. "Dilworth is the neighborhood where we are now. Unless I miss my guess, you live somewhere near here too, don't you?"

"Yes, but—"

"So I'm willing to bet you haven't been much farther than the restaurant and your house—right?"

"And my church. It's right around the corner there."

Brad made a disapproving face.

"I've been really busy getting used to my new job," Cori said defensively. "I haven't had time to see Charlotte."

"I figured as much." Brad extended his hand, palm up. "So come with me, Miss Cori, and let me show you my hometown."

Cori hesitated, remembering the slight uneasiness she'd felt riding in his truck. "I don't know . . ."

"I'm not going to take no for an answer. I want to take you on a walking tour of Uptown." Brad's voice lowered slightly. "I promise we won't go anywhere near the track."

"A walking tour?" She marveled at his sensitivity.

"We'll have to take the truck into town, but we'll park it somewhere and just explore Uptown on foot." Brad studied her closely. "Cori, I don't know what upset you so much yesterday, but it seems a pretty safe bet that it had something to do with racing or race cars. I just want to make it up to you, to show you another side of Charlotte—and me." He lifted his still extended hand slightly. "Won't you please join me?"

Cori was deeply touched by his sincerity. "Yes," she said softly, "that would be lovely." She placed her hand in his. The electricity was instantaneous. Cori suddenly realized

that despite the number of times her path had crossed
with Brad Marshall's, this was the first time they'd ever
actually touched. The current that pulsed between their
two hands was such a powerful force that she wondered if
it was visible to the naked eye.

Brad felt it, too. His palm tingled from a force he'd
never experienced before. It was even more powerful than
the feeling he got when he gripped the steering wheel of
his race car. It was several moments before he trusted
himself enough to speak.

"Can we go now?"

"Give me a minute. I need to get my purse." Reluctantly,
Cori pulled her hand away and headed to her office.

She paused in front of the mirror mounted on the back
of her door and considered releasing her chestnut hair
from its ponytail. *Mikey always teases me about this ponytail,*
she thought. *He says it makes me look about twelve years old.*
After a moment, she shook her head dismissively. *That's
silly—my ponytail is fine. Besides, we're just going to walk around
town.* She went to her desk and pulled her purse out
of the bottom drawer. Quickly, before she could rational-
ize the impulse away, she fished out her lipstick and applied
the wine color. Looking again in the mirror, she wished
she had other clothes to change into. Fortunately, she
was wearing flat walking shoes. But her khaki pants and
embroidered T-shirt, which were fine for work, were not
quite good enough for a date. *Date?!* She startled herself
with the word. *This is not a date. It can't be, because I don't
date. This is Brad Marshall trying to get me to sponsor his race
team.* She gave a stern look at the reflection in the mirror.
And don't you forget it. After a deep, steadying breath, Cori
prepared to leave her office.

But as she reached for the doorknob, not even the stern
warning could stop the giddy anticipation she felt building
in her chest.

Chapter 9

Brad smiled as he saw her approach. "All ready to go?" he asked cheerfully.

Ready as I'll ever be, Cori thought. But refusing to give in to any negative thoughts, she returned Brad's smile and nodded. "I'm looking forward to it. You're right. It's about time I saw Charlotte."

Brad gestured for Cori to lead the way and then followed her out to the parking lot. Michael entered the dining room from the back just in time to see the pair leaving the restaurant. *Where are they going?* He hurried over to Jasmine and grilled the hostess for information.

"I don't know," Jasmine insisted. "All I know is he showed up here, asked for Mrs. Justice, she came out of the kitchen, they talked, they left together. She didn't say where they were going, or when they'd be back."

Michael's brow furrowed. "That's completely out of character for Cori."

"Well, nothin' like a fine man to make a woman do something 'completely out of character'," Jasmine said wisely. "And that is one fine slice of manhood." She rolled her eyes heavenward.

Michael looked curiously at the hostess, then at the door that Cori and Brad had just passed through. "I wonder . . ." he mused.

After donning a pair of wraparound shades, Brad started the Blazer. "We'll park near the stadium and walk into town." He turned and regarded his passenger closely. "It'll be a lot of walking, from one end of Uptown to the other. Sure you're up to it?"

"Oh, please," Cori said easily, "you're the one who drives around for a living. Bet you haven't walked any farther than from the garage to the track in eons. You'll get tired before I do."

"That sounds like a challenge," Brad teased.

"What if it is? Up to it?" Cori was enjoying bantering with him.

"Okay, you asked for it. I was going to take you on the short tour, but now, it's the whole enchilada."

"I have to be back by five-thirty for the dinner rush," Cori reminded him.

Brad checked his watch. "That gives us about three hours—not much, but we'll make do." He flashed her a reassuring smile and eased the Blazer into the traffic.

Cori felt a momentary twinge of panic as the truck began to move, but she took a deep breath and pushed it away. *No ghosts are going to ruin this day,* she resolved.

Anxious to find a distraction, Cori tried to anticipate the route Brad would take to get to Uptown. She was familiar with the neighborhood around the restaurant, but beyond that she would be lost. The street he was driving down would take them right past her church.

"There's my church." She pointed at the sprawling white building. "See, I know my way around to a few places."

Brad recognized the church as one of the oldest in town. "I would be impressed that you knew your way to your church if it were a little farther away," he teased. "As close as it is to the restaurant, you'd have to be wearing a blindfold over your eyes to get lost going there. And even then, you could probably just feel your way down the street and around the corner."

She laughed in spite of herself.

A few short minutes later, they reached Ericsson Stadium, and Brad found a parking spot in one of the nearby lots. Since it was not a game day, parking was plentiful.

Brad leaned forward in the truck and pointed out the front window. "This, Mrs. Justice, is the home of the North Carolina Panthers, the new kings of the NFL."

"The stadium is very impressive, but 'new kings?' I don't think so." Cori shook her head. "New babies of the NFL is more like it. Wait until you have some history behind you, like the Chicago Bears, before you start claiming royal status."

Brad's head whipped around to look at her. "You follow football?" he asked, impressed.

"I've been to Solider Field once or twice," she allowed. "I follow football enough to know that those Panthers of yours are more lucky than good." She grinned, knowing her words were baiting him.

"We'll just have to arrange for you to attend a game this fall," he countered. "Then you can see for yourself how good the Panthers really are."

She smiled and said nothing, but her mind was churning. *This fall is a long time away, Brad Marshall. Do you expect to still be a part of my life by then?*

Brad climbed out of the Blazer and crossed to Cori's side to open her door. "Come on. We've got a lot of ground to cover."

The pair headed down Stonewall Street. They had only walked a short distance when Brad stopped and pointed. Following his finger, Cori sighted a stunning light sculpture. Concentric rings of holographic panels circled a neon spiderweb. As she watched, the light pulsated and changed in a rhythmic pattern.

"It's beautiful," she breathed.

Brad quickly consulted a folded paper. "That's the Duke Power Company's building. The sculpture is forty-eight feet high, and was created by an artist out of California." While Cori's attention was still diverted by the sculpture, he shoved the paper back into his pocket. "Come on," he urged, "lots more to see."

With an effort, Cori tore her eyes away from the hypnotic lights. They continued down the street another couple of blocks and then turned on what was the busiest street Cori had seen in Charlotte so far.

"Where are we?" she asked.

"This is Tryon Street, one of the main arteries of the city. If you ever get lost in Charlotte, just make your way to Tryon Street and you'll be able to get home."

"Oh, I don't know about that," she countered. "If I don't know how to get home from Tryon, I'll still be lost."

"Yes," he nodded, "but with so many people on the street there's bound to be someone who can direct you."

"Southern hospitality again?"

"Yes, Ma'am," he drawled. "We cain't have a purty little lady like you wanderin' around lost."

She laughed at his exaggerated accent. "Okay, so tell me more about Tryon Street."

They proceeded on down the street, Brad pointing out landmarks and office towers along the way. After a few blocks, they reached a busy intersection.

"This is the center of town, the corner of Tryon and Trade Streets." Brad stopped and pointed at sculptures which were stationed at the four corners of the intersection. Each bronze sculpture was mounted on a pedestal high above the sidewalk.

"They represent Charlotte," Brad explained. "That one of a railroad worker stands for transportation, the textile worker is industry, the gold miner and the banker are commerce, and the mother holding her child represents the future.''

"The future . . ." Cori's voice trailed off as she lost herself in the statue. "Children really are the future, aren't they?" After a few pensive moments, she pushed away the familiar pain that was gathering steam in her throat. With an effort, she turned to face Brad.

"You are quite the tour guide. How do you know so much about Charlotte?"

"I've lived here all my life," he explained. "I ought to know something."

"Yeah, but the details and the history . . . how do you know all that?" Cori was genuinely puzzled.

Brad paused for a moment, considering. "Okay," he said finally, "I'll 'fess up. Before I came to Foster's to pick you up, I stopped by Info Charlotte."

"Info Charlotte?"

"It's the visitor's bureau. They have all kinds of information for tourists. I got this brochure—" he fished the paper out of his pocket—"that details all the Uptown points of interest. I·just wanted your tour to be as thorough and as enjoyable as possible."

"That's really sweet of you." Cori smiled at him. "But I don't get it. Why have you been hiding that brochure all afternoon?"

Brad's face split into a self-effacing grin. "Because I've lived in Charlotte all my life. I'm supposed to know these things, but I didn't. Figured I'd better learn quick if I was going to show you around."

Cori laughed, touched by the effort he'd gone to. "Maybe you have lived here all your life, but I'll bet this is the first time you've seen the town as a tourist. Tourists see things that residents take for granted. It's that way in every city. There's nothing wrong with not having memorized the date a church was built or the name of the artist who designed a certain sculpture." She reached for his hand and gave it a firm squeeze. "I really appreciate all you've done to make this afternoon special."

He looked deeply into her eyes. "And is it?"

"It is." She smiled at him, hoping he could see her sincerity. "Okay, Mr. Info Charlotte, what's next?"

A full, rich laugh bubbled up from Brad's throat. "Well, my brochure says that Founders Hall across the street there has, and I quote, 'three frescoes depicting the themes— making slash building, chaos slash creativity, and planning slash knowledge'—end quote. And there are a whole lot of shops in there, too."

"A whole lot of shops? Does your brochure say that?" Cori teased.

"Nah, I added that part myself." Brad grinned. "Want to go in?"

Cori rubbed her hands together with exaggerated enthusiasm. "Frescoes and shops? I'm there!"

The pair crossed the street and strolled around on the retail levels of the imposing office tower. They stopped in front of the huge frescoes, admiring the artist's work.

Brad had been completely honest when he'd admitted that he'd never seen Charlotte as a tourist. Normally, the sum total of his exposure to Uptown was through the Blazer's windshield as he zoomed through on his way to somewhere else. This trip to Uptown was as enjoyable and enlightening for him as it was for Cori. It was the first time in a very long time that he hadn't been consumed with racing or sponsors or winning. He felt an unexpected bit of civic pride pointing out highlights and details of his city, attractions he had sped past on countless occasions, more concerned with reaching a destination than enjoying the journey.

He turned his attentions to Cori, who was busily examining earrings in one of the shop windows. Her smooth, caramel-colored face, though almost devoid of makeup, was hauntingly beautiful. For the first time since he'd known her, her eyes did not seem so deeply saddened. *I'm glad she agreed to come on this tour with me,* he thought. He was seeing a whole different side to Mrs. Corinthia Justice, and he was growing more entranced by the moment.

"What do you think?" Cori's question broke into his reverie.

"What do I think about what?'

"Those earrings." Cori pointed at a pair of tropical fish earrings, elaborately decorated with brilliantly colored rhinestones.

"Well," Brad hesitated, "if you like that sort of thing . . ." His voice trailed off. He was at a loss for words; he didn't want to hurt Cori's feelings, but he had never in his life seen such a gaudy pair of earrings.

"Not for me." Cori's eyes gleamed with mischief. "For you. I thought they'd be great for catching the spectators' eyes as you speed around the track."

Brad was stunned into momentary silence. The look on his face made it clear that he thought she'd suddenly taken leave of her senses. Finally, Cori burst into peals of delighted laughter.

"Oh, that was priceless!" Cori sputtered between giggles. "You should have seen your face!"

Brad recovered quickly. "Well, it's just that those fish don't really match my driving jumpsuit. I think those would present a more coordinated look." He pointed out earrings that looked remarkably like miniature rhinestone chandeliers. "Except, it might be hard to get my helmet on over them."

"Oh of course," Cori nodded, "why didn't I think of that?"

Their laughter mingled and filled the air around them.

As they continued their window shopping, Cori reevaluated her opinion of Brad. His sense of humor and the easy laughter they'd shared opened up new facets of his personality. She was pleasantly surprised to discover that her initial opinion of him—a self-centered speed demon— had been undeserved.

Brad checked his watch. "It's getting late, and I promised you I'd have you back at Foster's in time for the dinner rush. There's one more place I want to show you, though. Are you game?"

Cori checked her watch, too, considering. "It's not *that* late. What's up next on my tour?"

"A couple of blocks up is The Discovery Place. It's a museum—no wait." He consulted his brochure again. "It's one of the nation's leading hands-on science museums, with a three story rain forest, an Omnimax theater, and a planetarium."

"Sounds like fun," Cori nodded. "Which way?"

Brad pointed, and the pair headed toward the museum. As they drew near, Cori's step faltered. Lined up in front, fidgeting anxiously as they waited to be admitted, were several dozen children. A yellow bus was parked nearby, suggesting a school field trip. The children were laughing and talking, orderly but just barely. While Cori watched, a woman she presumed to be the teacher emerged from the museum doors and gave the children the signal to proceed inside. The teacher probably would have preferred an orderly procession, but the children broke into full throttle runs and poured into the museum.

The sight of so many laughing children, who appeared to be the same age Brianna would have been, stopped Cori in her tracks. Brad, assuming she was waiting for the entrance to clear before they proceeded, stood patiently next to her, unaware of her inner turmoil. Cori was waiting, all right, waiting for the tears she was sure would soon well in her eyes, waiting for the lump in her throat that would restrict her breathing, waiting for the ache in her heart that would force her to relive her loss.

But this time it was different. This time she was able to keep her thoughts firmly rooted in the present and maybe—dare she even consider it?—the future. This time nothing seemed as important as continuing the adventurous, discovery-filled day she was enjoying with Brad.

After a moment, Brad turned to her. "Ready to go in?"

Her smile was dazzling. "Absolutely."

Once Brad had paid the admission, the pair went on their journey of discovery. Dozens of science stations were set up throughout one level of the museum so that patrons could learn about everything from astronomy to how sound travels. Brad and Cori played as enthusiastically as any of the schoolchildren. One of the exhibits was designed to show how a series of single drawings becomes a moving cartoon. To get the full effect, the viewer had to spin a drum and peer through holes in the side of the casing. Cori wandered over to the spinning drum, waiting her chance to see the moving pictures. She happened upon a little girl who was trying to make the experiment work. The child began to cry, frustrated with her inability to spin the drum and look in at the same time.

Cori knelt next to the girl. "What is it?"

Between sobs, the girl managed to choke out an explanation. "I can't see it. Jaime said it was really cool, but I can't see it."

"Maybe I can help," Cori offered. "I'll spin the drum and you stand right here." She positioned the girl in front of the drum. "Keep your eyes on the hole."

Cori started the drum, speeding it up until the drawings began to seem alive.

"I see it! I see it!" The girl excitedly clapped her hands. "Jaime was right—it is way cool!" After a few more moments, the girl straightened up from her peering position. "Thank you, Lady!" She ran off in search of her friends, anxious to share the experience.

Cori watched her disappear into the sea of children. *She's almost as pretty as Brianna was.* Cori stood silently for a moment, lost to the memories.

"So this is where you wandered off to." Brad's voice startled her back to the present. "We need to hurry if we're going to catch the movie."

Cori smiled weakly, not yet trusting her voice.

"Remember?" Brad prompted, "The Omnimax show? I told you we were going to see it. It's called *The Living Sea*. I don't really know much about it—except it's an IMAX movie, which means a huge screen and booming sound system."

"Well, let's go," Cori said after finally shaking off the creeping memories. "I wouldn't want to miss a booming sound system."

They eased their way through the museum and got in the movie line. Inside the cavernous theater, they selected seats near the center of a row—Brad was confident those were the seats with the best view. They sat in companionable silence for a few moments, waiting for the show to begin.

Finally, the theater grew dark and the movie began. It was a spectacular production focusing on the sea and its importance to all life on earth. Because of the enormous IMAX format, several underwater scenes created the sensation of actually swimming with schools of fish.

Cori had expected to be overwhelmed by the "huge screen and booming sound system," but instead found herself strangely calmed and relaxed. The film's sound track, especially, added to her sense of peace. New age music ebbed and flowed in perfect synchronization with the film's images.

Brad, too, was strangely affected by the film. His previous exposure to the IMAX format had been a movie about flying and speed that seemed to put the viewer in the front seat of, among other things, a speeding roller coaster and a screeching jet fighter. That experience had given him an adrenaline rush and left him feeling exhilarated. When Brad bought the tickets for this film, he'd expected to have that same kind of experience. But this movie gave him an entirely different experience. He was awed by the beauty of the sea and its inhabitants. He was impressed by the simple dignity of the natives from a remote island who had learned to live in harmony with the surrounding sea.

Even the New Age sound track reached into his spirit and soothed him.

When the movie ended all too soon, a collective sigh went up from the audience. Cori and Brad sat in their seats for a few more quiet moments.

"Wow," Cori breathed finally. "That was ..." She paused, searching for the right word.

Brad supplied the adjective that came to his mind. "... extraordinary."

"Exactly." Cori smiled at him, still feeling the peace she'd found during the film. "Thank you for bringing me here."

Brad noticed that for the first time since he'd known her her smile actually reached her eyes. The shadows of sadness that seemed to be such an integral part of her expressive brown eyes were gone. He reached over and gently placed his hand on her forearm. "Thank you for agreeing to come." He smiled in return.

By the time they rose to leave, the theater was nearly empty. As they made their way through the museum heading toward the exit, Brad stopped abruptly. Changing directions, he reached for Cori's hand and led her to the Discovery Place gift shop.

"What are we doing here?" Cori asked, perplexed.

"I saw something in the window I want you to have. Wait right here." Brad disappeared into the shop.

Cori browsed through souvenirs for a few moments, wondering what he was up to. Shortly, Brad returned and handed her a small bag. Curious, she slowly looked inside.

"Oh, Brad," she breathed, "this is perfect." She pulled out a cassette of *The Living Sea* soundtrack. "How did you know?"

"You just seemed so totally relaxed and—oh, I don't know," Brad said, searching for the right word, "—*serene* after the movie. I wanted to give you something that would help that feeling to last."

She could only shake her head in mute wonder. It was

the second time that day she'd found herself marveling at
his perceptive sensitivity. It was the last thing she'd
expected to find in a man who raced cars for a living.
Unable to find words potent enough to express her grati-
tude, Cori rose up on her toes and planted a kiss on his
smooth, ebony cheek. "Thank you . . . again."

Brad's hand slowly moved to touch the still warm spot
on his cheek where her lips had been. "Anytime . . ." he
whispered.

Suddenly uncomfortable with the intimacy of the
moment, Cori tore her gaze away from his. "It's getting
late. We'd better go."

Brad nodded and motioned for her to lead the way out
of the museum. They headed back down Tryon Street,
making their way to Brad's truck. In deference to the hour,
they walked at a much brisker pace than before. Still, along
the way Cori paid close attention to the sights they passed,
as if trying to etch the details of Uptown in her memory.
Soon, they were back in the Blazer, getting ready to return
to Foster's. Before Brad could put the truck in gear, Cori
handed him the sound track tape.

"Would you play this, please?"

Sensing that she needed to relax during the ride back,
Brad easily agreed. He popped the tape in the player, and
moments later the truck interior was filled with evocative
music.

"Ready?" he asked.

Cori nodded and leaned her head back against the seat.
She knew Brad's driving style well enough by now to feel
comfortable with him at the wheel. Wrapped in her cocoon
of music, Cori closed her eyes.

Brad looked at her, secretly pleased that she was relaxed
enough to close her eyes while he drove. It was a dramatic
difference from the white-knuckled rider she'd been the
first time.

By the time they arrived at Foster's, Brad thought she

had fallen asleep. But when he turned off the truck, the sudden quiet made her instantly alert.

"Back so soon." Cori blushed. "I was really enjoying the music. A few miles more, and I'd have been asleep."

"See," he teased, "I warned you the walk might be too much for you."

"Oh, please. It's just that I got up really early this morning," Cori protested. "I could walk circles around you any day of the week, Brad Marshall."

"Okay . . . prove it. How about I show you some more of Charlotte tomorrow?"

Cori hesitated for the briefest of seconds before nodding. "After lunch—before dinner?"

Brad smiled. "I'll be here . . . with my walking shoes on."

Cori unfastened her seat belt and scrambled out of the truck, anxious to avoid that awkward moment when a date ends with a kiss. "Don't get out," she said, stopping him, "I'll just see you tomorrow."

Puzzled, he watched her hurry through the back door. Then he remembered the tape.

"You forgot your tape!" he called, but she was already inside. Shrugging, he decided to leave it in the player so he wouldn't forget to return it tomorrow. He started the Blazer and headed for home. Suddenly, he realized the sponsorship situation had not crossed his mind all afternoon.

Michael was waiting to pounce on Cori the moment she returned.

"Where have you been all afternoon?"

"Out . . . touring Uptown . . ." Cori's face beamed with a private smile.

"Alone?" Michael prompted, although he was fairly certain of the answer.

"Not exactly."

Michael waited, but more information was not forthcoming. "Aw, c'mon Cori. I know who you were with. How'd it go?"

"Just fine, Mikey. Your Mr. Marshall is a very charming man." The enigmatic smile broadened. "In fact, I'm going to see him again tomorrow."

Michael was stunned into momentary silence. Then, his face split into a huge grin.

"Cori's got a date, Cori's got a date." Michael's singsong words were deliberately childish.

I guess I do, Cori thought—and smiled.

Chapter 10

Wednesday afternoon, when Brad showed up at Foster's, Cori was ready. For the day's outing she had put on a pair of walking shorts, a bright yellow knit shirt, and comfortable athletic shoes. Although she'd considered it, it seemed too much of a change to wear her hair down, so she compromised: a ponytail with a few loose curls framing her face. She brushed just the slightest touch of blush to her cheeks, and applied her favorite wine-colored lipstick. She was trying very hard not to look as if she were watching the door, but every few seconds she caught herself craning her neck to see the front entrance.

Mikey caught her, too. "He'll be here, Sis. Relax." Mikey's grin was mischievous.

Cori mustered righteous indignation. "I'm not worried about whether or not Brad Marshall shows up."

Michael said nothing, but displayed a smile that said volumes.

"Don't you have some work you should be doing?" Cori asked, exasperated. She was slightly annoyed at herself for the level of anticipation she felt. She was feeling like a giggly schoolgirl waiting for her date to arrive. *That's ridiculous,* Cori admonished herself. *I'm thirty-four years old . . . too doggone old for this nonsense.* But the stern words did nothing to stop her from checking her watch and watching the door. They had not set a specific time—"after lunch—before dinner" was fairly vague—but Cori expected he'd arrive at about the same time he had the day before.

At promptly two-thirty, Brad sauntered into Foster's. Today, Jasmine was expecting him, and led him to the bar while she went in search of Cori. Not that she had to search far. Cori was in the kitchen, peering out through the hole cut into the door. When she saw Jasmine approaching, Cori quickly busied herself arranging clean plates.

"Mrs. Justice, he's here," Jasmine announced.

"Who's here?" Cori asked with carefully affected nonchalance.

Jasmine's smile was knowing. "Brad Marshall. He's waiting for you at the bar."

"Thank you, Jasmine. Please tell him I'll be right out." Cori returned to her pointless task.

"Girl, go on out there." Michael's tone was loving but impatient. "Why are you hiding back here? You've been looking for that man to show up all afternoon."

"Michael Foster, mind your own business," Cori snapped. "I'm going." Having completed her dish rearranging, Cori emerged from the kitchen.

Seeing her approach, Brad rose from his bar stool and smiled at her, displaying beautifully white, even teeth. Cori felt a shiver of anticipation course through her body at the sight of him, dressed in well-worn Levi's, a white No Fear T-shirt and athletic shoes, his bald head covered by a Carolina Panthers baseball cap. Smiling, she walked over to him

"Hello, Mr. Info Charlotte. Where to today?"

"Well, there are a bunch of malls and antique shops around Charlotte. Since you enjoyed shopping so much yesterday, I thought we'd try those."

"Well, only if there will be jewelry stores." Cori cocked her head to the side. "I'm determined to find you a pair of earrings that will fit under your helmet."

Brad laughed heartily. "Well, at least you have a mission." He grew serious. "Cori, I'm afraid we're going to have to do a bit of driving to get to the malls. Is that going to be okay?"

Cori nodded, touched again by his concern. "I'm sure I'll be fine. I trust you."

Brad reached for her hand. "Then let's go."

They headed out to Brad's truck and got strapped in for the ride. Once he started the truck, Brad pushed *The Living Sea* soundtrack into the tape player. "You left this yesterday. I thought you might like to hear it again."

Feeling immediately soothed by the New Age music, Cori nodded her agreement. "You were absolutely right. Which mall are we going to?"

"There's a place called The Marketplace at Mint Hill. My brochure says it's a hundred year old landmark that's been upgraded to house the most unique specialty shops and antique stores." Brad guided the truck into traffic. "It sounded like an interesting place."

"You've never been?"

"Lord, no. I hate shopping. My mom and my sister are always fussing at me to buy some new clothes. I'd just as soon wait for Christmas or my birthday, 'cause I know they'll buy me something to wear." Brad smiled, thinking about his overprotective family.

"I've never heard you mention your family," Cori said. "Tell me more about them."

Brad shrugged. "Not much to tell. My parents live here in Charlotte, actually a little north of town in Concord. They're both retired, and loving every minute of it. My sister, Julie, lives in Concord, too, with her husband Malcolm and their four-year-old twins, Tyler and Taylor. And my younger brother Dwayne lives in Atlanta."

"That's quite a family. You're lucky to have your family so nearby."

"Yeah, I suppose so. I don't get to spend the kind of time I'd like to with them, especially the twins, but it's good to know they're only a quick ride away."

Cori's brow furrowed. "Atlanta isn't so quick a drive away. You must not get to spend much time at all with your brother."

"The less the better." The words slipped out before Brad even realized he'd said them.

Cori heard an unusual harshness in Brad's voice when he mentioned his brother. "Sounds like there's a story there. Do you and Dwayne not get along?"

"Let's just say we have some very different views about life . . . my life."

"What does that mean?" Cori asked, intrigued.

Brad hesitated, not really willing to talk about his debates with his younger brother. "Dwayne thinks he's found the secret to happiness and success, and I don't agree."

"The secret for whom?" Cori wondered. "Isn't that 'secret' going to be different for each person?"

Brad smiled at her, impressed. "That's exactly what I keep telling Dwayne, but he doesn't seem to see it that way. Basically, my brother thinks I'm wasting my life trying to make a living racing cars. He thinks I'd be much better off if I got a 'real' job in some office, pushing papers around on a desk." The disgust in Brad's voice left no doubt about his opinion of that plan.

"I'm sure he means well," Cori offered. "Maybe he's just looking out for his big brother."

"You know, his big brother can look out for himself." Brad's mouth was set in a stubborn line. "I will make a career out of racing. Dwayne's big mistake is assuming racing is just some kind of hobby for me. It's so much more than that."

Cori, remembering the passion she'd witnessed when he'd explained his craft, had to agree. She'd admired his intensity and purposefulness, but now, remembering those qualities gave her a jolt. *He needs your sponsorship, and don't you forget it, a* little voice in the back of her head nagged. *Don't fall for this charming routine. All he wants is your sponsorship, and he'll do anything to get it.* Cori froze for a moment, shocked and annoyed by the cynical voice of her subconscious. Then, with an effort, she decided to put those thoughts aside. "I'm just trying to have a good time," she murmured.

"Well, good." Brad glanced at her curiously. "That's my goal, to show you a good time."

Cori blushed; she hadn't realized she'd spoken aloud. Wanting to quickly change the subject, Cori said, "You've told me about your family, so what about your friends?"

Brad considered his answer a moment. "Well, I suppose Vern is my best friend. He can be a mean old coot, but he knows racing better than anyone I've ever met. He really keeps me on track . . . and I mean that literally and figuratively."

Cori smiled, enjoying the affection with which Brad spoke of his friend. "And what about women?" Cori asked boldly. "Any girlfriends who are going to be mad at you for spending this much time with a new sponsor?"

Brad's easy laughter filled the truck. "Girlfriends—plural? Who has time for girlfriends? I'm always either working on my car or driving *in* my car. Haven't met a woman yet who's willing to put up with that." They had reached their destination, and Brad parked the truck in the mall lot. After shutting off the engine, he turned in the seat to face Cori. "And I like to think I'm spending time with a new friend, not just a new sponsor."

Cori blushed and looked away from the intensity in his eyes. *Very smooth, Marshall,* the cynical voice in her head responded.

Brad briefly thought about Lisa—the track groupie, according to Vern. *Lisa is most certainly not a girlfriend.* But even as the thought crossed his mind, he knew she would be angry if she knew about the time he was spending with Cori. Shrugging his broad shoulders, Brad climbed out of the truck and crossed to the passenger side to help Cori.

When their eyes met again, the anxiety and doubt they were both experiencing fell away. For this moment in time, the only thing that existed was their new friendship—no sponsorships, no track groupies, no cynical little voices. When their eyes met, those negativities shattered like crystal on a marble floor.

"Let's go find some earrings," Brad said.

Her face lit with a beatific smile, Cori climbed out of the truck to follow.

They wandered around the Marketplace mall, neither intending to purchase anything, just enjoying being together and getting to know one another. Window shopping, as it turned out, could be very revealing.

Cori stopped in front of an antique store. In the window were a pair of Louis XIV chairs with ornately carved backs.

"Those are beautiful," she enthused. "They'd look just perfect in my office."

Brad scowled at the chairs. "Those spindly little things? Soon as a man sat down on them, they'd fall apart."

"Brad," Cori said, amused, "those chairs are easily a couple hundred years old. They've managed to hold up so far."

"That's because nobody ever sits on 'em," Brad huffed. "Everybody just looks at them and says, 'Ooh they're so pretty.' Give me real functional furniture any day."

"Functional furniture? Like what?"

Brad looked around the mall. "Like that." He pointed in the direction of a furniture shop across the mall. On display were a sofa and chair with overstuffed plaid cushions set in knotty pine frames. "Now's *there's* furniture a man can live with. You can plop down on them without worrying about breaking anything, and you can watch television with a beer and not have to worry about spilling on them."

Cori laughed. "Is the reason you don't have to be worried about beer spills because the fabric is god-awful ugly?"

Brad pretended to ponder for a moment. "Well, I suppose that helps. But in truth, as long as a room has a big screen TV in it, a man will sit on the floor."

"So furniture is incidental?"

"It's certainly not as important as electronics. If I have to choose between getting a couch and getting a stereo system, I'm going for the sounds."

"I bet your apartment is a sight to behold."

Brad's smile was slow and sultry. "You'll have to see for yourself."

Cori was mesmerized by his sexy smile and inviting eyes. She felt like a fly caught in the silken strands of a spider's web. She sensed danger was lurking nearby, but somehow the sensation of the silken restraints was so enticing that she just couldn't break away.

Get a grip, Girl! The man is trying to work a game on you. Cori shook her head, scattering the disquieting thoughts.

Brad interpreted her head shake as refusal of his not-so-subtle invitation. He wasn't sure how to accept Cori's imagined rejection. *Well, we are, after all, business associates,* he thought. *She's just not going to let it become anything more than that.* Feeling surprisingly disappointed, Brad moved away from the furniture shop. He needed a moment to examine that disappointment. Did he want more from Corinthia Justice than her sponsorship support? It was an answer he wasn't ready to face. He stole a look at Cori, still lingering in front of the furniture store.

Sure, she's beautiful, he thought, drinking in her warm, caramel complexion, elegant profile, and long, shapely legs, *but 'beautiful' is a dime a dozen. What is it that makes*

Cori so special? What is it about her that has me wandering around a mall in the middle of the afternoon, picking out furniture?

He had tried to pretend it was just the looming sponsorship question that led him to these uncharacteristic activities, but in truth they had not talked of the sponsorship once during their excursions around Charlotte. What, then?

Cori walked up to him, breaking into his meditation. "Penny for your thoughts?"

"Trust me." He laughed shortly. "They're not even worth that." He quickly changed the subject. "Would you like to stop and get a cup of cappuccino?" He nodded toward a gourmet coffee shop a little farther down the mall.

"Sure, " she agreed and started in that direction. Brad followed a step or so behind her, noticing for the first time the graceful glide of her walk and the gentle sway of her hips. *Stop it Marshall!* he admonished himself.

At the shop, he bought two frothy, cinnamon-flavored cappuccinos and they settled in at one of the nearby cafe tables to enjoy their drinks.

"So, I've told you all about my family," Brad said, "tell me about yours?"

Cori shrugged and sipped her coffee. "Well, you've already met my brother, and my grandparents live in Dilworth, not very far from the restaurant."

"You live with them, right?"

She nodded. "For now at least. And my parents still live in Chicago."

"Is that where you lived before you moved here?" Brad was genuinely interested in knowing more about the intriguing Corinthia Justice.

"Yes." Her voice dropped slightly. "I had lived there all my life."

"So what brought you to Charlotte?"

Cori hesitated, not sure how to best answer that question. "I needed a fresh start," she said finally. "And Gram and

Poppy needed somebody to take over the restaurant so they could retire. It was the perfect solution for everyone."

"But it had to be hard to pick up and move from a place you'd spent your whole life," Brad observed. "Not to mention moving to a town where you didn't know anybody. That's very brave."

"It wasn't all that brave." She gave a self-deprecating laugh. "It was more self-preservation. Chicago was starting to haunt me . . . I had to get away."

"Haunt?" Brad's brow furrowed at the unusual choice of words.

Cori sat back in her chair and looked away for a moment. When she finally turned her attention back to Brad, he could tell that the shutters that closed her off from the rest of the world had returned. She looked as distant and pained as she had when he first met her.

She seemed to struggle to get the words out. "I had a wonderful life in Chicago, but when it ended I was left with a huge hole in my soul." She paused again, gathering strength. For some reason, she wanted to—no, needed to—share with Brad. "I tried to rebuild my life there, but there were too many memories. Charlotte was the best alternative."

There were a thousand questions Brad wanted to ask, but he knew now was not the time. The revelations Cori had made so far seemed to have drained her; to push for more now would be a mistake. He realized that, and was willing to wait.

They sat together in silence for a few moments. Cori was grateful that he seemed to respect her need for privacy.

After a bit, Cori finally broke the silence. "It's getting late. I should head back."

Brad nodded. They left the mall without looking at a single pair of earrings. This time when they arrived at Foster's, Brad got out and walked Cori to the back door. "I'm sorry if asking you about your past ruined the afternoon for you. " He looked a little like a wounded puppy. "That was the last thing I wanted to do."

Cori met his eyes. "Please don't apologize. My afternoon was not ruined. I've had more fun these last few days than I've had these last few years." Her sincerity seemed to reach into his soul. "I need to get to the point where my past doesn't hurt me anymore, where the memories are joyful, not painful. I get a little closer every day." A thought too intimate to put sound to flashed in her mind. *And I wonder how much of that is because of you, Brad Marshall?*

Emboldened by her words, Brad decided to press his luck. "Can I see you again tomorrow? To show you more of Charlotte, I mean."

Cori smiled. "You mean there's more?"

"How do you feel about zoos?"

Cori only laughed and nodded.

When Brad returned to his condo there were three messages waiting for him. The first was from his brother Dwayne: "Julie tells me you're back on the track. I don't know whether to send my congrats or my condolences. How much longer can you keep this up? Just remember, Brad, whenever you're ready to get a real job I can make a few calls for you."

Bite me, Dwayne, Brad thought caustically.

The next was from Lisa: "I haven't seen you all week. Why haven't you called? You wouldn't be trying to avoid li'l ole me, now would you, Sugar?"

Brad shook his head. *Not so much "avoid" as "ignore",* *Sugar.*

The final call came from Vern: "A couple of track officials came by the garage today. They're preparing the race program and want to know if you're going to be competing for the track championship. I didn't have an answer for them. Is Foster's in or out?"

It was the last call that gave him the most pause. Vern's

message reminded him that his racing future was still very much up in the air. He needed an answer from Foster's, and he needed it soon.

But what effect will that have on my new friendship with Cori? Do I dare mix business with pleasure? In reality, can I afford not to?

Chapter 11

Thursday morning found Michael lingering over his coffee. He had waited for days for Cori to bring up the sponsorship situation, but she seemed to have forgotten its urgency. So when their grandparents left for their morning walk, he pounced.

"We're running out of time here," Mikey warned. "We've only committed to sponsor the team through the race Saturday. After that, if we don't continue someone else will snatch up our car."

Cori waved her hand impatiently. "Oh, come on. What's the danger of that happening? I thought one of the main reasons you were so gung ho for this sponsorship was because Brad needed the support."

"That was before he won. Now that he's got the momentum, especially if he wins again this weekend, I'll bet he won't have any trouble finding a sponsor to replace us. If that happens, we'll be the only ones who lose."

"This is a huge commitment you're talking about." Cori shook her head slowly. "I need more time to consider it. Unlike you, I can't make snap decisions."

"Snap decisions?" Michael leapt from his chair. "Cori, it's been nearly two weeks! How much more time do you need?"

"I need more information in order to make a good business decision. Poppy warned me not to make any decisions based on emotions. I can't just sign off on this sponsorship without some proof that it's worth the investment."

"What proof would convince you? And what proof would we have after only a week?" Michael sighed in frustration. "You've seen business pick up. You even met a couple who said they came in because they saw the restaurant's name on the car."

"One couple is not enough proof. And who's to say business isn't picking up because of the changes in the menu?"

Michael rolled his eyes in exasperation. "I swear, Cori, if I didn't know better, I'd say you were dragging your feet just to keep Marshall coming around!"

Cori's mouth dropped open, and her eyes flew wide open with a mixture of astonishment and anger. "That's ridiculous! I am not manipulating this situation. Brad Marshall keeps coming around on his own accord."

Michael made a face. "Look, Cori. I'm thrilled to see you getting out and enjoying yourself. I don't want it to sound as if there's a problem with that. But at some point—very soon—you are going to have to separate business from pleasure and make a decision. You can't just keep dragging this out."

Cori's head snapped around and she glared at her brother. "I already told you I'm not doing that. So what are you saying, Mikey? That the only reason Brad Marshall is taking me out is to butter me up?"

Michael shook his head vigorously. "Where did you get that? Why wouldn't Marshall want to spend time with you? You're intelligent, beautiful, and intriguing. But that doesn't change the fact that a decision has to be made," he said doggedly.

Reluctantly, Cori nodded. "Soon, okay?" But even as she spoke, she had to wonder if Mikey was right. *Am I stalling to keep Brad around? And what's going to happen once the decision is made?*

Brad started his day at Vern's house. He needed his friend's advice.

"Mornin', Cowboy." Vern opened the door wide for Brad to enter. "You're out bright and early today. What brings you by?"

Brad entered the living room, a virtual racing museum. Normally, he loved to look at all the pictures and read all the clippings Vern had collected over the years, but today Brad was too distracted to even notice them.

"I got your message last night," Brad began, "and I honestly don't know the answer. I'm not sure where Foster's stands, so I don't know if we'll be able to compete for the track championship."

Vern cocked an eyebrow curiously at the younger man. "As much time as you've been spending with Cori Justice and you don't know where Foster's stands? What y'all been doing all this time?"

Brad hesitated, considering how to answer the question. "I've been showing her around town, letting her get to know a little about Charlotte."

"And a little about you as well, eh?"

Brad chuckled slightly. "You know Vern, you were absolutely right before. The rules are different this time. I've really just enjoyed being in her company." Brad surprised himself with the revelation.

Vern nodded knowingly. " 'Bout time you got interested in someone other than those track groupies who keep following you around."

Brad shrugged. "But you see, there is my problem. My association with Cori started out strictly business—she was a sponsor I was trying to sign, and that was all." Brad's voice grew softer. "But now, she's more of a friend—"

Brad stumbled slightly on the word—"and I don't want to mess up the friendship by bringing business back into it. She accused me once of trying to butter her up. I denied it, but at the time it wasn't totally untrue." He looked plaintively at his mentor and friend. "But things changed, and I'm afraid that if I bring the sponsorship up again, she'll go back to thinking that all I've been doing these past few days is indeed buttering her up."

Instead of responding, Vern walked toward the kitchen and motioned for Brad to follow. He poured two steaming mugs of coffee from the old-style percolator he had warming on the stove. He set the mugs on his battered Formica-topped table and indicated Brad should take a seat.

"Let me see if I've got this right," Vern said finally. "You got your basic Catch-22 here. If you ask her about the sponsorship she'll think you've been trying to use her, but if you don't get the sponsorship you won't be able to finish the season. Right?"

Brad nodded, a forlorn look on his face.

"Well, have you been? Using her, I mean?" Vern studied his driver carefully.

"No, Vern. I swear to you I haven't." Brad's deep voice rang with sincerity.

"So what if she says no? Would you still want to see her?"

Brad didn't hesitate. "Yes, I would. I would be very disappointed, but I'd still want to spend time with her."

Vern's grizzled, brown face broke into a smile. "Then you got no problem here, Boy. You've just got to be real careful to keep the business and the pleasure separate."

"But how?"

"I can't tell you that. You know the situation better than I do. But you're going to have to talk to her about the sponsorship. It can't wait any longer." Vern's tone was intense. "Today, Brad. You need to talk to her about it today."

* * *

At the 2:30 time that had become customary for their outings, Brad arrived at Foster's. Cori met him at the door.

"Right on time, I see." Her voice carried a slight edge that Brad didn't recognize.

"I wouldn't want to keep the animals waiting. Are you ready to go?"

Cori nodded and headed out the door. They barely spoke on the drive to the zoo, both replaying the conversations they'd had earlier in the day.

Brad knew Vern was right about needing to talk to Cori about business, but he was waiting for just the right time to bring it up. He desperately didn't want business to ruin the day he had planned for them, but the sponsorship, even unspoken, loomed over them like some ominous cloud.

Cori could sense his hesitation and uneasiness. *He's thinking about it, too,* she thought, the cynical voice in her head emerging. *He knows, better than anyone, that time is running out. Bet he thought he'd have an answer by now, what with all this attention he's been paying to me.* Cori took a deep breath, trying hard not to succumb to the negative thoughts. She allowed herself one more reflective thought—*please don't let all this have been just about the sponsorship*—and then forced her attention to their afternoon outing.

Their time at the zoo was more strained than any other time they'd spent together since their first outing to the track. The weather cooperated, but the clouds created by their anxieties darkened the otherwise gorgeous day. Both of them sensed what was causing the tension, but neither was willing to face it head-on. Eventually, it was time to return to the restaurant. When they arrived at Foster's, Cori realized she was unwilling to let the day end without tackling the issue between them. Even though she still had no idea what her answer was going to be, she knew it was time to face it.

"I'd like you to come in and have dinner with me," she offered. "We need to talk, and now is as good a time as any."

Brad nodded his agreement. He could feel his anxiety levels rising exponentially. *Am I more nervous about asking her, or about hearing her answer?*

Trying to project a casual air he did not feel, Brad followed her into the restaurant. As soon as they entered, Michael approached.

"Cori, may I speak with you a moment—privately?"

"Mikey, Brad and I were just about to get a table for dinner," Cori protested.

"This'll only take a sec," Michael assured her. "Have Jasmine seat him and you can join him in just a minute. Brad, you don't mind, do you?"

"Of course not." *It'll give me a minute to collect my thoughts.*

Cori shrugged apologetically at Brad and then followed Michael to her office.

She jumped on the offensive as soon as the door was shut behind them. "Look, Mikey, I know what this is all about. That sponsorship is all I've thought about all day, but I'm still not ready to decide."

"Well, maybe my news will help you decide." Michael pulled out her chair and motioned for her to take a seat. "While you were out today, a reporter from *The Charlotte Observer* called. A sports reporter, to be specific. He was at the race last week and saw Brad win. He wants to do a story on—wait a minute, let me remember his words exactly—'that exciting African-American driver.' "

"That's nice, but what does it have to do with us? Why did he call here?"

"Cori, you're being deliberately dense." Michael shook his head impatiently. "It has everything to do with us. He called here because part of his story is going to focus on Brad's sponsor. The way the reporter explained it, he wants to develop the African-American angle—driver and sponsor breaking into a predominately white sport. He sounded very enthusiastic about it all."

"Why now?" Cori asked skeptically. "I thought Brad had been racing for years. What makes this reporter want to write about him now?"

Michael's eyes shone with excitement. "That's the best part. The reporter said that Brad has created quite a buzz around the circuit, and is being considered by one of the major NASCAR Winston Cup teams. That's the big time, Sis. The reporter has followed Brad's career for a while, and he's convinced a big feature story will raise Brad's visibility, making him even more attractive to NASCAR." Michael leaned in closer to Cori. "And raising Brad's visibility can't help but raise his sponsor's visibility. Is this proof enough for you? Can you make a sound business decision now?"

"Does Brad know about this reporter?"

"I don't think so. The reason the guy called here was that he couldn't find Brad at his garage." Michael snapped his fingers as if remembering one final point. "Oh, and he wants to run this story in Sunday's paper. So you see, Sis, there simply is no more time. Are we in or out?"

Cori sat silently. Her eyes drifted to the picture frame on her desk. After an interminable moment, she nodded. "Okay, Mikey, we're in."

"Excellent!" Michael's whoop of joy could be heard out in the restaurant. "First, let's go tell Brad, and then we've got to have a party. Tomorrow night, we'll invite Brad's race team and that reporter to come to the restaurant, and we'll celebrate!"

"Whoa, Mikey. Slow down a minute." Cori put her hands up in front of her. "First, let *me* go tell Brad. If you don't mind, I want him to hear it from me." *I need to see his reaction,* she decided.

"Sure, Sis. Whatever you want. But we **are** going to have a party. Just leave it all to me. Tell Brad to plan to be here around six tomorrow evening. We'll get all the paperwork

out of the way first, and then we're gonna PAR-TAY!"
Michael practically danced out of her office, hurrying off
to attend to his plans.

Cori sat alone at her desk for a few moments longer.
She leaned back in her chair, her eyes staring at nothing
in particular. Having finally made the commitment, she
was now unsure how she felt about it. *It's not the speeding
car part of it all,* she decided. *I accept that racing is a legitimate
sport with a huge following. And it's not the money. I can see
that this sponsorship might ultimately make money for the restaurant.* She drummed her fingers on the arms of the chair,
trying to pinpoint the source of her uneasiness. After a
few moments of ruminating, her mind finally accepted
what her heart already knew. *This might very well be it,* she
mused. *After I tell Brad the "good news" this might be the last
I see of him. Except, of course, in the paper or in a burgundy
streak at the races.*

She pushed away from her desk and rose from the chair.
Mouth set in a determined line, she reached for the doorknob. *If that's the way it's going to be, then that's the way it's
going to be. Better to find out the truth now, before I get in too
deep.*

She took a deep breath, then went to face the music.

When Brad saw her approaching, he stood to greet her.
In her absence, he'd decided that he had to bring up the
sponsorship, however awkward that might be; he absolutely
had to know.

"Everything okay?"

Cori nodded. "Mikey had some news for us."

"For us?" Brad looked at her, curious. "What news?"

She watched him closely. His face held no guile or trickery. Whatever happened from this point on, Cori realized
she'd had a wonderful time with Brad Marshall and nothing would change that.

"Seems there is a reporter from the *Observer* who wants
to do a story on you and your sponsor. He called here

because he couldn't find you. Mikey says it's to be a feature story in Sunday's sports section."

"Oh?" Brad struggled to control his rising excitement. "A story on me *and* my sponsors?"

Cori nodded. "So Mikey pressed me for a decision on the sponsorship."

"And?" Brad could barely stand the suspense.

"And after careful consideration, I have decided that a race car with Foster's name on it is a good idea, after all." Cori beamed. "You can count on us."

Brad's whole body seemed to smile. He felt a thousand pounds lighter. A heavy burden had just been pushed off his head. He reached for her hands. "Thank you, Cori. You have no idea what this means to me. I promise you will never regret your decision." He pulled her close to him, wrapping her in a bear hug. Shafts of happiness and elation emanated from his very core, piercing through the armor Cori tried to maintain. Before she realized it, her arms slid around his firm midsection and she returned the hug. For a moment, she lost herself in the sensation of being so close to him. She took a deep breath and smelled his uniquely masculine scent, a mind-altering combination of cologne and "eau de Brad." A few moments later she regained control of her senses and released him. Brad held on to her for a second longer than necessary before he reluctantly freed her from the circle of his arms.

"Oh, I forgot to tell you." Cori was slightly breathless, "Mikey wants to have a party tomorrow night to celebrate the sponsorship, and he wants you and the whole crew here. The reporter will be here as well, since he wants to run his story in this Sunday's paper."

Brad shook his head in wonder. "I can't believe all this is happening," he murmured. *It's finally all clicking into place,* his mind celebrated. *It's going to work!*

Cori watched the play of emotions across his face. It seemed equal parts joy and amazement.

"I guess you probably want to go tell Vern and the team

the good news," she offered. She took a deep breath and steeled herself against the disappointment she was sure would come next.

It took Brad a moment to come down off his cloud and refocus his attention on her. Slowly, his face softened into an alluring smile. "That can wait," he said, his voice a throaty whisper, "right now I have dinner plans with a beautiful woman."

Cori returned the smile. *Maybe there* is *more to us than just a racing sponsorship, after all.* She sat at the table and prepared to enjoy her dinner.

Chapter 12

For the party Friday, Michael pulled out all the stops. Friday was typically one of the restaurant's busiest nights, but for the celebration of the association of Foster's Restaurant and Brad Marshall Racing, the dining room was especially full. For the party guests—which included the racing crew and their dates, the *Observer* reporter, and Mabel and William Foster—Michael had ordered the chef to fix a special selection of appetizers. Waiters circulated among the crowd with trays of crab puffs, bacon wrapped chicken livers, vegetable pizza, and caviar, among other things. Other waiters were charged with the responsibility of ensuring everyone always had a full glass of champagne.

"Quite a party, Son." William Foster complimented his grandson. "You must be spending a fortune tonight."

"My goodness, yes," Mabel agreed. "Caviar, Michael? Chips and dip wouldn't do?"

Michael grinned at his grandparents. "C'mon, Poppy. Weren't you the one who told me you've got to spend money to make money?"

" 'S'pose I did, at that," William agreed. "But are you sure all this is going to make money?"

"Poppy, I've never been more sure of anything. If you could just see those crowds at the races—" Michael caught sight of Brad. "But don't take my word for it. I want you to meet our driver." Michael waved for Brad to join them.

Michael made the introductions. "Mabel and William Foster, I'd like you to meet Brad Marshall, our driver. Brad, these are my grandparents and the founders of Foster's."

Smiling warmly, Brad extended his hand and greeted the Fosters. "This is a great restaurant you've got here. I've eaten here a couple of times and I've enjoyed it immensely."

"Thank you, Young Man," William replied. "Michael was just telling us what a great investment he's made in you."

"I hope he told you it would be great for all of us," Brad answered easily. "Stock car racing has a huge fan base around here. I'm confident the restaurant will get lots of exposure to new customers."

Mabel had watched Brad intensely during the men's conversation. She noted with approval the fine fit of his black pants and cream Henley shirt. "So you're the one who's been squiring our Cori around town, eh?" she asked shrewdly.

"Gram!" Michael protested, "What does that have to do with the sponsorship?"

"I don't know," she said slowly. "Mr. Marshall? What **does** it have to do with the sponsorship?"

"Not a thing, Mrs. Foster," Brad answered instantly. "I really just enjoy being in Cori's company. And it's been a lot of fun showing her around Charlotte. I've seen things this last couple of weeks while I was playing tour guide that I haven't seen in all my years of living here."

"Good." Mabel nodded her approval. "I mean it's good for Cori to get out more. She was working herself to death."

"Are you talking about me behind my back again?" Cori

walked up to her grandmother and kissed her lightly on the cheek.

"Not really. I was just thanking Mr. Marshall for getting you out of the restaurant every now and then."

"Uh-huh," Cori said skeptically. "Brad and Mikey, that reporter is ready for you now. He's over by the bar."

"Thank you." Brad turned to the Fosters. "It was truly a pleasure meeting you. I hope to see you again soon." He and Michael went to be interviewed.

Mabel watched his retreating back. "The pleasure was all mine." She grinned.

"Gram, what are you up to?" Cori asked.

Mabel mustered indignation. "Not a thing—stop being so suspicious. I can't help it if I admire that gorgeous man. I'm old, not dead."

After shooting an amused look to his wife, William added his observations. "He seems like a very nice young man, Cori. It's good that you're spending time with him."

"Don't push, you guys. Whatever will be, will be."

Mabel's hand fluttered to her chest. "What, us push?"

Cori was about to respond when she was interrupted by the dinging sound of silver against crystal.

"Ladies and gentlemen, if I could have your attention please." Michael stood up on a chair to be heard. "We are all here tonight to celebrate a new partnership. Foster's Restaurant and Brad Marshall Racing have joined forces, and together we're going to take the racing world by storm!" The audience applauded enthusiastically. "After we sign these contracts, it'll be official. Cori, Brad, would you join me at the bar?"

Approaching from opposite ends of the room, Cori and Brad reached Michael's side at the same time. Michael handed Brad a pen and pointed to the contract lying on the bar. "Brad, if you would, please." Brad applied his distinctive signature.

"Now you, Cori," Michael instructed.

Brad handed her the pen. Cori hesitated for the briefest

of seconds, and then, with a dramatic flourish uncommon for her, signed her name. She noticed Michael's signature was already there. *I wonder how long ago he signed?*

"It is now official—Brad Marshall is racing for fame, fortune, glory . . . and Foster's Restaurant." Michael led the audience in a round of applause. He signalled one of the waiters, and the man approached carrying a large box. "I have a little something for the race team," Michael announced. He reached into the box and produced a burgundy baseball cap with the oval Foster's Restaurant logo stitched in gold and a matching burgundy T-shirt. A cheer went up from the crowd.

"Thank you all for coming and sharing this celebration with us. Please feel free to stay as long as you'd like—there's plenty of food and drink left." Michael climbed down from his perch on the chair.

"Brad, would you mind passing out these hats and shirts to your crew?" Michael asked.

"Hey, no problem. Thanks again, Man. I promise I won't let you down." Brad grabbed the box and headed over to his crew.

"T-shirts? Hats? You had to have ordered these things a long time ago," Cori reasoned.

"Guilty as charged."

"You must have been really sure of yourself—or should I say sure you'd be able to convince me to go along with you."

Michael's smile was relaxed and confident. "I was sure that you are too good a businesswoman to pass up such an amazing opportunity." Michael leaned down and kissed her cheek.

"Oh, pretty smooth, Mikey." Cori grinned. "Pretty smooth."

By then, Brad had returned. "Cori, can I talk to you for a moment?"

Michael, taking the hint, left them to go rejoin the party.

"What's up, Brad?" Cori asked.

"Can we go to your office? I'd like a little privacy."

Cori cocked her head and regarded him curiously. She shrugged after a moment. "Sure. Right this way."

Cori held the door open for Brad to enter. She followed him inside and turned to make sure the door closed completely. Then she turned to face Brad and was immediately pinned against the door by his masculine presence. He reached for her, taking her face in his hands. Before she could draw a breath, his full, firm lips were pressed against hers, triggering all the electricity of a mega-watt lightning bolt. Her eyes widened in surprise. She wanted to protest, but Brad's tongue, warm and insistent, traced a pattern on her closed lips, urging them to open. Cori gave herself over to the warmth spreading from the center of her soul and radiating out to all parts of her body until even her fingertips felt the heat. Her eyes drifted closed, and her hands eased up his taut stomach until they rested on his heavily muscled chest. And slowly, sensuously, her mouth parted, welcoming the probing warmth of his tongue.

Suddenly, Brad's hands were everywhere—on her face, in her hair, down her sides. He pressed against her, pinning her between the solid hardness of the door and the growing hardness of his body.

Her hands traveled up his neck, caressing the smoothness of his shaven head. The kiss continued until it reached a blistering intensity. Their tongues and hands and bodies conveyed a message of need and urgency that neither could get their mouths to speak of.

Finally the kiss ended, leaving Cori dizzy and off balance. Slowly, she opened her eyes and looked at him with questions clearly etched in their brown depths.

"I should probably apologize for that," Brad said huskily, his breathing just returning to normal, "but I can't. I have been waiting to do that for so long. I was afraid I would explode if I didn't kiss you . . . and soon."

"And was it worth the wait?" Cori asked.

"It was beyond my wildest dreams," Brad answered honestly. "You move me to distraction, Corinthia Justice." He boldly pressed his body against her, leaving her with no question of his arousal. "Can't you tell?"

Cori smiled up at him, pleased to be the source of his stimulation. "Is this why you wanted to get me alone in my office?" she teased. "So you could seduce me?"

"Well, yes and no," Brad answered cryptically. "I definitely wanted to get you alone, but not to seduce you . . . well, not completely." He dipped his head and tasted her lips once again.

Cori swallowed deeply, trying to find her voice. "Where did all this come from?" She hoped her voice sounded normal. "One minute we're signing contracts and the next we're . . . we're . . ." She hesitated, unsure of how to characterize the last few minutes.

"And the next minute we're all over each other," he supplied helpfully. "I told you I couldn't wait another moment."

Cori ducked under his arms and moved away from the door. His nearness was compromising her ability to think rationally. "So was it the contract signing that caused you to lose your self-control?" She leaned against the corner of her desk and crossed her arms protectively in front of her chest.

"Hardly." He followed her to her desk, again closing the space between them. "I didn't kiss you beforehand because I didn't want you to think my kissing you was a part of some strategy to get your sponsorship." He reached for her hair and twirled a lock around his finger. "And I was afraid to kiss you after the contracts were signed, because I didn't want you to think that I kissed you because of the sponsorship." He leaned in close enough for his lips to leave featherlight touches on her cheek as he talked. "But then I decided that I wanted to kiss you—needed to kiss you—and to hell with how it might appear."

Cori nuzzled her face against his. "So, what now? Plan to do it right here on the desk?"

His voice was a sensual rumble in his throat. "I want you, Cori. I want you bad. But when I make love to you, it won't be a stolen moment locked in your office. I am going to take my time, and love you thoroughly from the top of your head to the bottom of your feet." He drew his fingers along her jawline and down her throat. "When I make love to you, it will be the most special night of my life."

Her skin tingled where his fingers had been, scattering her coherent thoughts. "You seem very sure of yourself, Mr. Marshall," she managed. "What makes you so confident that you are going to make love to me?"

"Because confidence is how I make my living. I can't be tentative or hesitant in my line of work. And I live my life that same way." He gently stroked her cheek. "When I decide what I want, it's really just a matter of time."

Cori found herself absolutely mesmerized by this ebony-skinned, baldheaded Adonis. She was unable to respond, so captivated was she by his touch.

"And I think," Brad's rumbling voice continued, "that our time is coming soon. Like maybe tomorrow, after the race."

Sanity returned to Cori. "Tomorrow? After the race? Wow . . . you really are confident. I had no intention of going to the race tomorrow . . . or of doing anything afterward."

Brad reached for Cori's hands and pulled them close to his lips. She could feel his warm breath graze her knuckles. He brushed her hands with a light kiss. "I know you don't like that kind of thing, but would you please come to the race tomorrow? You'll be my lucky charm."

Brad pulled her closer to him. Cori felt as if she were weightless, floating free in the air until her flight was stopped by the solid wall of Brad's broad chest. He released her hands and encircled her waist, gently crushing her against him. Her newly freed hands caressed his chest and slid up to his shoulders. She gently kneaded the firm cords of muscle across his shoulders. Brad bent closer to her, his eyes heavy-lidded with desire.

Cori experienced no anxiety, no guilty twinges, and no disquieting thoughts. All she knew as her head dropped back was that this beautiful man was about to kiss her again, and there was nothing she wanted more.

Brad gently pulled at her lips, tasting their sweetness. Their tongues mingled, exploring and experiencing each other. Cori's arms tightened around his neck, pulling him even closer, deepening the kiss even further. She felt transported out of her body; she was no longer a corporeal being, but a sensual mist existing only for this moment.

When finally the kiss ended, both Brad and Cori were shaken by its passion. When the power of rational thought returned to him, Brad realized there was still a question on the floor.

"Will you come to the race tomorrow?"

Cori looked up into his eyes, which were almost black with intimate intensity, and melted. "I wouldn't miss it for the world."

Chapter 13

"C'mon Cori! We're gonna be late!" Michael stood at the foot of the stairs urging his sister to hurry.

In her room, Cori heard Michael's call but was too engrossed in her preparations to respond. *What does one wear to a race?* she wondered. She stood in her underwear choosing from various articles of clothing strewn across the bed. The day was too hot for jeans, and a race was too casual for most of her work clothes. *The olive-colored walking shorts might work,* she thought, *but do I have enough time to shave my legs?*

Cori had a chuckle at her indecision. It was so unlike her to spend more than a couple of minutes deciding on clothes. Normally, as long as the clothes fit and were clean, she threw them on and went to tend to the business of the day. But for this occasion, Cori was agonizing over her clothing choice.

"This is silly," she said. Annoyed, she snatched the shorts off the bed and pulled them on.

"Cori, if you don't come on, I'm going to leave you!"

Michael's shouting cleared away the fog and forced Cori's attention to the matter at hand.

"Just wait a minute, Boy. I'm almost ready" A quick look at her long, caramel-colored legs convinced her that she wasn't in desperate need of a shave. She threw on a cream tank shirt and tucked the tail in the waistband of her shorts. She slipped on a pair of olive green mules and hurried over to open the door.

"I swear, Mikey, you act as if they can't start the race without us." Cori returned to her dresser and began combing her hair.

"Just come *on!*" Mikey tapped his foot impatiently. "I don't want to miss the beginning. That's when they announce the drivers and the sponsors."

"Okay, Okay, I'm coming." From force of habit, Cori began to pull her chestnut hair back into a ponytail. But then, the image of Brad releasing her hair from its restraints and reveling in its soft fullness flashed before her eyes. A slow, sultry smile spread across her face. Cori put the ponytail holder back on the dresser top and pulled the brush through her hair. After a few strokes, her hair emitted a healthy glow. Aware of Michael's impatience, Cori quickly finished up with her preparations and grabbed her purse.

"All right, let's go." She wagged her finger at her brother. "But I swear, Mikey, you'd better drive like you've got some sense."

An exasperated huff met that command. "Don't I always? Now, if you're through primping, come on!"

Cori opened her mouth to protest—*I don't primp*—but stayed silent. *Guess maybe I do, a little,* she allowed. With a private smile on her face and in her heart, Cori hurried out to her brother's car.

The CD that had been playing ended; the sudden quiet in the apartment jarred Brad back to the present. He checked a nearby wall clock. *Damn,* he muttered. *I'm going to be late.*

He hurried through the rest of his preparations. As he reached for the doorknob to leave his apartment, Brad paused and allowed himself one more personal thought. *This one's for you, Corinthia Justice.*

By the time Cori and Michael reached Carolco Speedway, the cars were already lined up in their starting positions. By virtue of having won the week before, the Foster's Chevrolet was in the pole position. Cori looked for Brad, but couldn't find him amid all the people milling around on the track.

Michael led her to the section reserved for sponsors and team owners, a section of grandstand near the track directly across from Victory Lane.

"Best seats in the house," he said proudly. "See, membership really does have its privileges."

"It's a little close, isn't it?" Cori asked anxiously.

"Don't worry." Michael motioned toward the fifteen foot high fencing in front of the stands. "That fence will protect us from any flying debris."

"Oh, thanks a lot, Mikey." Cori made a face at him. "That makes me feel much better."

Michael pointed across the track. "Look, there's Brad."

Cori felt her heart lurch a bit as she followed her brother's pointing finger. Then she saw him, and felt her heart lurch a lot. Brad's already commanding presence was made even more so by the fitted driving jumpsuit. She felt a surge of pride when he turned his back, and she caught a glimpse of the restaurant's logo emblazoned on his back.

It's sort of like my brand, she giggled to herself. *You're a marked man, Brad Marshall.*

He turned back to face the crowd and scanned the stands. For one electric moment, Brad and Cori's eyes met, and all the passion of the night before surged between them. There could be no denial of the almost visible current that linked their eyes and thoughts.

After a moment, he waved. The crowd cheered, responding to his acknowledgment. For her part, Cori simply nodded. It was enough; he saw.

Brad walked over to his car and retrieved his helmet from inside. He took a deep breath and cleared his mind. He forced his thoughts away from Cori and onto the business at hand. He stood next to his car, helmet tucked under his arm, head bowed. He looked for all the world as if he were praying. In his mind's eye he visualized the track, seeing himself steering through the turns and barreling down the straightaway. It was the exercise he usually did in the morning over his power breakfast, but this morning his visualizations had taken him someplace else.

Vern approached from Pit Road to run the last minute safety checks on the car. "Ready to go, Cowboy?" Vern's question broke into Brad's concentration.

"I was born ready, Old Man." Brad's voice rang with confidence. "How's my girl this morning?"

"You mean the car, right?" Vern chuckled slyly. "I only ask because I couldn't help noticing our new sponsors in the stands."

"Yes, Vern, the car." Brad chose to ignore the other observation. "How's my **car** this morning?"

Immediately, Vern put the teasing aside and became all business. "Boy, whenever I work on this car, she's gonna be in tip-top shape. What say you just keep her that way? I'm running out of Band-Aids to put on her."

"Relax, Old Man. I'll take good care of her. But I'm gonna give our sponsors their money's worth." Brad put the helmet on and adjusted the headset. He climbed into the driver's seat and fastened the various safety restraints. Vern reached in and made a few last minute adjustments. After assuring himself that everything was ready, Vern gave Brad a 'thumbs-up.'

Brad returned the gesture. "See you in Victory Lane."

Vern grinned, impressed as always by his driver's supreme confidence, and returned to his spot on Pit Road. He put on his headset and ran a test.

"Ready to rock and roll, Cowboy?"

Brad smiled. "I love it when you talk dirty to me."

Vern laughed. Brad's spirit and confidence were infectious. "Focus, Boy. It's almost show time."

Confirming Vern's warning, the starter's voice boomed over the loudspeaker. "Gentlemen, start your engines!"

Immediately, the roar of twenty-five stock car engines filled the air. In the stands, Cori resisted the urge to cover her ears. She sat very still, concentrating on remaining calm. She refused to allow a replay of her last visit to the track. Michael, also remembering how upset she'd been when she'd returned from her track tour, watched his sister carefully. After a moment, he reached for her hand.

"Okay?"

Cori nodded and squeezed his hand reassuringly. "Don't worry about me." Her jaw was set in a determined line. She was absolutely committed to seeing this race through to the finish.

The cars started their pace lap, the Foster's Chevrolet in front. When the pace car pulled off, the cars sprang to life. The roar was deafening as the cars accelerated to their racing speed. Cori watched, fascinated, as Brad pulled away from the traffic behind him. The crowd around her was on their feet, screaming their encouragement. Their actions struck Cori as odd. First of all, it seemed highly unlikely to her that the drivers could hear anything from the stands, and second, the race was scheduled for 150 laps. But those facts did not stop the crowd from roaring their approval as Brad passed in front of them. Cori craned her neck this way and that, trying to see the action on the track, but her view was blocked by the forest of fans standing around her. Finally, Cori rose to her feet.

If you can't beat 'em, join 'em. She sighed.

* * *

Out in front of the pack, Brad was able to floor the accelerator with no concerns about traffic. Moments later, he moved into The Zone, a sublime level of consciousness where he was one with his car. It was as if he could think a movement or maneuver and the car would execute it. Brad had often been called an instinctive driver, and it was these moments in The Zone that confirmed that assessment. His headset was silent. Even Vern could tell that Brad needed no coaching right now.

Twenty-five laps into the contest, Brad was still out in front. He was beginning to lap the slower cars. Suddenly, his headset crackled to life.

"There's a crash coming out of turn two," Vern warned. "You'll have to come around on the inside to avoid it."

"Got it." Brad did as he'd been instructed and was able to get around the debris without incident. The yellow flag came out, signaling a caution on the track. Brad, along with most of the drivers on the lead lap, took that opportunity to come in for a pit stop. As soon as Brad pulled in to his pit area, a team of men swarmed around the car, adding gas, checking tires, and cleaning windows. Vern handed Brad a sipper bottle filled with a sports drink.

"Looking good out there, Cowboy," Vern said. "You're gonna need to watch out for turn two now. It's gonna be slick after that crash."

Brad nodded and returned the bottle. Within seconds, the team was finished and Brad peeled out of the pits.

In the stands, Cori had missed seeing the actual crash; her eyes were following Brad around the track. All she saw was the aftermath as the remaining cars deftly avoided the debris. That sight was enough to cause her jaw to tighten and her fists to clench. She could feel the familiar panic begin in her throat. *NO!* she screamed in her mind. *Go away!* She unconsciously lifted her fists, ready to battle some unseen foe.

Out of the corner of his eye, Michael caught the subtle movement. He turned to look at his sister and saw a look on her face he did not recognize. He expected the pained, haunted expression that had become so much a part of her during these last five years, but that was not what he saw. Etched on Cori's face was grim determination. She looked ready to do battle if necessary.

Michael reached for clenched fists. "It's okay, Cori. Look, Brad is fine. That wasn't his car in the crash."

Cori felt the tension drain from her body. The panic had passed and she'd come out on top. "Yes, I know," she whispered. "Brad's fine, and so am I." Feeling more relaxed than she'd ever thought would be possible around cars again, Cori settled in her seat to watch the rest of the race.

The track was cleared and the green flag came back out. Brad pushed his car further into the lead, anxious to put more distance between him and the rest of the pack. He felt the car fishtail slightly as he accelerated through the turns, but quickly brought it back under control.

Brad shifted into the highest gear and aired out the engine. He sailed past the grandstands, oblivious to the cheering crowds. In his rearview mirror he saw one of the rival cars closing in on him.

"Car number twelve coming up fast!" Vern's voice confirmed Brad's observation. "Stay low on the turns and you should be able to hold him off."

Brad grunted in response. He was pushing his car as hard as he dared, and there was still nearly half the race left to go. In a split second, Brad made a strategic decision. He eased up on the gas, drawing the number twelve car, driven by his friend Cliff Roberts, even closer. He allowed Cliff to pass him on the outside, and then pulled in behind the number twelve.

"Drafting, eh Cowboy?" Vern's voice filled his head.

"Aren't you the one who taught me two cars can move faster than one?" Brad yelled the response.

"Well, yeah, but who knew you were listening?"

The race continued, with the lead changing hands every few laps. Although Brad periodically dropped out of the lead, he was never any further back than fifth. The race was almost picture perfect. Except for that earlier crash, there were no other incidents. Soon, it was time to run the last few laps.

"Okay, Cowboy," Vern alerted his driver. "Five laps left. Time to go for it."

"With five laps left to go?" Brad's voice held a teasing reprimand. "Vern, that's not very exciting for the fans. I've got a little time left before I need to bring it on home."

"Don't play out there, Boy. Just wrap it up and finish it off."

"Patience, Vern. Patience."

Vern huffed his disapproval but held his tongue. He'd worked with Brad long enough to trust the driver's instincts.

With three laps to go, Brad decided it was time to make his move. He pulled to the outside and pressed the accelerator, calling up the power he'd held in reserve. Quickly, he moved from fourth place up to second, right on the bumper of Cliff Roberts's number twelve Ford. Two laps left found Brad and Cliff jockeying for position. Cliff weaved across the track, trying to block Brad from passing. As they zoomed past the starter's position, the white flag was waved, signaling the last lap.

Traveling at speeds in excess of 130 mph, Cliff and then Brad approached the treacherous turn two. As he had done all afternoon, Cliff eased up on the gas, expecting Brad to do the same. But Brad, who had practiced for just this moment, floored the accelerator, headed for the outside lane, and screeched past a flabbergasted Cliff Roberts. After that, it was just a question of speed. Brad held off the challenge, crossing under the checkered flag milliseconds ahead of the second place finisher.

The crowds in the grandstands went wild. The race was

more exciting than anyone had anticipated. Cori and Michael were jumping up and down as enthusiastically as everyone else.

"We won!" Michael shouted, hugging Cori. "We won!"

The announcer blasted the race results over the loud-speaker, creating the kind of moment that had convinced Michael of the value of racing sponsorships.

"And the winner is tonight's pole sitter, Brad Marshall, in car number thirty-four, the Foster's Restaurant Chevrolet!" Brad took a celebratory lap around the track before heading to Victory Lane.

"Come on Cori." Michael pulled on her hand. "Let's go down and congratulate our driver."

Cori resisted his tug. "We can't go down there," she protested.

"Of course we can, we're the sponsors. That's our car! Come on!" Michael led the way through the crowd down to Victory Lane.

Brad parked the car and was immediately surrounded by well-wishers. As he climbed out of the car Vern ran up to him and heartily slapped him on the back. "Nice driving, Cowboy! That was a pretty gutsy move there at the end. One of these days . . ." Vern's voice trailed off.

"But not today, Old Man!" Brad hugged his crew chief. "Not today!" Brad looked around the growing crowd, try-ing to spot one particular caramel-colored face framed with shining, chestnut hair. Then he spotted her, trailing behind Michael. He smiled in anticipation of her reaching his side.

A tap on his shoulder pulled his attention away from Cori. He turned to see who was behind him. Then sud-denly, unexpectedly, arms were flung around his neck. Before he could protest, a warm pair of lips locked with his in a passionate kiss. Startled, Brad stared wide-eyed into the face of the kissing bandit.

Lisa! The name exploded in his mind. *What is she doing?*

The catcalls of his crew urged Lisa on. The kiss lingered,

seeming to last for much longer than necessary. Finally, Brad was able to break away.

"Congratulations, Sugar." Lisa's voice was a husky whisper.

Brad smiled weakly, feeling cornered by Lisa's audaciousness and the good-natured cheering of the surrounding crowd. He looked around for Cori, desperately afraid she had seen Lisa's performance.

She had. Cori stopped dead in her tracks, the smile melting off her face. The sight of Brad locked in a passionate kiss with this unknown woman shook Cori to her very essence. *Less than twenty-four hours ago, those lips were kissing me, talking about making love to me,* she thought, outraged. *How could he?*

Told you he was running a game on you, girl. The cynical voice in her subconscious had resurfaced with a vengeance. *He was after your money . . . got that, and a whole lot more . . . and now it's back to business as usual.*

Cori experienced a feeling that was totally foreign to her, even with her intimate knowledge of pain—the pain of betrayal. Tears stung at her eyes. *It took me five years to find a man who could make me feel again,* her mind screamed, *and now look at him!*

Michael, who hadn't seen the kiss, was steadily trying to work his way to Victory Lane. He checked to make sure Cori was still behind him and saw her, standing stone still in the middle of the milling crowd.

"What's up? Why aren't you coming?"

"Take me home, Mikey."

"What?" Michael regarded her with a stunned look on his face. "Why?"

"Never mind why. Just take me home right now, or so help me I'll walk." Cori's mouth was set in a thin, stubborn line.

"Well, at least let's go congratulate Brad before we leave," Michael pleaded.

"No, Mikey. Now. I want to go now." Cori turned on her heel and started toward the parking lot.

Michael's head spun between his sister's retreating back and the celebration happening in Victory Lane. He didn't know what had set Cori off, but he knew his sister well enough to know she would make good on her promise to start walking if he didn't drive her home. Frustrated, Michael changed directions and hurried after her.

Trapped in Victory Lane by the ardent Lisa and a throng of celebrating well-wishers, Brad could only watch in despair as Cori stalked off.

Chapter 14

Brad awoke early Sunday morning, restless from his uneasy sleep the night before. He'd come right home after he left the track, in no mood for a victory party. Not even Lisa's impassioned coaxing could persuade him to go out. Normally after a race, especially a winning effort, Brad Marshall was the first one in line for an all-night celebration. But after what happened with Cori, a party was the last thing on Brad's mind.

The question that had kept him from sleep assailed him yet again. *What must she think of me? I have to see her,* he decided. *I have to explain.*

After a quick check of his clock, Brad knew it would be several hours before he could catch Cori at the restaurant. Since it was Sunday morning, she wouldn't come in until early afternoon. *After church. . . .*

In his mind's eye, he could see the sprawling white church Cori had pointed out to him during one of their sightseeing trips. Even as the thought occurred to him, Brad knew what he had to do.

* * *

Cori went through her preparations for church woodenly, her heart filled with equal parts sadness, hurt, and anger. The sight of Brad locked in a passionate kiss with that beautiful stranger kept flashing in her mind.

But I guess she isn't much of a "stranger" to him, Cori thought ruefully. *They obviously know each other.*

The whole scene seemed to confirm all her worst fears about Brad Marshall and his intentions. *Just as I suspected. I was a means to an end for him. And to top it all off, he must have been lying when he said he didn't have a girlfriend. . . .*

Cori shook her head sadly. *And I was beginning to really like him, too.* Seated at her vanity table, studying the brown eyes that stared back at her, Cori shrugged.

"The contracts have been signed, and the restaurant is committed, so I'll make the best of that." Cori spoke the words with a conviction she didn't quite feel. "But from here on out, Brad Marshall is strictly business to me."

Resolution made, Cori hurried through the rest of her preparations. She did not want to be late to church today. There were some special prayers she wanted to send up.

Brad didn't know what time services began, so he decided to get to Cori's church as soon as possible and just wait. If luck was with him, he would be able to catch her before she went inside. If not, he was ready for that, too.

He stood in front of a mirror in his bedroom, straightening his tie. He felt slightly uncomfortable in the black, double-breasted suit; he hadn't worn it since his grandfather's funeral a year before. Brad wasn't much of a suit man; this was one of the few he owned. He was infinitely more comfortable in jeans and T-shirts. But he was committed to seeing Cori today, and if that meant wearing a suit and going to church, so be it.

After slipping into his suit coat, he was ready. *Hope the sight of me coming to services doesn't cause that old church to collapse.* He grinned ruefully.

By the time he arrived at the church, services had already begun. Brad entered the vestibule and found himself with a group of about a dozen latecomers. The doors leading to the sanctuary were closed. He fidgeted for a moment, unsure of what to do next. Then he was greeted by one of the ushers.

"Welcome to First Baptist," the smiling older woman said. "Is this your first visit with us?"

"Yes, Ma'am." Brad smiled at her gratefully.

"Then would you please fill out one of our visitor's cards?" She handed him a postcard-sized form and a pen. "When you've finished, I'll take care of it. You'll be able to go inside in just a minute. Pastor is praying right now."

"Thank you." Brad accepted the card and went over to a nearby table to fill it out.

The usher watched his fluid movements admiringly. *If I were twenty years younger. . . .*

Brad quickly filled in the blanks on the card. One space, however, gave him pause. *Guest of. . . . Can I be her guest if she doesn't even know I'm here?* After a moment's hesitation, Brad scrawled in the name Corinthia Justice.

He returned the card to the waiting usher. She scanned it quickly.

"Oh, you're a friend of Cori's?" Her voice betrayed her surprise.

"Yes, Ma'am. Could you tell me if she's here yet?"

"Well, I haven't seen her, but I'm sure she's here somewhere," The usher replied. "Cori has been very faithful since she joined church."

'Been very faithful. . . .' The image from Victory Lane of Cori's shattered expression rose once again to haunt Brad. *What must she think of me now? What can I say to make this right?*

Finally, the doors were opened from within and the

latecomers were admitted. Although the church was nearly filled, there were a few seats scattered about. Brad craned his neck as subtly as he could, trying to find Cori in the crowd, but he didn't see her. Disappointed, he took a seat near the back of the sanctuary. Because he was late, the aisle seat was already claimed. He had to step over a few people to get to a seat in the middle of the pew. He tried to make as little commotion as possible, but being unobtrusive was impossible for a man of his height and build.

Several pairs of appreciative female eyes watched every move of the darkly handsome, bald stranger. One of the observers watched, not so much with appreciation as with anxiety.

What is he doing here? Cori had to make a conscious effort not to scream the question out loud.

Once all the latecomers were seated, the service resumed. Still unable to locate Cori, Brad decided to concentrate on the proceedings for now. *If she's in here I'll find her,* he promised.

He found the services surprisingly inspirational. The main reason for his appearance in church this morning was to speak to Cori; in his mind, the program was incidental. But then the choir sang a soul-stirring song about grace and mercy, followed by the pastor's powerful sermon on personal responsibility and faithfulness. Before he realized it, Brad had been moved.

The morning services were nearly wasted on Cori, however. The peace and serenity she regularly found in church were compromised by the presence of Brad Marshall. She tried to concentrate on the pastor's message, but she couldn't stop her mind from wandering—to the back of the church, to be exact. She kept trying to hold on to the righteous indignation she'd so carefully nursed ever since the end of the race, but seeing the strikingly handsome figure Brad cut in that black, double-breasted suit stirred her in ways that had nothing to do with religion.

Soon, the sermon ended, and it was time for the part of the program where announcements were read and visitors were officially welcomed. The smiling usher who had initially greeted Brad came up to the front of the sanctuary and read from the visitor cards she'd collected. There were six visitors other than Brad. As each name was read, that person was asked to stand and say a few words to the congregation. Brad watched the proceedings with growing panic. Having to stand and speak before a room full of strangers was the last thing he had expected. All too soon, his name was called.

"Pastor Henry," the usher announced, "our next visitor is Brad Marshall, the guest of Sister Corinthia Justice."

After taking a deep, calming breath, Brad stood. "Good morning. My name is Brad Marshall. I came to visit your church today because of my friend, Mrs. Justice. I could see the joy she feels here on her face, and I wanted to experience it for myself. Thank you for the kindness you've shown me in welcoming me to fellowship with you." Relieved, Brad sat down amid a hail of "amens" and a round of applause.

"Welcome, Brother Marshall." The pastor's voice boomed down from the pulpit. "I read an article today in the *Observer* about an up-and-coming stock car racer. Are you that Brad Marshall?"

Suddenly, Brad was feeling very exposed. He had completely forgotten that article was coming out today. Slowly, he stood again to answer the pastor's question. "Yes, Sir."

"The article also said Foster's Restaurant is Brother Marshall's major sponsor," Pastor Henry announced to the congregation. He turned to Cori, in her customary seat about four pews from the front. "Bless you, Sister Justice, for looking after not just this man's business, but his soul as well."

Still standing, Brad looked in the direction where Pastor Henry had addressed Cori. He finally saw her. Their eyes locked, and a torrent of emotions was unleashed. The mixture of anger, remorse, betrayal, and contrition that passed between them was almost palpable.

Slowly, reluctantly, Brad took his seat. The remainder of the program passed fairly quickly, and soon the congregation was milling about, socializing on their way out of the church. Several members approached Brad with good wishes and words of welcome. He smiled, nodded, and charmed everyone who took the time to speak to him, but a part of his attention was always on Cori. Once he'd located her in the sanctuary, he'd kept an eye on her movements. He was not going to let her avoid talking with him.

As it turned out, his vigilance was unnecessary. After the pastor's announcement linking her with Brad, Cori decided it would generate too much gossip for her to leave without speaking to him.

After the crowd around him thinned, Cori walked up to Brad. "I hope you enjoyed the services."

Brad looked at her closely. "The services were very inspirational. But that's not the only reason I came."

Cori lifted her chin. "Well, if you came for any other reason, then you've wasted your time."

"But it was my time to waste. Besides, a couple of hours in fellowship can never be a complete waste of time, can it?"

Cori nodded, conceding the point. "Well, I'm sure you'll be welcomed back for fellowship any time." She made a move to leave.

Brad's hand shot out and grabbed her arm, stopping her departure. "Welcomed back by whom?" His voice was low and intimate. "What about you, Cori? Will you welcome me back?"

Cori blushed and lowered her lashes as the double meaning behind Brad's words became clear.

Brad pressed his advantage. "I'd like to talk to you."

Eyes blazing, Cori snatched her arm from his grasp. "What else do you want from me?" she hissed. "You already have my money. That's all you were after anyway, so why won't you just leave me alone?

Brad looked hurt. "That's not true. And this has nothing to do with the sponsorship. This is about you and me."

"There is no you and me. You drive a car with my business's name painted on the side, and that's where it ends."

"Maybe that's where it ends for you," Brad said, "but that's not where it ends for me. This isn't over . . . not by a long shot."

"Just do your job, Mr. Marshall. Drive real fast and win a lot of races so you can keep making that trip to Victory Lane. I know how much you enjoy that." Cori spun on her heels and stalked away. Dejected, Brad left the church.

Once he got home, Brad's phone rang off the hook. Seems everyone in Charlotte had seen the article, and they all wanted to congratulate him. But Brad, in a black mood, didn't want to speak to anybody. Actually, there was one person he desperately wanted to talk to, but couldn't. To avoid subjecting everyone else to his foul mood, Brad turned on his answering machine and let it handle all calls.

He sat slumped in the leather recliner in his den. The big screen TV was on, but muted. Absently, he flipped through the channels, looking at but not seeing the images that flickered before him.

The phone rang again and he heard the machine pick up. After the beep, his sister Julie's voice filled the air.

"Congratulations, Sweetie! That was some article! I bought some extra copies and I'm going to send one to Dwayne. I want him to see how well you're doing. Call me later."

Brad scrambled to reach the phone before she hung up. Hearing Julie's voice made him suddenly not want to be alone anymore.

"Julie, Julie. I'm here—don't hang up."

"Brad? You're screening calls?" Julie sounded confused.

"It's been a little crazy here today, what with that article and all. Are you going to be home later?"

"Yes. . . ." Now Julie was curious. "Malcolm's out of town on a business trip, so the kids and I were just going to hang out here and probably barbeque later. Why? What's up?"

"I think I just need a hug." Brad smiled, thinking about his niece and nephew. "Tell Taylor and Tyler that Uncle Brad is on his way."

Brad hung up the phone and grabbed his keys. He'd changed out of his "Sunday-go-to-meeting" clothes earlier and was dressed in a T-shirt and jeans. *Perfect for wrestling with the kids.* He smiled. He checked his freezer and found a pair of T-bone steaks. *My contribution to the barbeque.* He tossed the steaks into a plastic grocery bag. With an unexplained sense of urgency, he slipped his feet into a pair of sneakers and hurried out to the Blazer.

All the way out to his sister's house, he kept his mind deliberately blank. *I'm tired of thinking about Mrs. Corinthia Justice,* he decided. *It's giving me a headache!*

Soon, he turned onto the cul-de-sac where Julie and her family lived. It was a picture-perfect suburban setting: split-level house, manicured lawn, colorful flower beds, children's toys scattered about the yard. For just a moment, Brad was wistful. As he approached Julie's house he couldn't help wondering what his life would be like now if he had chosen a different path. Then, as if they were living entities with a consciousness separate from his own, his thoughts wandered back to Cori. A picture formed in his mind with his truck parked in front of the two car garage and Cori coming out to greet him. His brow furrowed as he forced the unsettling vision away.

Having regained his equilibrium, Brad pulled into Julie's driveway and honked the horn. Immediately, the door flew open and his four-year-old niece and nephew spilled out.

"Hi, Uncle Brad!" The twins raced out to meet him.

Brad climbed out of the truck and dropped to his knees.

He wrapped the bouncing twins in a bear hug. Their matching faces nuzzled each side of his. He could feel the love radiating from their little bodies warm his soul and wipe away his disappointment from earlier in the day.

Julie leaned against the door frame and watched her brother and her children. *What is going on with you, Brad?* she wondered silently. It was fairly uncommon for Brad to drive all the way to her house in Concord on the spur of the moment. And she couldn't remember the last time he'd admitted to needing a hug. After a few minutes, she headed out into the yard to join them.

"Got a hug for me?"

Brad tried to stand to hug his sister, but the energetic twins had climbed onto his back. He took a moment to secure them on either hip and then stood. "Hi, Julie. My arms are a little full right now. Will you settle for a kiss?"

Julie laughed and presented her cheek for his lips. "Come on in, Little Brother, and take a load off." She pinched her daughter's smiling cheek. "And I mean that literally."

Brad laughed and followed her into the house. Even though Julie's married name was Crawford, it was clear from looking at her that she was a Marshall through and through. Though not quite as dark as her brothers, Julie's complexion was a beautifully rich chocolate. She wore her black hair natural and carefully trimmed in a box-shaped Afro. Julie was a little round through the hips—"baby fat" she still called it, despite the fact the twins were four years old. Julie's face was marked with the same chiseled cheekbones and piercing eyes that made her brothers' faces so distinct. And when she smiled, which was quite often, Julie's perfectly straight, brilliantly white teeth gleamed.

"All right, Brad," she said after he'd put the children down and settled on the couch, "what brings you all the way out here? And what's this business about needing a hug?"

"I've had a really hard couple of days, and I needed to

forget about it all for a while." Brad's voice held a pleading note. "Can we not talk about it right now? Right now, I just want to play with my niece and nephew."

Although she was burning with curiosity, Julie decided to respect her brother's privacy. "Whenever you're ready, you know I'm here."

Brad nodded gratefully.

"Why don't you grab the kids and meet me out back?" Julie suggested. "I'm going to fire up the grill and start dinner."

For the rest of the evening, Brad distracted himself with the demands of family. He and the twins wrestled and played in the grass until the children were so exhausted they could barely keep their eyes open. In between rounds with the kids, Brad tended to the grill, keeping a close eye on the steaks until they were cooked to perfection.

After dinner, Julie hustled the children upstairs for their baths. Brad grabbed a beer from the refrigerator and settled in on the sofa to await her return. He was channel surfing with the remote when Julie finished the bathing detail.

"Taylor and Tyler swear the only way they're going to go to bed is if Uncle Brad tucks them in," she announced. "Do you mind?"

"I'd love to." Brad followed her up to the kids' room. At the doorway, she stepped aside and allowed him to enter.

He walked over to the bunk bed and reached for the covers on the top bunk. "Good night, Tyler." Brad pulled the Power Rangers bedspread up to the boy's chin. "Sleep tight." Tyler rolled onto his side and scrunched up into a ball. " 'Night, Uncle Brad."

Brad then kneeled next to the lower bunk. Taylor already had her Beauty and the Beast coverlet up around her chest. She reached for Brad and wrapped her arms around his neck. " 'Night, Uncle Brad. I love you."

Brad felt his heart swell against his ribs. "I love you too,

Sweetheart. Now get some sleep. I'll see you soon." He kissed his niece's forehead. He stood and headed out of the room.

Julie, who had stayed at her position at the entrance, turned off the lights and closed the door. Thoughtfully, she followed her brother into the family room. He plopped back down in his previous spot and resumed his channel surfing. Julie changed directions and went into the kitchen to pour herself a glass of wine. Glass in hand, she returned to the family room and took a seat at the other end of the couch from Brad.

"Okay," she said finally, "ready to talk about it now?"

For a moment, Brad considered feigning ignorance—*Talk about what?*—but then he decided he really was ready.

"I took your advice about my new sponsor, Cori Justice," he began. "I spent some more time with her, and we really started to connect."

"That's a good thing, isn't it?"

"Yeah, but. . . ." In terse tones, Brad told Julie about the incident at the track.

"So who is this Lisa, anyway?" Julie asked. "Why haven't I heard you mention anything about her?

"Why would I mention anything about her?" Brad demanded, irritated. "She's not anybody special. Vern once called her the Flavor-of-the-Month."

Julie's eyes widened in shock. "Brad! that's awful. Is that how you treat women?"

Brad made a face. "Aw c'mon, Julie. Lisa and I are both consenting adults, and I never made any promises. I am what I am—free, single, and over twenty-one."

"And you really wonder why Cori's upset?"

"Cori overreacted," Brad snapped. "She never even gave me a chance to explain."

"Explain what? About track groupies and Flavors-of-the-Month?" Julie shook her head. "Believe me, Brad, that would not win you any points with Cori."

"But it's not like that between Cori and me." Brad

hesitated for a moment, trying to sort out and explain his feelings. "There's more to us than that . . . at least there could be . . . I think."

"Let me tell you what I think. Cori is feeling used and betrayed. From where she sits, it looks like you just used her to get a sponsorship and now you're back to your old habits."

Brad opened his mouth to protest, but Julie cut him off. "Let me finish. It's going to be up to you to make things right between you two again. You're going to have to prove your sincerity, or else that relationship is dead in the water."

Brad sat quietly, processing her advice. "I don't know, Julie. Maybe it's not worth it. I mean why should I expend all this effort trying to square things with Cori when there's a ready supply of Lisas out there?"

Julie looked at him for a long, hard moment before answering. "Brad, it's so obvious that you want more than that out of life. I mean—look at you. You came all the way out here because when you were down, you needed a hug. You've spent the whole evening playing with the kids and enjoying a taste of family life. You don't want to spend your life in meaningless associations with Lisas. You have to try again with Cori, Brad. If you don't, you'll regret it for the rest of your life."

Brad lowered his head and ran his hands across his smooth scalp. He took a deep breath as he grappled with Julie's words. Finally, he raised his head, looked his sister in the eye, and nodded.

Chapter 15

The Monday lunch rush at Foster's truly lived up to its name. The restaurant was packed, both in the dining room and out on the verandah, and there was even a waiting list for tables.

Michael was nearly bursting at the seams from excitement. "See Cori, I told you the sponsorship was a good idea. All of these people came to check out the restaurant because of that article in yesterday's paper."

But Cori, busily handling cash register duties, couldn't share his enthusiasm. "It sure seems to be paying off," she conceded. "Let's hope this keeps up and it's not just a fluke."

"Ah, that's where the food comes in," Michael pointed out. "You've always said if we could get people to eat here just once, they'd be customers for life. Well, now's your chance to prove that theory."

Cori nodded.

"By the way," Michael asked, "what time is Brad coming by today? I'll bet some of these people would love to meet him."

Cori turned her back to him and busied herself with the cash register. "I don't imagine Mr. Marshall is coming by today. Or any other day, for that matter."

Michael looked confused. "Why?"

Cori whirled around to face him, her eyes blazing. "Why would he? He got his sponsorship. What else would he be coming around here for?"

Michael was stunned by the vehemence behind her words. "What's going on with you two? You have been acting funny about Brad ever since the race Saturday. What happened? I thought you two were getting along so well."

"Nothing happened, Mikey," Cori said flatly. "Mr. Marshall was trying to close a business deal. Once the deal was made, his business here was completed."

Michael made no attempt to hide the skepticism on his face. "I don't believe that, and neither should you."

"Okay, fine." Cori said shortly. "You keep your eye out for him. Just don't expect him to show." She slammed the cash drawer with more force than necessary and walked away.

Puzzled, Michael watched her departure. *What on earth is going on between Cori and Brad?*

Out at the track, the same question had formed in Vern's mind. He watched Brad go through the motions of practicing, but it was obvious his heart and mind were elsewhere.

"Bring 'er in, Boy," Vern radioed to Brad. "You're just wasting time and gas."

As Brad pulled the car into the garage, Vern impatiently tapped his foot. When finally Brad climbed out, Vern lit into him.

"What's going on with you, Boy? You drove that car like my grandmother today."

Brad shrugged shortly. "It was just an off day, that's all. My mind's somewhere else."

"Well, you damn well better get it back in that car before this weekend. Because of that article yesterday, some scouts from a couple of the NASCAR teams are planning to come to see you perform." Vern turned a stern eye on his protégé. "This could be it for you, Cowboy. Your invitation to the big show. But you could blow it completely if you don't get your head together."

"I hear you, Vern." Brad tossed his helmet onto the driver's seat. "I'm wiped today. I'll see you tomorrow." Brad turned and walked away, leaving a frustrated and concerned crew chief behind.

As he was pulling out of the track parking lot, Brad considered heading to Foster's to try again to speak with Cori. He sat in the truck at the track gates undecided. In his mind's eye, he could see Cori as she had looked yesterday morning at her church. He involuntarily recoiled, remembering the anger and hurt he'd seen blazing in her eyes. *Not today . . . I'm not up for it today.* Shaking his head, he started home.

Closeted in her office, Cori watched the relentless march of time on her digital clock—2:20, 2:25, 2:30, 2:35. *Mr. Marshall's customary arrival time has come and gone,* she noted grimly. *Just as I thought. All that time together, all that touring around town—just a means to an end.*

Disgusted, Cori grabbed her purse out of the bottom drawer of her desk. She jerked the door open and headed out into the restaurant. The main crush of the lunch rush had passed. *I'm not just going to sit around here all afternoon waiting for him to appear,* Cori decided. She found Michael behind the bar.

"Mikey, I'm going out for a while. I'll be back by dinner."

Michael smiled and looked around the dining room. "Is Brad here? I didn't see him come in."

"No," Cori snapped, "Brad is not here. Why would you ask me that?"

"Well, you said you were going out. I just assumed—"

"Assuming. That was your first mistake. I'm going out alone. Is that all right with you?" Without waiting for his answer, Cori turned away and stalked out through the kitchen.

Somebody's in a mood today, Michael mused.

Cori walked home, using the short distance between the restaurant and the house she shared with her grandparents to cool off. When she arrived at the house, Mabel was in the den watching her soap operas.

"Who's there?" Mabel called.

Cori stood in the doorway of the den. "It's only me, Gram."

"Cori? Girl, what are you doing here this time of day?"

"I just needed to get out of the restaurant for a while. We were really busy today, and I needed a break."

"Oh, I see," Mabel said slowly. "Really busy, eh? You suppose that article about your racing friend in yesterday's paper had anything to do with it?"

"I wouldn't know," Cori said shortly. "Mikey certainly seems to think so."

Mabel regarded her curiously. "Come on in here and talk to me, Girl." She clicked off the TV and patted a spot on the sofa. "Come on . . ."

Cori heaved a sigh and did as her grandmother instructed. "What do you want to talk about, Gram?"

"You tell me. You've obviously got something on your mind. It's not like you to come home in the middle of the day like this."

Cori hesitated, unwilling to talk about Brad's duplicity. But the more she thought about it, the more sense it made. Cori had always trusted her grandparents' opinions. She was sure that once Mabel heard the whole story about Brad she would agree that Cori had been used. Then she could use her grandmother's support to reinforce the armor she was trying to erect around her heart.

"I guess I do have a lot on my mind, Gram," Cori began. "It's about Brad."

Mabel nodded. "I figured as much. What happened?"

Cori gave Mabel the condensed version of the previous week's events. When she came to the encounter in Victory Lane, Cori's voice cracked slightly. Gulping in a gasp of air, Cori was able to finish her story.

"So you see, Gram, he was just using me all along. All he wanted was that sponsorship, and he was willing to do anything to get it." Cori shook her head in disgust. "And to think, I almost fell for him."

Almost? Mabel thought, but wisely kept that to herself. "So why are you so upset? I mean, since you didn't fall for him?"

"Gram! Because he used me. Can't you see that? He pretended to be interested in me as a woman, when in truth he was only interested in me as a payday."

Mabel shook her head. "I talked to that young man at the party, and that was not the impression I got. He seemed very sincere, and he genuinely seemed to have enjoyed the time you two spent together."

Cori made a snorting sound. "Well, of course he seemed sincere. That's what makes this whole situation even worse. He tricked me."

"You know, Cori, maybe he could trick you. But he couldn't have tricked me." Mabel looked her granddaughter square in the eye. "I'm a lot older than you, and a lot less susceptible to a handsome man's charms. When I spoke with him at the party, I asked him point-blank if the sponsorship and your apparent relationship were connected in some way. Sweetheart, I can tell you with all confidence that the man I talked to was not trying to trick you."

"But you didn't see him at the track Saturday," Cori protested. "You just don't know him like I do, Gram,"

"Maybe you don't know him like you should. And maybe you're blowing whatever happened at the track that day all out of proportion."

"Gram, you just don't understand . . ."

"Oh, I think I understand just fine," Mabel said shrewdly. "You are mad at this Mr. Marshall because you saw him kissing another woman, and you felt like he was betraying you by doing so. Am I understanding so far?"

At Cori's silent nod, Mabel continued. "You believed you were building a relationship with this man, and yet you have not given him the opportunity to explain what happened at the track. You have drawn your own conclusions and convicted Mr. Marshall without the benefit of a trial. Am I still understanding?"

This time, Cori's nod was slow in coming.

"Notice, Darling, that I have kept the sponsorship out of my understanding of the situation. I don't believe the sponsorship has anything to do with this. That's business. This is personal." Mabel's voice softened. "Brad seems able to keep the two separate, and so should you."

Cori sat quietly for a moment, lost in thought. "You're right, Gram. I will keep the two separate." Cori's eyes took on a determined gleam. "From now on, Brad Marshall is just an employee to me. Hopefully, the restaurant will profit from the association, and that will be the extent of my involvement with Mr. Marshall." She leaned over and kissed her grandmother's cheek. "Thanks, Gram. You've been a big help." Cori stood and left the den, leaving Mabel sadly shaking her head.

"That's not what I was trying to get at," Mabel mumbled.

For the rest of the week, Brad and Cori busied themselves with the myriad details of their daily lives, but neither one completely blocked out thoughts of the other.

Vern tried desperately to get his driver to focus. The night before that weekend's race, he went to Brad's condo for one more pep talk.

"It's really going to happen, Cowboy," Vern said enthusiastically. "I've talked to the track owners and the scouts from NASCAR are definitely coming this weekend. Now, he didn't say they were coming to see you, but that's where the smart money is." Vern watched him for a reaction. "Well, Cowboy, what do you think?"

"That's great, Vern. I'll try to do my best." Brad's response was lackluster at best.

"I don't get it. I thought this was what you wanted."

Brad nodded. "It is, Vern." He paused, reconsidering. "Or at least it was." He sat up from his slumped position on the couch and looked Vern directly in the eye. "There was a time when making NASCAR was the center of my existence. It was all I lived and breathed for. But now, it's not quite so important anymore. Now, I want things that have nothing to do with racing."

Vern shook his head. "Boy, I have watched you mope around like a lovesick puppy all week, and it just doesn't make sense to me. I've seen you with lots of women, but I've never seen one get under your skin quite like this one has."

Brad recoiled. "Under my skin? I don't know if that's it. I respect Cori, and care about her opinion. I can only imagine what she must think of me after the last race. And that bothers me."

"Cowboy, that's the very definition of 'under your skin.' " Vern's mouth was set in a straight line. "But tomorrow is for racing, and you need to focus on the goal. Understand?"

"Understood."

"Not a chance Mikey," Cori said flatly. "There's no way I'm going to that race today."

"But why? I thought you enjoyed the race last time." Michael had assumed that since Cori had gone to the previous week's race, she'd want to go this week, as well. He was stunned to come down for breakfast and find her still in her bathrobe puttering around in the kitchen.

"I did enjoy last week's race," Cori agreed. *To a point.*

"I'm just not interested. I never planned on going every week, you know." She turned to the coffeemaker and began fixing a second pot.

Michael tried again. "Don't you want to support our race team?"

"Not interested," she responded over her shoulder. "Think I'll go shopping today. For earrings. You go on to the track without me."

Michael threw up his hands and left the kitchen, muttering under his breath. From under her lashes, Cori watched his departure. She was not feeling nearly as casual as she pretended. Part of her wanted to go to the race, but the bigger part of her couldn't face the possibility of another Victory Lane celebration. With an effort, she returned to her coffee making chore.

Since Cori wasn't going to be joining him, Michael decided to take Brad up on his standing offer to view the race from the pits. By the time Michael arrived at the track, the cars were being placed in their starting positions. For some reason, the entire pit road was buzzing with a peculiar energy.

"Hey, Vern," Michael greeted the crew chief, "what's going on?"

"Everybody's excited about the NASCAR scouts. They're here in the stands, come to check out the talent. Somebody's liable to get an invitation to The Show."

Michael nodded, impressed. "You think it could be Brad?"

"Could be," Vern nodded. "He's the hot driver around here these days. At least he has been up until now."

Michael looked around the pit area. "Where is he?"

"Over in the lockers getting dressed. He should be out soon."

Confirming Vern's words, Brad walked toward them, his

helmet tucked under his arm. At the sight of Michael, Brad's pulse raced a little faster. *Could she be here, too?*

"I hear NASCAR's in the house," Michael greeted him cheerfully.

"So they say." Brad extended his hand. "Glad you could make it today. Is, uh, your sister here, too?" He injected a note of indifference in his voice.

"Nah." Michael firmly shook the extended hand. "Said she was going shopping for earrings today."

An image flashed in Brad's mind of him and Cori giggling at the gaudy tropical fish earrings in that store window days ago.

Vern watched the play of emotions across his driver's face. "Focus, Boy," he growled. "Today's for racin'."

Brad nodded shortly and pulled his helmet on. He left the pit and climbed in his car. As he strapped in, he took several deep breaths, clearing his mind of all external noise and directing all his attentions and energies to the task at hand.

"Gentlemen, start your engines!" It was time for the race to begin.

"Show 'em what you're made of, Cowboy." Vern's voice boomed across the headset radio.

Brad gripped the steering wheel tightly. When the pace lap began, he tried to force some of the tension out of his body. He wove the car slightly across the track, warming up the tires for the race ahead. Then the pace car pulled off, and the race was on.

Brad's starting position was near the middle of the field. He gunned the engine, trying to improve his placement. He moved ahead of several cars, but was still trailing the leaders after ten laps.

From his spot in the pits, Vern watched with amazement as the race unfolded. *What is he doing?* The question screamed in Vern's mind. As much as he fussed at Brad about his aggressive driving style, Vern had always admired the younger man's courage and instinct. But today, his driving was almost tentative. "You should be closer to the lead by now. Pick up the pace," Vern yelled through the radio.

Annoyed, both at Vern's instruction and his own lackluster performance, Brad gunned the engine, determined to overtake the lead cars. The Foster's Chevrolet gained momentum, easing past cars on its march to the front. Brad kept his foot pressed mercilessly on the accelerator, and his attention focused on the cars in front of him. He was not watching his instrument panel, so he didn't realize how dangerously close to the red zone his tachometer was climbing.

Even though he wasn't in the car, Vern realized the car was heading for trouble. "Your RPM's! Watch your RPM's!"

The command came too late. Suddenly, Brad heard a cracking noise and a cloud of black smoke coughed out the back of the car. Immediately, he knew what that sound meant. He looked down at the tachometer and saw the needle buried in the red zone. The engine cut out, and the car began to slow. The yellow caution flag came out, signalling the drivers that there was trouble on the track. Most of the drivers used the caution lap to make their pit stops. But for Brad, the race was over. He'd blown the Chevy's engine.

Fortunately, he was able to coast into his spot on Pit Road. Once he was off the track, the caution ended and the green flag restarted the race. Brad climbed out of the disabled vehicle. The crew came over and pushed the car out to the garage.

"What happened?" Michael demanded.

"Your 'Ebony Warrior' here just blew the engine," Vern said in disgust. "Nice going, Cowboy. No chance the NASCAR boys are gonna want to talk to you now."

Angrily, Brad snatched the chin strap loose and pulled his helmet off. "Gimme a break, Vern. It's not like I blew that engine on purpose. Maybe you didn't have it tuned

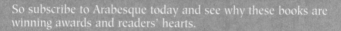

WE HAVE 4 FREE BOOKS FOR YOU!

ARABESQUE

FREE BOOK CERTIFICATE

Yes! Please send me 4 *Arabesque* Contemporary Romances without cost or obligation, billing me just $1 to help cover postage and handling. I understand that each month, I will be able to preview 4 brand-new *Arabesque* Contemporary Romances FREE for 10 days. Then, if I decide to keep them, I will pay the money-saving preferred subscriber's price of just $16.00 for all 4...that's a savings of almost $4 off the publisher's price with no additional charge for shipping and handling. I may return any shipment within 10 days and owe nothing, and I may cancel this subscription at any time. My 4 FREE books will be mine to keep in any case.

Name _____

Address _____ Apt. _____

City _____ State _____ Zip _____

Telephone ( ) _____

Signature _____ AR0498
(If under 18, parent or guardian must sign.)

ZEBRA HOME SUBSCRIPTION SERVICE, INC.

120 BRIGHTON ROAD

P.O. BOX 5214

CLIFTON, NEW JERSEY 07015-5214

right. Maybe you didn't have the car ready for a real race today."

"And maybe you weren't tuned right," Vern shot back. "Maybe *you* weren't ready for a real race today." The argument was uncharacteristic, and both Vern and Brad knew it.

"Blew the engine?" Michael sputtered. "Engines don't come cheap! What is it? Now that you have our sponsorship, you're gonna start driving like some rookie? We've got an investment in you, and we expect you to do your part."

"Look, Michael," Brad said shortly, "shit happens. It's part of the race game. All we can do is try again next week."

"NASCAR won't be here next week," Vern reminded him.

"Whatever." Annoyed, Brad threw up his hands and stalked off.

Chapter 16

By the following Friday, Vern had had enough. *It's been two damn weeks! I can't take anymore of this mooning around,* Vern thought. *Something's got to be done.* Vern leaned back in his chair, considering. After a moment, he made a decision. Reaching for the phone, he quickly punched out a number.

"Michael Foster, please. Tell him it's Vern Ramsey calling."

A few minutes later, Michael hung up the phone thoughtfully, mulling over the conversation he'd just had with Vern. *The man's right,* Michael decided. *Seven o'clock?* He checked his watch. *That doesn't leave me much time.* He took a deep breath, squared his shoulders, and headed for Cori's office. Without knocking, he charged into the room.

"Hey, Sis. I want to take you out to dinner." Michael's voice brimmed with enthusiasm.

Cori looked up from her paperwork, astonishment

etched on her features. "Mikey, it's Friday night and the dinner rush is in full swing. What makes you think I could leave now? For that matter, what makes you think *you* can leave now?"

"Why couldn't we go out? C'mon, Cori, it's not like either one of us is going to wait on any tables or cook any meals. That's why we hired staff." Michael crossed over to her desk and sat on its edge. "You need a break from this place," he reasoned. "You're working yourself too hard. The restaurant will run just fine without us for one night. Come on and let me take you to dinner—my treat."

"I'm sorry, Mikey. That's just not possible." Cori's attention returned to the notations she had been making to the forms on her desk.

Michael reached for her pencil and pulled it out of her fingers. Startled, Cori looked back up at her brother.

"I'm not taking no for an answer," he said flatly. "You're not going to keep hiding out in here. It's time for you to get a life."

"I resent that," Cori protested. "I already have a life, and it's running a restaurant."

Michael decided to try a different approach. "Okay, the place I want to take you is one of the hottest restaurants in Charlotte. Look at this dinner as a chance to scope out the competition. Maybe we can pick up a few ideas that we can bring back here."

"That might be a good idea any other time, but not on a Friday night," Cori said. "We really shouldn't be away from the restaurant on one of the busiest nights of the week."

"But we can learn more from our competition on a Friday night," Michael coaxed. "We can see how they handle the rush, and what they do for people who have to wait. Honestly, Cori, Friday night is the absolute best time for a fact-finding mission like this one."

Cori sat silently at her desk, mulling over Michael's words. Sensing her weakening, Michael pressed his advantage. "Come on, Sis. It'll be a lot of fun. You deserve a little break from this place. And I promise you the restaurant won't collapse if you're not here."

Cori looked at him skeptically. "You're treating?"

Michael nodded.

"Well, then, I can't possibly refuse. If for no other reason than to see you pick up a check," she teased.

Michael's laughter filled the office. "Well then, Miss Cori, let's go home and get changed. Our reservations are for seven."

"Reservations? You were pretty sure of yourself."

An irresistible smile spread across his face. "I told you I wasn't taking no for an answer."

The unexpected sound of his doorbell startled Brad. He had just settled in for what he planned to be a night of concentration and preparation. After his performance in last week's race, Brad couldn't afford to be off his game again. The bell rang again, more insistent this time. Irritated, Brad snatched the door open. He half-expected to find Lisa on the other side. The last face he was prepared to see was Vern's. Confusion furrowed Brad's brow. Vern was the one who always emphasized the importance of rest and concentration the night before a race.

"Vern? What are you doing here?"

"Hey, Cowboy. I need to talk to you. Can I come in?"

"Oh, of course." Brad quickly stepped to the side. "I'm sorry. I'm just so surprised to see you here." He closed the door behind Vern and led the way into the living room. "Have a seat. Can I get you a beer or something?"

Vern sat on the edge of the black leather sofa. "No, thanks. Just come sit down. We need to talk."

Curious, Brad did as he was bid.

"Something's been eating at you for the last couple of weeks, and I'm pretty sure I know what it is. Or should I say, *who* it is? You've been mooning around like some lovesick puppy because of Cori Justice."

Brad opened his mouth to respond, but Vern held up his hand to stop him.

"Let me finish. It's obvious something is going on, and I'm willing to bet it has everything to do with Little Miss Track Groupie's performance the other week."

Brad's jaw fell open in amazement. He had no idea Vern knew about that.

"Clearly, you need to talk to Cori and air this thing out once and for all," Vern continued. "I was going to come over here with some excuse to get you to go to dinner with me, but on the way over I decided I just don't have the time or the energy for that kind of thing. So here's the deal," Vern watched Brad closely, "I called Michael Foster, and he's going to get Cori to go to a restaurant in Uptown at seven. You need to meet them there. You need to go and talk to her and work out your problems. You need to do it tonight . . . before the race tomorrow."

Brad sat in stunned silence as the import of Vern's words sank in. Thoughts formed in his mind faster than he could get them out. "Why did you do that?" he managed finally.

"Because somebody had to do something," Vern snapped. "You keep moping around like you've lost your best friend and you *will* make a mistake on the track—a mistake that could kill you." Vern's tone softened. "Besides, I can tell you care about this woman. You owe it to yourself and to her to talk out your problems."

Brad shook his head slowly. "I don't know, Vern. What could I say to her? I haven't seen her in almost two weeks. She must hate me by now."

"That's all the more reason for you to go," Vern insisted. He stood and prepared to leave. "Look, I've set the wheels in motion. It's up to you to cross the finish line. Michael and Cori will be at the Mimosa Grill at seven. She doesn't know you're supposed to be coming, so if you decide not to go they'll just have a nice dinner together and she'll be none the wiser.'' Vern walked into the hall and opened the door. ''But don't be a fool, Brad. You *need* to go.'' Vern left the condo and closed the door behind him.

Brad had remained glued to his seat the whole time Vern talked. Now, as he watched the door close, Brad wondered what his next move should be. He was uncertain what he could say that would fix things between him and Cori. In his mind, the more time that passed the less chance there was that their relationship could be repaired. But as he thought more about it, he knew Vern was right. He needed to go. Brad looked up at the wall clock.

Seven o'clock? I'd better hurry.

When Michael turned the car onto Tryon Street, a flash of supressed memories exploded in Cori's mind. She recognized several of the buildings and landmarks Brad had pointed out to her during their long ago tour of Uptown. Remembering that day now, Cori smiled in spite of herself. *It really* was *a wonderful* day, she mused.

Michael parked the car alongside the curb near the corner of Second and Tryon. A valet appeared instantly and opened Cori's door.

''Nice place, Mikey,'' Cori observed as she alighted from the car. ''How'd you find it?''

''Uh . . . a friend told me about it,'' Michael hedged. ''And by the way, you look fabulous tonight.''

Cori was wearing a black mini dress with a flirty hemline, black hose encasing her long, caramel-colored legs, and a pair of high heeled black sandals.

''Well, thank you, Mikey, but you did insist that I wear this dress.'' Cori grinned, remembering how her brother had gone through her closet looking for ''just the right outfit.''

''I know, but it's not just the dress. Everything about you looks especially lovely tonight.'' Michael smiled and held out his arm. ''I'm real proud to be your escort.''

Cori smiled and nodded, graciously accepting the compliment. She took his arm, and they headed toward the restaurant.

The Mimosa Grill was located on the ground floor of one of Uptown's office towers. To reach the entrance, patrons had to cross a beautiful plaza. The plaza had chairs and tables scattered about; it was no doubt one of the premiere "people watching" locations in Uptown. There was a fountain in the plaza with different levels that created a waterfall effect. In the fountain were bronze statues of children at play. The life-sized statues were meticulously detailed, and so lifelike that Cori half-expected to be able to hear their laughter.

Michael and Cori passed through the plaza and entered the restaurant. It was a fairly small space, about half the size of Foster's. But the view more than compensated for the lack of space. A wall of windows looked out over the plaza. Michael walked a little ahead of his sister, carefully scanning the restaurant's interior. He approached the maître d's stand. "Reservations for Ramsey, party of two."

Cori reached his side in time to hear the last bit of his words. "Reservations for Ramsey? Vern Ramsey?"

"Um, yeah . . . Vern's the friend who told me about this place," Michael said smoothly. "He made the reservations for me."

The maître d' led them to a quiet table next to the wall of windows. Cori settled in her chair and accepted the menu. She scanned through the menu selections.

"Mikey, I don't know if this place can fairly be considered a competitor of Foster's. They're serving a completely different cuisine." Cori looked at Michael, waiting for his reaction.

Michael, however, wasn't listening. His attentions were focused on searching the restaurant. He'd taken the chair facing the entrance, but still he kept craning his neck to look around.

"Mikey? Did you hear what I said?"

"What? Oh, I'm sorry, Cori. I guess I wasn't paying any attention."

"Obviously," she said shortly. "Who are you looking for? Afraid one of your honeys will see you with me and think you're cheating on her?"

"Don't be silly. That's the last thing on my mind."

"Then what is it? Who are you looking for?"

Michael, again scanning the restaurant, didn't answer.

Brad rushed up to the maître d's stand, slightly flushed and out of breath. He'd run through the plaza and up the stairs to the restaurant, trying not to be any later than he already was.

"I'm meeting some friends here," he told the maître d'. "The Foster party?"

The maître d' checked his reservations list. "I'm sorry, there's no one here by that name."

Brad looked crestfallen. "Are you sure? What about Justice? Anyone here by that name?"

Again, the maître d' checked, and again he came up empty. Brad's concern was growing. *Vern did say Mimosa, didn't he?* Then a thought occurred to him. "How about Ramsey? Is there a Ramsey party here?"

This time the maître d' nodded. "Yes, Sir! They're right this way."

Brad followed him through the restaurant. By the time Michael saw him, Brad was almost at the table. Smiling, Michael stood to greet him. A confused expression appeared on Cori's face as she watched Michael stand up. Curious, she turned to see who was coming.

At first, all she noticed was the belted waist. Then, slowly, her eyes travelled upward, taking in the muscled chest and broad shoulders. Her breath caught in her throat as she realized who it was. Standing before her, dressed in an olive-colored linen sport coat, tan mandarin collar shirt and olive linen slacks, Brad cut an impressive, handsome figure.

Electricity crackled in the air around them as Brad and Cori's eyes met. For that sensory-charged moment, all the hurt and anger and anxiety fell away and there was only chemistry between them.

The maître'd's apology shattered the moment. "I'm sorry, I thought this was to be a table for two. If you'll wait just a moment, I'll get another chair and place setting."

"No, that won't be necessary," Michael said. "I was just leaving."

Perplexed, Cori looked at her brother. "What are you doing, Mikey?"

"Just looking after my sis," Michael responded. He leaned over and kissed her cheek. "Don't be mad at me, Cori," he whispered in her ear. "I only did this for your own good." He straightened and extended his hand to Brad. "I trust I can count on you to get my sister home safely?"

Brad shook Michael's hand gratefully. "Don't worry about a thing."

Then Michael and the maître d walked away, leaving Brad and Cori alone.

"May I join you?" Brad gestured to the now empty chair.

"It doesn't look like I have much choice," Cori observed dryly.

"That's not true. I'm sure I can still catch Michael if you want me to. I don't want you to feel forced or pressured in any way."

Cori tilted her head slightly and considered. "No," she said finally, "that won't be necessary. Please have a seat."

Brad released a breath he hadn't been aware of holding as he sat down. "Thank you. I wasn't sure how you'd feel about all this."

"Well, I'm not sure, either. Did you put Michael up to this?"

Brad chuckled shortly. "Actually, no. Vern cooked up this whole scenario."

"Vern? Why?"

Brad paused, picking his words carefully. "He's been concerned about . . . about . . . things," Brad said finally. "He believes that if we can talk, we might be able to work out our . . . differences."

Cori cocked an eyebrow. "Do we have differences to work out?"

"I think so. I'm not ready to leave things the way they are."

"And how are they, Mr. Marshall? What are our differences?"

Brad heaved a sigh. "You're not going to make this easy for me, are you?"

"Make what easy for you?" Cori placed her elbow on the table and propped her chin in her hand, fingertips drumming impatiently on her cheek.

The thought occurred to him to play the game and adopt a "What me, worry?" posture. For one alluring moment, it seemed like a great idea to take the easy way out and not attempt to break down the wall that had sprung up between them. But then Julie's advice came back to him, with clarity so real that it felt as if someone had slapped the back of his head.

"It's going to be up to you to make things right between you two again. You're going to have to prove your sincerity, or else that relationship is dead in the water."

"Cori, I owe you an explanation and an apology, and I'm not going to let this evening end without having given you both." Brad's eyes radiated honesty and contrition, so much so that Cori was moved by their intensity.

She leaned back in her chair and placed her hands in her lap. "I'm listening."

Brad took a deep breath. "First of all, I want to explain about Lisa, that woman you saw kissing me after the race."

"I'm not sure if her kissing you is how I would describe

what I saw. It looked more like the two of you kissing to me."

Brad shook his head. "I was certainly not kissing Lisa. But I guess that's beside the point. Lisa is just a friend. Maybe she wants to be more, I don't know, but it's not what it seemed."

"What it *seemed* is that you were very publicly, very passionately kissing this Lisa less than twenty-four hours after you had been very passionately kissing me. It doesn't matter if she's just a friend or more than a friend." Cori's eyes bored into him. "Your actions make you a wandering playboy at best, and a duplicitous cheat at worst."

"That's not a fair assessment. I was standing in Victory Lane looking for you . . . waiting for you. Lisa just appeared, and before I knew what was happening she was kissing me."

"Then you must have the type of relationship with Lisa that would make her believe that surprising you with a kiss would please you."

Brad heaved a sigh. "Cori, I'm thirty-five years old. There **were** women in my life before I met you. But believe me when I tell you that no woman has ever mattered to me the way you do."

"What?" Cori asked sarcastically. "Am I the first woman sponsor you've ever had?"

"This is not about the sponsorship," Brad ground out through gritted teeth. He was struggling to control his rising anger; she was being so obstinate! But if he accepted Julie's advice, he knew he'd have to go the extra mile. "I don't care about the sponsorship, not nearly as much as I care about our relationship. And if I need to tear up the contracts to prove that to you, I'm willing to do that." Brad reached across the table and held her hand. "Cori, I have spent my whole adult life moving from one meaningless relationship to another. I never met anyone who made me think there might be more to life. Never until now. This past week without you in it has been miserable for me. I tried to ignore it, I tried to deny it, I tried to get over it, but the simple truth is you have gotten under my skin, and I need you."

Tears welled in Cori's eyes. *Can it really be? Is it possible that this man feels this way about me?* Cori found herself speechless in the face of Brad's words. During their week apart, she had surrendered to the cynical voice in her head that convinced her Brad was using their friendship to achieve his own ends. But now, faced with the obvious evidence of his sincerity and longing, Cori was forced to reconsider.

She finally found her voice. "I don't know what to say. I have missed you this past week. More than I had any business missing you."

"What does that mean?" he asked softly.

"I don't know if I can trust you . . . if I dare trust you." Cori met his eyes. "I fell for you, Brad Marshall. I fell hard. And then I saw you with that woman, and I hurt—bad. I don't want to hurt like that ever again."

"Cori, I swear to you I would never knowingly hurt you." Brad's eyes pleaded with her. "You can trust me. I will never hurt you again."

Cori looked deeply into Brad's expressive brown eyes. "I'm ready to go now."

"But we haven't eaten yet. You want me to take you home?"

"Yes . . . your home."

Brad reached for her hand and held it to his chest. "Can you feel how fast my heart is beating? That's because I want you, Corinthia Justice. Please don't ask me to take you to my home if you don't want me, too."

Cori flexed her fingers and gently massaged his firm chest muscles. "I do," she whispered. "I want you, too." She leaned in close and locked him in a searingly passionate kiss—one that left no room for doubts.

That was all the encouragement Brad needed. Cori and Brad hurriedly left the restaurant. In what seemed to be

one fluid motion, Brad opened the passenger door, helped
Cori into the seat, and then climbed into his own. Neither
of them spoke. Words seemed superfluous at that point.
His condo in East Charlotte was not terribly far, but even
so Brad desperately wished they were already there. He
resisted the itching urge to speed home; he understood
enough about Cori by now to know that riding in a speeding truck would terrify her.

Cori's mind was blissfully, peacefully blank. She had
wrestled her demons from the past to the ground, and she
was now confident that this time—and this man—were
right. She looked over at Brad, studying his proudly African
features. His beautifully shaped bald head drew most of
her attention. After a moment, she decided that she had
to touch him. She stroked his scalp, reveling in the feel
of warm smoothness against her palm.

Her unexpected movements both pleased and startled
Brad. It took every ounce of his driving skill and concentration to keep from running the truck off the road. His head
tingled under the rubbing of her fingers; he experienced a
pleasure dangerously close to pain when she gently scraped
her nails along the back of his head and down his neck.

A red traffic light delayed their journey. Temporarily
stopped, he turned to face her. Reaching for the hand
that stroked his head, he pulled her closer. They kissed,
tongues tentatively exploring, testing, tasting. When the
kiss ended, he was frustrated to see the light was still red.

Change, damn you! his mind growled.

Although Cori shared his impatience, she was nervous.
It had been a very long time since she'd given herself to
a man—not since her husband died. For a long time she
was in mourning, and even when her grief began to ease
she couldn't imagine sharing intimacy with anyone else.
She had come to accept that *that* part of her life was over.
Until now.

No man had ever stimulated her—emotionally, physi-
cally, and spiritually—like Brad Marshall. She resisted the

pull at first, but the more she knew about Brad the more she was convinced that this was a man she could trust with her body and soul.

The light finally changed. With as much speed as he dared, Brad covered the distance to his home. He parked the truck in front of his condo and turned off the engine. He reached for Cori and pulled her as close as he could. With one arm wrapped firmly around her waist, he used his free hand to smooth away an unruly lock of hair that had fallen in front of her eyes. Her skin tingled like a living entity everywhere his fingers touched. Brad took a breath and looked deeply into her eyes.

"It's not too late." His voice rumbled in his chest. "I can still take you home if you want."

Cori nestled her cheek in the palm that was still caressing her face. "What I want, I can't get at home," she said softly.

Brad kissed her again. In the heat of that kiss all questions were answered, all doubts erased.

Brad climbed out of the truck and hurried to Cori's side to help her out. She wrapped her arms around his neck and they kissed again. The look of love that passed between them transcended words. Arms wrapped around each other's waists, they walked the short distance to his condo. After fumbling briefly with his keys, he flung open the front door. Cori stepped past him into the room.

Closing the door behind him, Brad flipped on the lights. Cori was impressed by her first look at his home. They were standing in his living room, a masculine collection of a black leather pit grouping, a big screen TV, and an impressive stereo system housed in a black lacquer entertainment unit.

"Can I get you anything? A glass of wine, or maybe something to eat?" Brad was uncharacteristically nervous.

Cori shook her head. She walked up to him until their bodies were nearly touching. Brad stood perfectly still, letting her set the pace. Cori placed her palms on his chest and slowly ran her hands over the broad expanse. She gently pulled at the buttons of his shirt until they were released and the shirt hung open. Brad sucked in a quick gasp of air as her fingers found the hair on his chest. Slowly, methodically, Cori eased her hands up his body until they reached his shoulders. Then, she pulled him to her. Her lips parted slightly in anticipation of his searing kiss.

Eagerly, Brad bent to claim her waiting lips. This kiss burned with more fire and passion than any that had passed between them. This kiss moved them to a place where nothing mattered but each other.

Suddenly, Brad swept her off her feet. Never breaking the kiss, he carried her into his bedroom. Her lips sought his hungrily as he laid her gently on his bed. He stood and shrugged out of his jacket and shirt. Looking down at her, Brad was almost overcome with emotion. It was a stunning sensation for him. Never had his emotions mattered more than his body, but somehow, some way, things were different now.

He kneeled at the end of the bed and gently pulled off her sandals. Then, with agonizing slowness, he eased his hands up her legs to remove her panty hose. Cori moaned softly as Brad's hands caressed her legs. Before she was even aware of it, her hose were in a ball on the floor. Then his hands were back again, smoothly gliding over her legs, leaving a trail of fire in their wake. He eased his hands along the insides of her thighs and gently slid them apart. His fingers touched her warm, wet flesh. He touched and teased the button of her passion until she thought she would burst from within.

"Brad, no, please, not yet."

"Shh," he whispered. "There is much more where this comes from. We have all night."

He continued to touch her, moving his fingers faster and more insistently. Cori thrashed on the bed, her whole being centered on the spot where Brad's magic hands worked her to a frenzy. Then he felt the shudders of her fulfillment. Smiling, he climbed onto the bed next to her.

"Why did you do that?" she asked breathlessly.

"Just because," was the enigmatic answer.

She rolled on her side to face him and reached for the waistband of his pants. "I want to feel you, now," she urged.

Nodding, Brad kicked off his shoes and unfastened his belt. When he stood to remove his pants, Cori sat up and whipped the mini dress off over her head.

Soon, they lay facing each other, their naked bodies touching from waist to toe. Cori marveled at the absolute sculpted beauty of him. She had seen glimpses of his physique through his clothes, but nothing prepared her for the reality of his firm thighs, muscled arms, and taut backside.

They kissed again, more relaxed this time but still insistent. Hands roamed over bodies, exploring and learning. Cori wrapped her hand around his erection. Brad gasped through gritted teeth at the fire her touch caused. She rubbed her hand up and down the length of him.

Abruptly, Brad rolled away. Cori's face sagged with disappointment. "What's wrong? Did I hurt you?"

"Yes," Brad ground out, "but not the way you mean." He reached in a nightstand drawer and fished out a foil package. "If I don't feel you around me soon, I think I'm going to die."

Cori laughed. "Well, please don't die right now. How would I ever explain it?" She stretched across his body and pulled the package out of his hand. "Let me," she ordered.

Brad rolled on his back and surrendered himself to her ministrations. With infinite slowness, Cori rolled the condom down his shaft. Brad was barely breathing, trying desperately to maintain some modicum of control. Once the condom was in place, he quickly moved over her. Their eyes met and there was a spark that existed outside of the act of lovemaking, a spark that was love itself.

Then Brad could contain himself no longer. With one powerful thrust, he entered her wet and willing body. That moment of intimate contact between their two hungry bodies was blistering in its intensity. He began to move, in the age-old dance of passion. Their bodies took over and Cori and Brad became one soul, climbing together to the peak of fulfillment. The dance became faster, more intense with each passing moment.

Then, just as they thought they could take no more, an explosion engulfed them. It started at the joining of their bodies, and quickly spread until their entire beings were consumed by the white hot burst.

Brad collapsed against her. Cori wrapped her arms around his neck, holding him close to her. A fine sheen of sweat covered them both. Slowly, their breathing and pulses returned to normal.

"I never . . . that was amazing." Brad found his voice first.

Unexpected tears flowed down Cori's face onto the pillow.

"Why are you crying?" Brad's face was etched with concern.

"I just . . . I don't . . ." Cori paused, trying to find the right words. "I have never felt anything like that before," she managed finally. "I am just so . . . so . . . overcome."

Brad lightly kissed her forehead. "I know," he murmured. "I know."

He moved to lie next to her, cradling her to his chest. "I know . . ."

Much, much later, they were in Brad's truck heading for Cori's house.

"I wish you would stay the night."

"I couldn't," she insisted. "Besides, you have a race tomorrow. I'm sure you need to get to the track early."

"You are coming tomorrow?"

"Again?" She teased.

It took a moment for her meaning to reach him. "To the race, Cori," he responded with mock exasperation. "I want you to come to the race."

She leaned over and kissed him—a deep, soul-mingling kiss that left them both breathlessly wanting more. "I wouldn't miss it for the world."

Chapter 17

Brad went through his race day preparations on automatic pilot. He barely tasted the power breakfast shake, and paid almost no attention to the music pumping from his stereo. His thoughts were consumed with memories of the previous night. He'd broken his cardinal rule banning sex the night before a race. Brad was just superstitious enough to believe that making love prior to a race would sap the strength and concentration he needed to win. But oddly enough, he felt more energized than drained.

Brad had certainly had more than his share of intimate encounters with women, but last night with Cori touched him in places that had nothing to do with sex. He kept reliving their passion in his mind, experiencing that magical moment when all Cori's inhibitions seemed to fall away, and she gave herself over to him. It was a moment he had never experienced before. Never in his life had a women put so much of herself and her soul into lovemaking. Brad was moved to distraction because of it.

He shook his head, banishing the intimate memories to a corner of his mind. There would be time for them later.

Now, he had a job to do. This was going to be a race to end all races. He could feel it in his bones. Focused on his objective, Brad finished his rituals and headed for the track.

"Out kinda late last night, weren't we?" Michael subjected his sister to some good-natured grilling during the drive out to the racetrack. Today, he hadn't needed to hurry her along. Today, she was anxious to get to the race.

Cori blushed slightly. "Mind your business, Michael Foster. And how would you know what time I came home, as late as you stay out?"

"That's how I know. When I got in last night—or should I say this morning—your bed was still empty."

"You checked in on me?" Cori demanded indignantly.

"Oh, yeah," Michael said easily. "I wanted to see if my hunch was right. I guess it's safe to assume that you and Mr. Marshall made up."

Cori wanted to hold on to her righteous anger, but she was so filled with joy that she couldn't. "Oh Mikey, he's such a wonderful man. We talked it over and were able to put our differences behind us."

"Talked it over?" Michael stole a sideways glance at the glow on his sister's face. "Is that all you did?"

"Michael! A gentleman would never ask such a question."

"Maybe a gentleman wouldn't, but a nosy younger brother sho' would. So, you going to answer?"

Cori gave him a disapproving look.

"Never mind. I can see for myself." Michael grinned from ear to ear. "Good for you, Sis."

You have no idea exactly how good it was for me. Cori smiled and said nothing.

"I sure hope our driver is as rejuvenated as you seem to be," Michael continued. "He stank up the track last week with his driving. He damn well better make a better showing this week."

"I'm sure this week will be completely different," Cori said enigmatically.

Today's race was being held at Highland Speedway, about twenty miles outside of Charlotte. Brad had raced here dozens of times before and was almost as familiar with its twists and turns as he was with Carolco's. The cars were lined up in their starting postions on the track; their crews were making their last minute adjustments. By virtue of his leading times in qualifying runs earlier in the week, Brad was in the pole position for today's contest.

Sitting in his car, waiting for the race to begin, Brad closed his eyes and began his visualization exercises. He ran through the track in his mind, seeing the mile long oval from ground level. He pictured the groove he would follow, planning to stay low on the straightaways and high on the turns. His breathing was slow and measured as he moved closer to The Zone.

"Almost show time, Cowboy. You ready?" Vern's question broke into his concentration.

"I've told you before, Old Man, I was born ready." Brad stretched and flexed his fingers, readying them to grip the steering wheel. He tried to return to his track visualization, but a much more intimate vision forced its way into his mind. A tingle worked itself down Brad's spine as he remembered, yet again, the passionate night he'd spent with Cori.

He shook his head violently, trying to loose the visions from his mind. *Not now,* he admonished himself. *Keep your mind on the track. A loss of concentration out there could be fatal!*

"Gentlemen, start your engines!" The track announcer blared the starting signal. The engines roared to life. The pace car began the show lap around the track. In the pole position, Brad followed closely behind. After two laps, the pace car pulled off and the race was on.

Brad drove with supreme confidence. Almost immediately, he was in his Zone. There was much jockeying for position behind him, but Brad rode unchallenged in the front of the pack.

In the stands, Cori cheered for her driver. She chuckled, remembering when she'd thought cheering at a race was a dumb waste of time and energy. She now understood that the cheers were as much for the spectators as they were for the racers. She watched as Brad smoothly covered the turns and flew down the straightaways. *That's it, Brad,* she silently urged him on, *win one for me.*

The race progressed almost routinely. Brad made his scheduled pit stops with no incidents. He was able to easily resume the lead after every stop. Even Vern was unconditionally pleased with the performance of both the car and the driver.

Midway through the race, Brad had passed one of the slower cars, putting it a lap down. "There's a crash coming out of turn two," Vern screamed into the radio. "There's debris all over the track. You're going to have to come in low to avoid it."

"Understood," Brad replied tersely. He was fast approaching the accident site. All he could see was a cloud of smoke obscuring the track. As he had been told, Brad moved down to the bottom of the track, planning to burst through the smoke and come out in the clear on the other side. But it wasn't clear on the other side. The crash was a multi-car pileup and two of the battered cars had slid to the bottom of the track. By the time Brad saw them, it was too late. He stood on the brake, trying to stop the car, but his efforts only caused the car to skid into a spin. He slammed into the two wrecked cars broadside, taking the impact on the driver's side. The crash caused his car to

go airborne, over the other cars, and flip several times
before slamming to a stop against the track wall.

In the stands, Cori watched in complete horror as Brad's
car sailed through the air. After what seemed an eternity,
his car finally stopped flipping and smashed against the
track wall. For a terrifying moment, the world was in a
state of suspended animation. Cori and the fans around
her were frozen by their collective concern for the downed
warriors. Then, the track sprang to life. Ambulances and
tow trucks rushed onto the track. Paramedics quickly freed
the drivers from the smoking wreckage.

Cori sprang to life, as well. She rushed out of her seat
in the sponsors' section, single-minded in her determination to get to Brad. Michael, who had been sitting next to
Cori, was still frozen in place when she bolted from the
stands. When he looked around to check on her, Cori was
already halfway down to track level. He hurried after her.

A security guard stopped her at the track gate. "I'm
sorry, Ma'am, you can't go out there."

"Like hell." Cori's voice was a low growl. "I am that
driver's sponsor. I have every right to be out there. Now
get out of my way." Cori began to push past him.

"Wait a minute, Ma'am. You are not allowed. I don't
care if you're a sponsor or not."

"Get out of my way," Cori growled. "I need to be out
there."

Something in Cori's eyes convinced the security guard
that discretion was the better part of valor. Slowly, he
stepped aside and held the gate open for her.

By the time Michael reached the gate, the guard was
back in control. "Sorry, Sir, you can't go out there."

Frustrated, Michael could only watch while his sister ran
to Brad's pit area.

When Cori reached the pit, the crew was standing stone
still, watching as the paramedics cut Brad out of the wreckage. As she watched, saws whirled and metal screamed in
protest as what was left of the Foster's Chevrolet was ripped

away. Finally, they got a look at their driver as Brad's limp, lifeless body was lifted onto a gurney. The medics fitted him with a cervical collar and gently removed his helmet. Brad did not stir during their ministrations.

Cori stood with her arms wrapped tightly around her body, rocking gently back and forth. *Oh God, not again . . . not again.* The words ran together in her mind until they were no longer separate, but one long anguished sound. When the paramedics began to wheel him into the ambulance, Cori vaulted from the pit and ran out to the ambulance. Vern saw her darting across the track and ran after her.

Cori attempted to climb in the ambulance with Brad, but the paramedics stopped her.

"You can't go in there, Ma'am. You'll have to follow in your car."

"No!" Cori screamed. "I have to go with him. He needs me. Please, you don't understand." Tears filled her eyes. "I have to go."

Vern was at her side by now. "It's okay, Cori. I'll drive you to the hospital." He gently pulled her arm, attempting to move her away from the ambulance. Suddenly the present fell away, and all Cori could see was Tony's bloodied body as the ambulance doors closed. Suddenly, it wasn't Vern leading her away, but a Chicago police officer, guiding her to his patrol car.

"NO!" She yanked her arm out of his grasp. The screech seemed to be wrenched from the depths of her soul. "I have to go. Please Vern, make them understand. I have to go!"

Shock drained the color from Vern's face. He had never seen someone so close to the edge. He turned to the paramedics. "Looks like you'd better let her ride along."

The head paramedic nodded shortly. Cori scrambled into the back of the ambulance. Within seconds, with sirens blaring and lights flashing, the ambulance left the track.

Cori huddled in a corner of the ambulance, trying to

stay out of the way. She was vaguely aware of all the terse directives being issued around her, but the words did not penetrate. Instead, all she could focus on was Brad: perfectly still, barely breathing, and covered with blood.

HoldonBrad,I'mhere,pleasedon'tleaveme. There were not so much words as a string of barely coherent emotions that swirled around in Cori's mind.

When they reached the hospital, the paramedic crew burst in through the emergency room doors. They had radioed ahead, so the medical team was ready for Brad. As soon as they entered the hospital, the emergency room erupted into a flurry of activity. Brad's gurney was whisked away; Cori could only watch through the windows cut in the emergency room doors. She wrapped her arms around her waist in a fruitless effort to quell the shivers that wracked her body. Slowly, she backed away from the doors. *Oh God, not again.* Tears streamed down her face. *Please, not again.*

Vern and Michael raced through the hospital door. Seeing Cori, they hurried to her side.

"Cori, what is it? How's Brad?" Vern's voice was tight with urgency.

"I don't know," Cori choked out. "They just took him in there. He was still unconscious."

"C'mon, Honey." Michael gently led her to a nearby waiting room. "Let's sit down. We might be in for a long wait."

Michael's prediction turned out to be true. Early on, one of the doctors told them that Brad was being rushed up for emergency surgery. Several hours had passed since then while Vern, Cori, and Michael waited for word on Brad's condition. Each of the trio dealt with the wait in his or her own way. Vern replayed the accident in his mind, trying to figure what directions he could have given Brad that would have steered him around the crash. Michael's worries were split; he was deeply concerned about Brad, but he was almost as deeply concerned about Cori. She had not spoken more than ten words in the hours they had been waiting. She was off in her own world—remembering, Michael knew.

She *was* off in her own world—or more accurately, in her own past. She couldn't stop the memories that flooded her mind. The screech of twisting metal, the scream of the ambulance siren, the medicinal smell of the waiting room, were all visceral reminders of the accident many years before.

Finally, one of Brad's doctors approached them. Instantly, they were on their feet, meeting the doctor halfway.

"How is he, Doc?" Vern asked. "How'd the surgery go?"

"The surgery went quite well. He suffered extensive head injuries, not to mention several broken bones. During surgery, we were able to relieve the pressure on his brain, and set the bones."

"Will he be all right?" Cori's voice shook, so it was hard to understand her.

"The next forty-eight hours will be critical. We'll monitor him closely, but only time will tell."

Michael squeezed his sister's hand. "Can we see him?"

"Yes, of course, but one at a time, please. And just for a few minutes. I'll have one of the nurses take you to him." With a curt nod, the doctor disappeared down the corridor.

"Cori, you go first," Vern offered. "I need to call Brad's family. I wanted to wait until we had some information before I called them."

Cori nodded gratefully. A nurse walked up to them. "The doctor asked me to show you to Brad Marshall's room. Follow me."

Cori approached the door of Brad's room with an overwhelming feeling of dread. She couldn't quite place its source, but she felt deeply apprehensive about entering the ICU room. She placed her hand on the knob. The smooth cool metal helped her gather her courage. She nodded her thanks to the nurse and turned the knob.

Upon entering the room, she was immediately assaulted

by the sight of Brad lying on the bed. The beautiful bald
head she had come to love seeing was covered with ban-
dages and propped up on two pillows. Someone had pulled
a sheet up to his chest. His sculpted ebony arms stood out
in stark relief against the white coverings and the pale
hospital gown he was dressed in. An IV line in his arm
pumped fluids and medicine into his system. He was so
stone still that, for a moment, she feared the worst. But
then the reassuring bleep of the hospital machinery confirmed that Brad Marshall was holding his own.

Tentatively, Cori approached the bed. Her vision
blurred as tears brimmed in her eyes. "Oh Brad," she
murmured. Cori felt guilty, thinking about how short and
distant she'd been to him the last few weeks. Not even the
memory of Brad locked in a kiss with the woman she now
knew to be Lisa could muster the indignation Cori had
cloaked herself in until recently. All she could think about
was the time they'd spent together, getting to know Charlotte and getting to know each other. She remembered
his unabashed pride as he walked her through Uptown,
his hearty laughter as they window-shopped at the mall, and
she remembered the intensity of the passion that flowed
through him when they'd made love.

She was standing by the side of the bed. Gently, she
reached for his hand and found it warm but lifeless. Cori
took his hand in both of hers and stroked it lightly. "You're
going to be all right, Brad. I know it . . . You just have to
be." She crooned the words until they were not so much
words as comforting sounds.

Suddenly, Brad's chest heaved as he gasped for air. The
steady beep of the hospital monitors turned into a shrill
scream of alarm. Buzzers reverberated throughout the previously quiet room. Cori looked around in confusion.
Within seconds the room was swarming with medical per-
sonnel.

"He's crashing!" Someone yelled.

"Get the paddles—set to a hundred fifty."

A nurse pulled Cori away from the bed. "You'll have to step back, Miss."

Cori found herself standing forgotten in a corner of Brad's room. It was almost surreal: she could feel the urgency and tension in the room, but the activity that swirled around her all seemed to be happening in slow motion.

Oh God, please, she silently prayed, *not him, too. Please, not him, too.*

A voice rose above the din. "Charging. Clear!"

Brad's body leapt from the bed as the paddles sent an electric jolt to his heart.

"Still flatlining," one of the nurses called.

Please God, I'll do anything, Cori prayed desperately. *I'll walk away if that's what you want. Just please don't take him, too.*

"Set it at two fifty!" The doctor yelled, "Clear!"

Again, Brad's body jumped on the bed. For one electric moment, the room was perfectly still, all eyes trained on the monitor, willing it to begin the rhythmic beeping that signaled life.

Finally, the monotone beep filled the room. A collective sigh of relief went up from the medical staff.

"He's back," the doctor declared. "Heartbeat strong and steady." The doctor proceeded to issue a series of instructions to the attending nurses, but Cori could hear nothing but the beeping of the heart monitor. Each beep confirmed that her prayer had been answered, and each beep sealed the bargain she'd made with God. With one last look at the motionless ebony figure on the bed, Cori backed out of the room.

When he saw her emerge from Brad's room, Michael hurried out of his chair to meet her. "How is he?"

"Mikey, please take me home." Cori's anguished voice cracked at the words.

Michael looked questioningly at her. "Now? Why do you want to leave now? Is Brad out of the woods?"

Cori hesitated before answering, thinking about her "deal." "Yes, Mikey," she said tonelessly, "Brad is out of the woods. He is going to be fine."

"How do you know?" Michael persisted. "Did you speak with his doctor?"

"Not exactly."

"Then what exactly?"

"I've prayed over it, Mikey. I've made a deal with God."

Although they had been raised in the same way and taken to the same church as children, Michael did not share his sister's absolute faith. But out of respect, he had never questioned it. Never until now.

"Made a deal with God? What does that mean?"

Cori looked away, busying herself with gathering her things. "I offered to stay away from Brad if God would spare his life, and God agreed."

"WHAT?" Michael jiggled a finger in his ear as if to clear away the obstruction that had to be blocking his hearing. "You did what?"

Cori gave him an exasperated look. "You heard me, Mikey. It's because of me that Brad is in this shape, so it's up to me to make him better."

"That's nuts! How is Brad's accident your fault?"

"It just is, Mikey. I was getting too happy, too compla-cent. Brad had to crash to shake me up."

Michael looked at her with bug-eyed disbelief. "Do you have any idea how ridiculous that sounds?"

Cori rolled her eyes. "You don't understand."

"No joke."

"Don't you see? This is just like when Tony died."

"WHAT? This is nothing like when Tony died! Tony was dead before they even got him to the hospital. What do you mean?"

"I mean me . . . how I was feeling . . . it's just the same. The day Tony died, I was as happy and content as I had ever been. I thought my life was perfect. Tony's death shattered that illusion and made me see that life ain't no crystal stair.''

"You think Tony died to teach you a lesson?'' Michael was incredulous. He had no idea his sister had been carrying around that kind of pain. "Brianna, too? You think Brianna's death was somehow directed at you?''

"I don't know!'' Cori shouted. "All I know is I was happy and complacent and then my whole world was shattered. All I know is everything happens for a reason, and maybe the reason they died is because I'm not meant to be happy.''

"Cori, you're talking crazy!'' Michael yelled. "God does not want you to be unhappy! You haven't done anything to deserve that.''

"I don't *know* that, and neither do you. All we do know is that as soon as I found someone I might be able to be happy with, he was snatched away, too.''

"But Brad did not die.''

"Exactly. And do you know why?'' Cori's eyes bored into her brother's, pleading for understanding. "Because I promised God if He spared Brad, I would leave that man alone. I'm telling you, Mikey, it's just not my destiny to be happy.''

Michael tried a softer approach. "Cori, you're exhausted. You haven't left this hospital ever since Brad was brought in. You aren't thinking rationally. Please, Honey, don't do this. You need this man.''

"You don't have to understand, Mikey. You do, however, have to respect my decision. I made a deal with God. He did His part, and now I'm going to do mine.''

Chapter 18

As the doctor predicted, the next forty-eight hours were critical. Brad fell into a coma after the surgery. The doctors assured Brad's anxious friends and family that a coma was not uncommon, given Brad's injuries.

"All we can do is monitor him and wait for him to wake up," the family was told.

The waiting room near the ICU was command central for the "Brad Watch." Brad's parents, Edgar and Frances Marshall, his sister Julie, Vern, a few of the pit crew, and Michael all alternated between staying in the small area waiting for news of Brad's improvement and sitting by his bedside. Even his brother Dwayne came up from Atlanta. The only person missing from the gathering was Cori.

Julie asked Vern about the missing sponsor. "When do I get to meet this Corinthia Justice my brother couldn't stop thinking about? I expected she'd be here."

Vern shrugged. "I expected she'd be here, too. She was here that first day, and for some reason she hasn't been back since."

That's odd. Julie pondered. "Maybe she wasn't as involved as he wanted her to be, after all."

Vern shook his head. "I don't know why she's not here, but I do know she was plenty involved with him. You didn't see her that day at the track. She nearly went ballistic when the paramedics wouldn't let her ride in the ambulance. Something's going on, but it's not that she doesn't care about him. I'd stake my life on that."

Julie looked across the waiting room at Michael slumped in a chair, thumbing aimlessly through a magazine. "Think he knows?" She nodded in Michael's direction.

"Could be."

Julie stood and started toward Michael. She was stopped in mid-step by the return of her mother from a brief dinner break.

"Julie, have the doctors been back? Have they said anything?" Frances Marshall walked over to her daughter's side. At five-foot six inches, Frances was about the same height as Julie, but that was where the similarity ended. Frances was fair and thin. She wore her silvering hair in a neatly cut bob that didn't quite reach her chin. The family had always joked how such a thin, light-skinned mother could create three such strapping, dark-hued children. One would only have to look at the ebony physique of Edgar Marshall to understand that. All three Marshall siblings took directly from their father.

"No, Ma'am. Nothing's changed." Julie placed her arm around Frances's shoulders and pulled her close. "I would have called you immediately if anything happened."

Frances sighed. "I know you would have, Honey. It's just that this waiting is making me crazy. How much longer can he go on like this?"

Julie thought about the accounts she'd heard of patients lingering in comas for years. But she decided not to mention it; that knowledge would only upset her mother further. Instead, she hugged Frances again. "He's going to be okay, Mom. Brad is the strongest man I know. He'll be fine."

"Fat lot of good all that strength is doing him now." The snorted comment came from a nearby chair. "I kept telling him this racing would be the death of him."

"Now is not the time, Dwayne," Julie said sternly. "Let it go. We need to concentrate our energies on Brad's recovery."

At an inch or two shorter, a pant size larger, and a shade lighter, Dwayne was a slightly modified version of his older brother—sort of "Brad Lite." Gold-toned, wire rimmed oval glasses projected the air of seriousness Dwayne worked hard to cultivate. He was clean-shaven and kept his black hair closely trimmed.

"Of course Brad is going to recover," Dwayne said matter-of-factly. "The question is, what will he do then? He can't keep racing. I would think this little incident proves that beyond a shadow of a doubt."

"Why wouldn't he be able to keep racing?" Julie demanded. "If racing is what he wants, who are you to say he can't do it anymore?"

"Who am I? Looks like I'm the only sensible one here." Dwayne sat bolt upright in his chair. "Are you overlooking the fact that Brad nearly died because of that damn racing? He can't just keep putting himself in that kind of danger. And for what? A cheap plastic trophy and a few dollars?"

Frances shook her head tiredly. "Dwayne, it's Brad's life, and his choice. You have to let him make it."

"Yes, Ma'am." Dwayne fell back into a sullen silence.

The two days they'd spent waiting at the hospital were beginning to wear on all of them.

Vern, who had observed the whole Marshall family drama, shook his head in disgust. *That Dwayne has always been jealous of Brad,* he thought. *He'll damn well hold his tongue when Brad wakes up. The last thing he'll need is that boy raggin' on him.* Vern decided to go check on Brad before he said something he'd regret.

Vern slowly pulled open the door to Brad's room. The blinds were closed, darkening the room. Brad lay in exactly the same motionless position he'd been in for the last two days. His rich complexion seemed sallow in the dim light. There was an oxygen tube in his nostrils, feeding him a steady supply of pure air. Several IV bags hung from a stand near the bed; there were IV needles taped to both his arms. The room was still except for the quiet gurgling and beeping of the hospital machinery.

Brad's father, Edgar, was sleeping in a chair at the foot of the bed. Vern approached the sleeping man.

"Ed." Vern shook him gently. "Ed. Why don't you go on home and get some rest?"

Ed Marshall looked up at Vern groggily. "I'm okay . . . I wasn't sleeping."

Vern laughed shortly. "Yeah, right. At least go to the cafeteria and get yourself a bite to eat."

Ed nodded and rose from the chair. He stretched, working the kinks out of his back. "Are you going to stay with him?"

Vern nodded. "I promise I'll come get you if there's any change."

"Thanks, Vern. You've always been such a good friend to my son." Ed patted Vern's shoulder and left the room.

Watching the elder Marshall's departure, Vern had to wonder if he really had been so good a friend to Brad. *Maybe if I were a better friend, or at least a better spotter, he wouldn't be lying here battered and comatose.* Vern collapsed in the chair Ed had just vacated. He concentrated on pushing away the disquieting thoughts and focusing on Brad, as if somehow he could will his friend to awaken. The two of them stayed that way, each still and in his own world, for nearly an hour. Vern had dozed off when he heard a sound coming from Brad's bed.

Brad's head turned from side to side on the pillow. "Cori? Cori?" The words were whispered, barely audible over the sounds of the machinery.

Vern was instantly alert. "No, Cowboy. It's me—Vern."

Fighting through layers of haziness, Brad was slow to respond. "Vern? Where am I? What happened?"

"You're at the hospital. You had a pretty bad crack-up. Do you remember any of it?"

Brad struggled to recall. "I remember there was a crash ahead of me . . . I came in low to miss it . . . but it was there." His voice trailed off at the end. "That's the last thing I remember. What day is it?"

"It's Monday, Cowboy," Vern said gently. "You've been in a coma for two days."

"Two days? I've lost two days?" Brad's eyes closed again. Then he was suddenly alert again. "No, wait, I remember one more thing. I remember seeing Cori, after the accident . . . in the ambulance?" Brad focused on Vern. "Where is she, Vern? I want to see her."

"Tell you what," Vern said, deftly avoiding the question, "there's a whole lot of people out there who are going to be jumping for joy that you've come around. I'm going to go get them." Vern hurried to the waiting room.

Within seconds, Brad's room was swarming with family and friends, some with tears in their eyes.

"Hey, Guys," Brad managed weakly, "how's tricks?"

Brad's mother was the first to reach his bedside. Frances bent to kiss her son, her tears of joy wetting both their cheeks.

"Mama, don't cry." Brad tried to lift his arms to comfort her but the effort took too much out of him.

"I can't help it, Baby." Frances brushed at the steady stream with her fingers. "We almost lost you. I was so scared."

"I'm not going anywhere, Mama. I promise you that."

As Frances sat on the side of his bed, Brad looked around the room, taking in the concerned faces of his family. The Marshall clan gathered around the bed, drawing strength and comfort from each other. No one said anything. Even

Dwayne managed to still his tongue, because they all knew now was not the time.

Brad could feel the love of his family nourishing him, bolstering him for the tough days of recovery that lay ahead. In the circle of his family, he felt supported and loved. Only one thing was missing.

"Cori? Somebody, where's Cori?"

"I'll find her for you, Cowboy." Vern's mouth set in a determined line. "Don't worry about a thing."

Instead of rushing into the room, Michael had stayed back. There were two reasons: first, he didn't want to intrude on the Marshall family at this time of joy, and second, he wanted to call Cori right away with the news.

In her office at the restaurant, Cori was ecstatic. "Oh, Mikey, I knew it! I knew he'd pull through."

"So when are you coming down? Everybody's wondering where you are." Michael had overheard Julie and Vern's conversation.

"Mikey, you know I can't do that."

"Not that stupid deal again." Michael snorted. "When are you going to quit acting crazy?"

"It's not crazy—it's real. You're the one who just said Brad is out of his coma."

"But that had nothing to do with any deal."

"How do you know?" Cori asked pointedly. "You don't. And I'm not going to risk it. A deal's a deal. Thank you for giving me the update." She hung up the phone before he could respond.

Alone in the quiet of her office Cori thought, yet again, about Brad and the hospital. These last two days had been hell. Her mind was never far away from Brad; her prayers never addressed anything else. She was deeply relieved that Brad had awakened from his coma, but in her mind that just reinforced her commitment to her "bargain".

I know Mikey thinks I'm acting crazy . . . maybe I am . . . but

I can't risk it. She looked at the picture of Tony and Brianna. All the guilt and uncertainty that had become an integral part of her makeup gurgled and swelled inside of her until she thought she'd choke on bile.

What if I'm right? What if Brad's recovery was *God keeping his end of the deal?* The thought tortured her. In her heart, she knew she desperately wanted to see Brad, wanted to stroke his smooth, ebony face, wanted to feel the power of his muscled shoulders and arms under her hands. The longing was so powerful that she felt a tingling sensation in her hands. And now that she knew he was awake, she ached for him even more. But some force deep in her consciousness, some power that defied reasoning and logic, kept her from going to be by his side.

She pushed herself out of the desk chair and paced the small office with all the coiled tension of a caged panther. Her heart ached, perhaps even more than when Tony died, because Brad was still within reach . . . just a phone call or a short ride away. But in her mind, Brad was just as lost as Tony.

"I could have loved him." Her forlorn voice was barely a whisper. "We could have had a future together." Cori's shoulders sagged from the weight of her loneliness. "I cannot go to the hospital," she muttered, resigning herself to the notion that Brad's recovery was contingent on her leaving him alone. "I promised. . . ."

After a few minutes, the pain in her soul became too intense to ignore. Cori left her office, in search of a diversion. The restaurant was fairly quiet; the dinner rush had not yet begun. She wandered into the kitchen, but her staff had everything under control. She checked with the hostess, but again found that her assistance was not required.

Shrugging, she turned back in the direction of her office. That's when they caught her eye—dozens of colorful bottles lined the counter behind the bar, inviting Cori to seek solace in their depths. Without having made a conscious

decision, Cori found herself walking into her office with
a half-full container of vodka under her arm.

Michael slowly replaced the receiver of the pay phone.
Cori is acting like one class A lunatic. She's being so stubborn!
Michael shook his head sadly. *And what am I going to say
to Brad? I can't make any excuses for Cori,* he thought, *and I
don't want to tell Brad where her head is, not until I have a
chance to talk her out of this nonsense.* After a few moments,
Michael decided his only option was to leave the hospital
without seeing Brad. Michael returned to the chair where
he'd spent so many hours hunkered down and picked up
a few things he'd left nearby. He'd almost made it to the
exit when Vern stopped him.

"Did you call her? Is she coming?" Concern was etched
on Vern's grizzled features. "He's been asking for her."

"Unfortunately, Vern, she isn't coming," Michael said,
"at least not yet."

"What? Why? I don't get it."

"Yeah, well take a number in that line," Michael muttered. "I can't really explain it, Vern, but something's
going on with Cori, and I need to talk to her."

"Look, you tell that sister of yours that this boy needs
her, so she'd better get her tail down here right away. I
don't care what's going on with her. Brad's recovery is all
that matters now," Vern said, uncharacteristically angry.
"Tell her to get down here, Foster, or I'll come and bring
her down here myself!"

Unconsciously, Michael took a step back from Vern's
wrath. "Whatever's going on with with Cori, I don't believe
threats are going to be the answer," Michael said. "She's
going to have to make the decisions that are best for her."

"No, she's not . . . not if she loves that boy like I think
she does. She's going to have to make the decisions that
are best for Brad, regardless of how it effects her."

"I think maybe that's exactly what she's doing." Michael thought about Cori's misguided sense of sacrifice.

"You're talkin' in circles, Foster," Vern snapped. "I don't know what you mean, and I don't care. All I care about is that boy's recovery. He wants to see your sister, and I'm going to make that happen for him." Vern's voice broke slightly, and he had to swallow a lump in his throat before he could continue. "That's the least I can do for him. I let him down before at the track . . . I'm not going to let him down again." Vern's eyes glinted with unshed tears. "Get her here, Michael . . . please."

Nodding, Michael hurried out of the hospital.

Chapter 19

When Michael arrived at Foster's, he marched straight
to Cori's office, determined to get her to go to the hospital.
Without knocking, he threw open the door. What he saw
inside the office made his blood run cold.

Cori was sitting, arms folded on the desktop, her chin
resting on the backs of her crossed hands. She was at eye
level with a clear liquor bottle, staring vacantly into it. On
the desk next to the bottle was a highball glass filled with
ice. Condensation had formed on the outside of the glass,
and rivulets of water were rolling down the sides, making
a ring on Cori's desk blotter.

Michael stopped dead in his tracks, his mission forgotten. "Oh, Honey, no. . . ." His voice was a strangled
whisper.

"Come on in, Mikey." Cori didn't move from her position. "Pull up a chair. You might want to get your own
glass, though. This one's mine." She continued staring
into the vodka bottle.

Michael pushed the door closed behind him and went
to kneel next to Cori's chair. He stretched one arm across

the back of the chair and reached for the bottle with the other. "Cori, please tell me you haven't been drinking. Please tell me you didn't go *there.*"

"Why shouldn't I, Mikey?" The question was flat and absent. "What earthly reason would I have for not taking this drink?"

"Don't you remember, Honey? Don't you remember how drink almost ruined your life?" Michael eased the bottle off the desk, out of her line of sight.

Still, Cori didn't move. "What I remember is how completely the pain was erased when I drank. Nothing hurt anymore. I could forget all about Tony and Bree and the accident. That's what I remember."

"I'm surprised you remember that," Michael mumbled. "Cori, that was the blackest period of your life, even worse than the accident, because you were doing it to yourself. Nothing hurt anymore because nothing mattered anymore."

Cori shrugged. "Maybe that's where I should be again . . . in that place where nothing hurts or matters anymore."

"What's wrong with you, Girl? Have you completely lost your mind?" Michael snapped. "I have been trying to be understanding and supportive, but I am not going to sit by and watch you destroy your life again! I love you too much for that. Now answer me—have you had a drink?"

With agonizing slowness, Cori lifted her head from the desktop and turned to look her brother square in the eyes. "No, Mikey. I haven't. But I was closer than I've been in years."

Michael breathed out heavily. "Why? I don't understand—why now?"

Cori looked away, unable to offer an explanation.

"It's because of Brad, isn't it? And this ridiculous 'deal' you think you've made." Michael's voice was heavy with contempt. "Look, Sis, I don't have the same kind of relationship you do with God, and I'll be the first to admit that, but I can't believe God wants you to be drunk and alone. Is that what you think He wants for you?" Michael demanded. "Well, is it?"

"Of course not." Cori's eyes widened in shock. "That's a dumb thing to say."

"And yet I find you closeted in your office staring into a vodka bottle."

"That was my choice," Cori admitted, "not a directive from God."

"So you are still making some choices for yourself." Michael nodded. "Good. Because I need you to come to the hospital, and I need you to come now."

Cori sat in stunned silence for a moment, processing her brother's words. "You know I can't do that," she whispered.

"No, Cori. I know that you *have* to do that. Brad needs you—and you owe him some kind of explanation. You can't just disappear from his life without a trace." Michael reached for her hands. "If you are determined to honor this 'deal' of yours there's nothing I can do about that, but Brad loves you. You were the first person he asked for when he regained consciousness. Walk away if you feel you must, but not before you talk to Brad. You owe him that much—hell, you owe yourself that much."

Cori shook her head in protest. "I can't—"

"You have to," Michael insisted. "Obviously your decision is not a done deal in your mind. Otherwise, you wouldn't be sitting here contemplating making the worst mistake of your life. So you have to see him. Think of it as closure if that'll help—but you have to go." Michael stood and gently pulled her up with him. "Now."

Cori again shook her head. "You just don't understand, Mikey. It's not that I don't want to see Brad. My heart aches I want to see him so much. I just can't." She pulled her hands out of his grasp.

"What is it you want, Cori?"

She pushed a lock of chestnut hair away from her eyes,

stalling while she pondered the question. "I want Brad to recover."

Michael nodded. "Okay. Then believe me when I say that seeing you will speed his recovery like no medicine can." He held out his hand. "How about it?"

Cori looked deeply into his eyes. She was seeing her brother in a whole new light. No longer could she regard him as a ne'er-do-well who needed constant supervision. Somehow, since they'd arrived in Charlotte, little Mikey had become a man. "When did you get so wise, Little Brother?"

Michael shrugged. "I'm just looking out for my big sis." He moved his still outstretched hand closer to her. "Are you coming?"

After heaving a heavy sigh, she placed her hand in his. "I'm just going to make sure he's all right," she said stubbornly. "This doesn't change a thing."

"Whatever you say, Sis. Whatever you say."

After an examination, the doctor pronounced Brad well on the road to recovery.

"He's got a long way to go," Dr. Bennett warned, "but the prognosis is good.'

A collective sigh of relief whooshed through the room. The elder Marshalls, Julie, Dwayne, and Vern were all crowded into Brad's hospital room. Although they had made room for the doctor, no one had wanted to leave since he had regained consciousness. Julie and Dwayne stood next to each other near the window, across the room from the bed. Frances and Ed had stations next to the bed, and Vern, having completed his business with Michael Foster, stood with his back against the door.

Brad sat patiently throughout the doctor's examination. "So how soon can I get back in my race car?" To Brad, not racing was not an option.

"Let's just wait and see about that, Mr. Marshall," Dr.

Bennett replied. "For now, let's focus on getting you back on your feet. . .the race car can wait."

"Permanently, if you ask me," Dwayne muttered.

"Back off, Dwayne," Julie hissed softly. "This is not the time."

Dwayne turned to face his sister. "Well, when *is* the time, Julie?" Dwayne demanded. "Brad almost died this time. What more is it going to have to take?"

Julie rolled her eyes at him. "Not now." She left Dwayne fuming and went to stand by Brad's side. She bent to kiss his cheek. "You gave us quite a scare."

"Aw, Julie. I've told you before, it's not my destiny to die in a race car." Brad managed a semi-cocky smile. "You need to trust me."

Everyone in the room, with the exception of Dwayne, shared a tension-breaking laugh.

"Now, Ladies and Gentlemen," Dr. Bennett began, "I know how concerned you are about him, but for now, I must ask you to leave his room. Brad needs to rest and regain his strength. You can all come back tomorrow."

Frances Marshall huffed, preparing to protest the doctor's orders, but her husband intervened.

"Come on, Frannie, the doctor's right. Besides, you need your rest, too, or else you'll wind up here in a room next door." Ed gently pointed his wife toward the door.

"Okay," Frances agreed, "I'll go for now, but I'll be back first thing in the morning." She bent to kiss her son. "Get some rest, Darling. I love you."

Brad smiled, warmed by the power of his mother's love. "I'll see you in the morning, Mama."

Ed reached for his son's hand and gave it a firm squeeze. "Boy, you and that racing are going to be the death of me," he chuckled.

"Well, since I drove them here, I guess I've got to go, too," Julie said. "Besides, the twins have probably driven Malcolm crazy by now."

"Kiss Tyler and Taylor for me?" Brad asked.

"Of course. And they'll be so happy to hear that Uncle Brad is going to be all right." Julie smiled. "Maybe I can bring them out later." She brushed another kiss on his cheek and then followed her parents out the door, which Vern was holding open.

Brad turned to Dwayne, who was still standing near the window. "Thanks for coming up here, Man."

Dwayne snorted shortly. "Where else would I be?" He walked over to the bed. "I'm just glad you're going to pull through. We had some scary moments these last couple of days."

"Nothing to be afraid of," Brad assured him. "I'm just a little banged up. No big deal."

"No big deal?" Dwayne's voice rose. "Man, you almost died! How much bigger a deal could it be?" Dwayne took a deep breath. "Look, Brad, everyone around here has been telling me that now is not the time, but I can't think of any better time."

"Time for what?"

"Time to talk to you about giving up this racing nonsense." Dwayne ignored the threatening looks he was getting from Vern. "Brad, it's time to quit. You can't keep putting your life at risk like this. And for what? Cheap plastic trophies and a few dollars? Isn't your life worth more than that?"

Vern stepped up to him. "You've been singing that same tired old song for the last two days, Dwayne, and it's just as much none of your business now as it was as when you started. Get off his back."

"Wasn't nobody talking to you, Old Man," Dwayne ground out. "This is between my brother and me."

"Like hell it is," Vern growled. "Your brother is my friend, and I'm not going to sit back and let you rag on him about his career choice."

"If you really were his friend, you would make him see how dangerous and stupid his 'career choice' is." Dwayne met the grizzled crew chief toe-to-toe. "But maybe it's a moot point, anyway. Where is your sponsor, Brad? Now that you're out of commission, have they just kicked you to the curb like yesterday's trash?"

"That's stupid and mean," Vern said, quick to respond. "You're just so jealous you can't think straight. Brad is more of a man, living more of a life than you'll ever know, and it makes you crazy, doesn't it, *Dwayne?*" Vern spat out the name.

"Insult me all you want to, Old Man, but that still doesn't change the fact that Brad's sponsors have not been around here." Dwayne turned questioning eyes on Brad. "What's up with that?'

Brad looked plaintively at Vern. Of all the things that had been said around him, the question of his sponsors— Cori in particular—rattled him the most. "Yeah, Vern. What *is* up with that?"

Vern was just opening his mouth to answer when a knock on the door cut him off.

"Can we come in?" Michael stuck his head in the door.

"We?" Vern asked hopefully.

A broad smile spread across Michael's face. "Yes—we." He pushed the door open completely and gently pulled Cori into the room.

Cori strode over to Brad's bed, oblivious to the presence of others in the room. "Thank God," she breathed, "it is true. You are awake." Her hand moved of its own accord, and before she knew what was happening she was stroking his warm, smooth cheek. The tingling sensation she'd felt earlier, yearning to touch him, was replaced by the undeniable current that pulsed between them. Tears sprang to her eyes.

"Oh, Brad," she said, her voice barely more than a whisper, "I don't know what I would have done if you'd died, too."

Too? The question exploded in Brad's mind.

"Who are you?" Dwayne demanded, looking from Cori to Michael.

"Where are my manners?" Vern interjected. "Dwayne Marshall, allow me to present Michael Foster and Corinthia Justice—Brad's sponsors." A satisfied smirk colored Vern's features. "Michael and Cori, this is Dwayne, Brad's baby brother."

The look of confusion on Dwayne's face hardened into a mask of sheer loathing. "So you're the ones financing Brad's little suicide trip, eh? Bet this accident has been worth a boatload of publicity for you."

Cori recoiled, visibly shaken by the disdain she felt emanating from Dwayne.

"Hey, Man, what's your problem?" Michael could feel muscles tensing as if preparing for a fight.

"My problem is my brother seems determined to kill himself, and I'm standing in a room full of people who keep providing him with the loaded gun!"

"Chill, Dwyane." The directive came from Brad, issued with quiet authority. "These people are my friends, and I won't stand for you talking to them like that. Racing is my choice . . . it's what I want out of life. You don't have to understand or like it or support it, but you do have to respect it." Brad leaned up on his elbows as best he could, mustering power to put behind his words. "I think you ought to go now. You have caused enough tension for one evening."

"For one lifetime, you mean," Vern muttered.

"Brad, you've got to know that I'm only upset like this because I love you and I care what happens to you." Dwayne turned pleading eyes on his brother. "I'm sorry if I was out of line, but I can't just sit by and watch while you drive yourself into an early grave!" He turned to go, pausing with his hand on the doorknob. "Just think about what I've said, Bro. I'll be in town for the rest of the week, so if and when you decide you're ready, I'd be happy to make a few calls for you."

"I'll keep that in mind," Brad said dryly. "Talk to you later, Dwayne."

After nodding a grudging apology to Cori, Michael, and Vern, Dwayne made his exit.

"I'm really sorry about Dwayne." Brad sighed. "He's a little intense."

"A little?" Michael shook his head. "Man, that brother of yours is wired to blow."

Brad lay back on his pillows, exhaustion taking its toll. Vern noticed the movement.

"Foster, why don't we leave these two alone? Won't be long before our buddy is out for the count, and I know he'd like to spend a few minutes with Cori before it's lights out."

"Good idea." Michael nodded his agreement. He walked over to his sister and wrapped her in a hug. "Don't make any decisions you're going to live to regret," he whispered in her ear.

Cori nodded briefly, not trusting her voice to speak. Within seconds, Vern and Michael were gone. It seemed to Cori as if the room were filled with crackling electricity.

"Come sit next to me," Brad invited. "You don't know how happy I am to see you."

"I'll bet I do know," Cori said, nodding her head, " 'cause I know how happy I am to see *you*." She reached for a nearby chair and pulled it up to the side of his bed. Settling in the chair, she clasped his hand between hers. The rugged texture of his palm felt like a loving massage to her hands.

"The last time I saw you, you weren't looking so good. What does the doctor say about your condition?"

"Aw, you know doctors . . . always being overly cautious." Brad shrugged. "He says I'm doing better, but I've still got a long way to go. He says it's amazing I wasn't banged up worse than this. I guess God's been very good to me."

"More than you realize, Brad. You have been blessed." She looked earnestly into his eyes. "You're going to have to take it easy for a while, but I know you'll make a complete recovery."

Brad yawned, joking lightly, "From your mouth to God's ear."

His innocent words sent ice through her veins. "Brad, I need to talk to you," she began.

"Kiss me first," Brad commanded.

"Wha—" Cori hesitated, startled by the request. "What did you say?'

"I said, kiss me first." He tried to stifle a yawn. "Whatever you want to talk to me about will have to wait until you kiss me."

Cori sighed. *This is going to be harder than I thought.* She lifted the hand she was holding to her lips and brushed the back of it with an airy kiss. "There. Now can we talk?"

"Cori," he said, his voice full of gentle reproach, "you're not getting shy on me now, are you? That's not the kind of kiss I had in mind." His dark eyes grew even more intense. "Kiss me like you mean it," he purred.

"Brad, you just woke up from a coma," Cori protested.

"All the more reason to kiss me like there's no tomorrow." His hand tightened around hers as he pulled her closer.

What can it hurt? Cori thought. *One last kiss, and then I'll be ready to let go.* She rose slowly from her chair and leaned over Brad. He raised his arms to wrap her, pulling her into an intimate hug. She moved closer to him, feeling his breath hot against her lips. Her eyes closed, and a shiver of anticipation rolled down her back. Then their lips met, and all the worry, anxiety, and fear of the past two days evaporated like a drop of water on a hot griddle. The kiss was tender at first, but mushroomed in urgency and intensity. His tongue probed her mouth, tasting, seeking to lay claim on her soul. She met his searching tongue with a hunger that took her by surprise. For the moment, nothing existed, nothing else mattered, but this man and this kiss. She felt herself on the edge of a precipice, with no desire to stop her fall.

After a moment, rational thought struggled to be heard.

Cori pulled away, ending the magical kiss. Breathless and confused, Cori turned away from his searching eyes and settled herself back in the chair. She used the moment in an effort to compose herself, an effort that was strained at best. *I shouldn't have done that,* her mind screamed. *I've got to be stronger. I'll never be able to get through this otherwise. But Lordy, how that man can kiss!*

"Mmmm," Brad purred, unaware of her turmoil. "Now that's what I call a kiss." His eyes closed as he drifted toward sleep.

"Brad, I need to talk to you," Cori insisted. "Please don't fall asleep yet."

"I'm really beat now, Cori." Brad's voice grew increasingly groggy. "Can't you talk to me tomorrow?"

Cori's eyes widened. "No, Brad. It has to be today." *I don't know if I'll be able to tomorrow.* "Just listen for a few minutes. I can't see you anymore," she blurted out. "I have to leave you alone."

"No . . . you don't," Brad mumbled, misunderstanding her intentions. "I can sleep with you here. I'm just really tired now . . . stay with me?" For all intents and purposes, he was asleep as soon as he finished the sentence.

Cori heaved a frustrated sigh. *I don't think I'll be able to go through this again tomorrow. It's just too hard.* She sat by his bed, watching the rhythmic rise and fall of his chest, contemplating her decision. *I tried to tell him,* she reasoned stubbornly, *but he wouldn't listen. He'll just have to accept it. There's no other way.*

She rose from her chair, scraping it across the floor. The movement stirred Brad.

"Are you leaving?" he managed.

"Yes, I've got to go."

"I'm sorry I'm not good company tonight." His sincerity was touching. "I'll feel better tomorrow."

Cori nodded. "You're going to feel a little better every day, I promise you that. In time, you'll be as good as new." She was only partially talking about his injuries.

He shifted on the bed, settling into a more comfortable position. "G'night, Cori," he mumbled.

She brushed a kiss on his forehead and gently stroked his cheek. "Good-bye Brad," she whispered.

Chapter 20

Almost immediately, a black cloud settled in on Cori, a cloud through which no one could penetrate. The change in Cori started the moment she left the hospital that last time. All the way home in the car with Michael she was sullen and incommunicative. Her family and the staff at the restaurant sensed her loneliness and isolation, but Cori deliberately closed herself away. The few brave souls who tried to reach her experienced the sound and fury of Hurricane Cori.

Only Michael knew the source of her pain, and he chose to keep his own counsel about the situation. Cori knew, better than anyone, how he felt about her choice, but out of love and respect for his sister, Michael held his tongue.

Cori went through the motions of her day, but she was never completely there. On the third day after she left Brad at the hospital, her emotions had reached the breaking point.

She was in her office, ostensibly working on a produce order form. In truth, she was having great difficulty focusing on the paperwork spread on her desk.

A knock at the door startled her. "Come in," she barked.

Jasmine stuck her head in the office. "I'm sorry to bother you, Mrs. Justice, but he's on the phone again—"

"And?" Cori snapped. "Have you forgotten what I asked you to do when this happens?"

"No, Ma'am." Jasmine hesitated. "But he sounds so sad and upset. I just thought—"

"See, there was your first mistake. Don't think, Jasmine." Cori's voice was uncharacteristically harsh. "Just do. I don't want to talk to him. I haven't wanted to talk to him all week, and nothing has changed. Please don't bother me with anything like this again."

"Yes Ma'am!" Jasmine dared a mock salute before she beat a hasty retreat.

Instantly, Cori was sorry for her behavior. *It's not Jasmine's fault,* she reminded herself. *You made this choice. It's not fair to take it out on everyone around you.* She braced her elbows on the desk and held her head in her hands. *But I cannot talk to Brad. I know he must be confused, but I'm just not sure I'm strong enough to stick to my decision.* A heavy sigh escaped her lips. *With each passing day, this seems less and less like a good idea.*

Her musings were interrupted by another knock. This time it was the bartender, Darrell, who dared to invade her privacy.

"Mrs. Justice." Darrell stood in the doorway with one hand on the knob, ready to quickly escape if the situation warranted it. "I was just taking inventory of our supplies and we're running low on cocktail napkins."

"Running low? How low? And why have you waited until now to tell me about this?" Cori practically growled the interrogation.

"We're just low, Mrs. Justice. We're not out," Darrell defended himself. "I thought you'd need to know so you could order more, but it's not an emergency or anything." Darrell had inched further out of the office as he talked.

The sight of Darrell's discomfort leeched all of the anger

and annoyance out of Cori. "Darrell, I'm so sorry. I had no reason to speak to you like that. I hope you can forgive me. I guess I've got a lot on my mind these days."

Darrell nodded. "Don't worry about it, Mrs. Justice. Please let me know if there's anything I can do for you . . . or if you just need to talk, I'm only a bar stool away."

"I'm staying away from those bar stools," Cori muttered under her breath. "Thanks for the offer, Darrell. And I'll get those napkins ordered right away."

Darrell nodded and left her alone with her thoughts again.

I've got to get out of here for a while. I'm driving myself and everyone around me nuts. She checked her watch. *I've got a few hours before dinner. Maybe I'll take a little walk, try to burn off some of this energy.*

Cori fished her purse out of a desk drawer and headed toward the door. At the hostess's stand, she stopped to offer her apologies.

"Jasmine, please forgive me for being such a bear earlier," Cori said. "I've been in a funk lately, and I had no right taking it out on you."

Jasmine nodded. "That's okay, Mrs. Justice. I know what it's like to deal with a broken heart. It'll get better eventually."

Cori was momentarily taken aback by Jasmine's assessment. *A broken heart? Is that what I've got?* "Well, whatever it is, it's not your fault, and I was wrong to snap at you." Cori took a deep breath. "I'm going out for a while, Jasmine. I just need a little fresh air to clear my head."

"Sure. No problem, Mrs. Justice." She smiled encouragingly. "Take as long as you need."

Cori left the restaurant with no destination in mind. She just knew she needed to get away—away from that booth where she had first encountered Brad's proudly bald, ebony presence; away from that office where Brad first claimed her lips in a torrid kiss; and mostly, away from that ever-present threat behind the bar.

Cori walked without really seeing the scenery around her. She walked, hoping to forget, but her thoughts still churned with memories of Brad and what they shared.

After several minutes, Cori stopped to get her bearings. Gleaming in the sunshine a block ahead was the steeple of First Baptist Church. Cori smiled at the realization that her wanderings had led her to her sanctuary.

I wonder if Pastor Henry is here. She paused, considering. *I sure could use someone to talk to.*

Her stride quickened as she approached the church doors. The parking lot next to the building was empty. Disappointment washed over Cori.

Pastor Henry makes it a policy to have the church open during the day, she remembered. *He says it's the church's job to be available when the people need it, so the secretary ought to be here, at least.*

She decided to try the doors, anyway; even if she couldn't talk to Pastor Henry, she could still find a little comfort and a few minutes peace inside. Much to her relief, the doors were unlocked. She pulled them open and slipped inside.

The large church seemed cavernous when it was empty. Cori tiptoed through the vestibule and entered the sanctuary. The walls were painted white, but with the sun streaming through the stained glass windows the room seemed more colorful. Rows of polished, dark, wood pews lined the sides of the room. In front, the pulpit was in the center of the church, with choir stands on either side. A row of potted plants lined the floor immediately in front of the pulpit. And hanging on the wall behind the pulpit was an enormous wooden cross.

Cori went to the front pew and sat down quietly. "Lord, I need some help." Her voice echoed in the empty room. "I just don't know anymore if I'm doing the right thing." She sat on the edge of the pew and leaned over the front railing. The beginnings of tears welled up in her eyes. "I'm so confused."

Suddenly, footsteps broke the quiet of the church.

"Sister Justice? What a pleasant surprise!" Pastor Henry approached her, a broad smile stretched across his face. "I thought I heard somebody in here."

Cori looked up, startled by his appearance. "I didn't think you were here, Pastor. I didn't see your car in the lot." Of average height, Pastor Henry somehow managed to seem taller, even without the benefit of his pulpit. His dark-skinned face held expressive, brown eyes that missed nothing that went on in his church. He was in his mid-fifties and had tended to the needs of First Baptist for the last fifteen years.

"Well, Mrs. Henry has it today. Said she had some errands to run, but I suspect it was really some shopping to do." He winked. "So I'm stranded here without a car, which suits me just fine because I get a lot more work done when people don't think I'm here."

"Oh." Cori was dismayed. "I'm sorry. I don't want to interrupt your work." She stood. "I can just go now."

Pastor Henry took her hands. "Corinthia, my people are my work," he said gently. "Obviously there's something on your mind. Why don't you sit back down and talk to me about it?"

Cori hesitated for the briefest of seconds and then nodded. She took her seat on the pew and scooted over to make room for the pastor.

"I don't know where to begin." Her voice was barely more than a whisper. "I've made a decision for what I thought were all the right reasons, but now I'm not so sure."

Pastor Henry nodded and waited for her to continue.

Cori took a deep breath and plunged in. "It has to do with that race car driver who visited church last month, Brad Marshall. See, he is . . . was . . . more to me than just a driver I helped sponsor. Brad and I became very close. It has taken me a long time to find a man I wanted to be with . . . a man who could help me leave my past behind me. I really thought I could fall in love with him.'' At first, the words hung up in her throat, but as she talked the story came easier. ''I don't think I've ever admitted that before, not even to myself.'' She tested the words again. ''I think I was falling in love with him.''

''So what went wrong, Cori?'' Pastor Henry prompted.

''I don't honestly know. Brad had a horrible accident a week or so ago.'' Cori's eyes glazed over as she remembered. ''His car flipped over and over . . . I thought for sure that he was dead. But he wasn't . . . and I rode with him in the ambulance to the hospital. At first, the doctors wouldn't let me be with him.'' Her voice trembled and tears clouded her view. ''It was just like Tony all over again.''

''Tony was your husband who died?'' Pastor Henry nodded. ''I remember you talking to me about him and your daughter when you first arrived here.''

Cori nodded. ''Yes, Tony was my husband and the doctors wouldn't let me see him, either. When they finally let me in, Tony was dead. She lost her composure completely as the threatened tears came. Pastor Henry got a box of tissues from the choir stand and handed it to her. ''It was different with Brianna. She held on for two days before her little body gave out. I was holding her when she died. . . . I rocked her right into heaven.'' Cori tried to dry her face, but the tears kept coming. ''Pastor Henry, I wanted to die, too. I have never been that low before. And on top of everything else, I felt guilty. Why did I live, and not them? Why wasn't there something I could do for Tony? I never even got to say good-bye.''

Pastor Henry gave her hand a reassuring squeeze. ''I can only imagine what that must have been like for you, but you have to know that God doesn't give any of us more than we can handle. I not quite sure, though, how that fits in with your problems with the race car driver.''

Cori drew in a cleansing breath and continued. ''When I saw Brad's accident, all I could think about was what happened with Tony, that I couldn't fail Brad the way I'd failed Tony. The doctors finally let me in Brad's room, and he was unconscious but alive. I was just reaching out to touch him when he went into cardiac arrest. Doctors and nurses raced into the room, scrambling to save his life. At that precise moment, I prayed, harder than I ever remember praying before. I asked God to save Brad's life and I promised that if He did, I would stay away from Brad. It was a scary couple of minutes, but the doctors were able to revive him. I took that as the answer to my prayer." Cori smiled, reliving the relief she felt when Brad was revived. "I'm trying to keep my promise and stay away from him, but Pastor, it is so hard. I miss him so much. But I'm afraid to go to him, because I promised." Cori's voice trailed off uncertainly.

Pastor Henry was silent for a moment, trying to pick his words carefully. "I think you have misinterpreted what happened that day. It was not your promise that led to Brad being healed. It was your faith in God's power that made it happen. All God asks of us is that we believe in Him, that we have faith in His power and His love for us. By turning to Him at your moment of greatest need, you have demonstrated your faith. He's not holding you to any promise, because He knows you believe—just because you asked."

Cori looked hopefully at her pastor. "Can that really be? Am I really not bound by this promise?"

"Only you can answer that, Cori," Pastor Henry said. "But I am curious about one thing. Why did you even make such an offer to begin with? Why would you think the way to save Brad's life was to stay away from him?"

"You're going to think I'm acting foolish," Cori muttered, looking away. "My brother has flat-out called me crazy."

"I am absolutely positive you are not crazy. Now tell me."

"I guess I don't think God intends for me to be happy.

I mean, before Tony and Bree died I was as happy and contented with my life as I've ever been, before or since. And then they died, and I fell into a black hole. When I finally climbed out and began to feel again with another man, then he's struck down, too. It just seems to me that it's not my destiny to be happy," Cori finished sadly.

"That's simply not true." Pastor Henry's voice was suddenly stern. "God wants the best for all His people. He has promised us that. And there's something else you should know. The Lord gives us joy through the people He brings into our lives. Joy doesn't just fall into our laps like manna from heaven. There must be a reason this Brad Marshall has been placed in your life. Remember in all things God works for the good of those who love Him."

Cori sat silently, rendered speechless by the simple truth of the pastor's words. "What do I do now?" she asked finally.

"I don't have that answer for you, Cori. You're going to have to find it for yourself," Pastor Henry said kindly. "But whatever you decide, just remember that God loves you."

Cori hugged him. "I can't thank you enough for talking with me today. You've given me a lot to think about."

"I'm always here for you." Pastor Henry returned the hug.

Cori caught a glimpse of her watch. "I had no idea how late it was! I've got to get back to the restaurant." She rose from her seat. "Thank you again, Pastor Henry."

He nodded. "I'll see you Sunday?"

"Count on it." Cori hurried out of the church, her heart lighter than it had been since Brad's accident.

"What do you mean, she's not in'? It's almost time for dinner. How could she not be there?" Brad snarled into the phone.

"I'm sorry, Mr. Marshall, but she left earlier this afternoon and she hasn't returned yet." Jasmine's apology sounded hollow. "I can tell her you called."

"Again, you mean. You can tell her I called again." Brad heaved an exasperated sigh. "And tell her I'm going to keep on calling until she talks to me. Got that?"

"Yes, Sir," Jasmine nodded. "I'll give her the message as soon as she comes in. You have my word on it."

Brad slammed the phone down in disgust. Julie, who was just entering his hospital room carrying a potted plant, jumped at the loud cracking sound the receiver made.

"Problems?" she asked mildly, placing the plant on the windowsill.

"You could say that," Brad grumbled. "I have been trying to reach Cori for the better part of a week. I think she's avoiding my calls."

"Why would she do that?" A confused look covered Julie's face.

"I have no idea. The last time I saw her, she'd come here to the hospital. We talked a few minutes, kissed, and then she was gone. I haven't seen or talked to her since." Brad's frustration was evident.

"Did you argue when she was here?"

"No." Brad shook his head vigorously. "We had a wonderful visit. I just don't get it." He angrily pushed the bed tray aside. "And I can't get any answers because I'm being held prisoner in this damn hospital!"

"Brad," Julie soothed, "I hardly think the doctors are holding you prisoner. They'll release you when you're fit and ready to go."

"I'm ready to go now," Brad fumed. "I need to talk to Cori, and obviously it's not going to be on the phone."

"Well, if it'll make you feel any better, I just spoke with your doctor out in the hall." Julie smiled. "And he says you're making excellent progress." Julie's smile broadened. "As a matter of fact, he said he may release you tomorrow."

"Really?" Brad's face brightened with the prospect. "Tomorrow?"

Julie nodded. "That's right. By this time tomorrow, you could be at home."

Home will not be my first stop, Brad decided.

Chapter 21

Somehow, Cori managed to get through the dinner rush. She was actually grateful for the activity, as it kept her mind off her predicament. She wasn't kidding when she'd told Pastor Henry he'd given her a lot to think about; she just wasn't quite ready to face it yet.

So after the restaurant closed for the night, Cori went directly home and collapsed on her bed, too tired to think or feel.

The following morning, when her alarm went off, Cori decided to turn it off and ignore its call. *Let Mikey handle the restaurant this morning. I'm sleeping in.*

"Where's your sister this morning?" Mabel asked her grandson. "She usually beats you down for breakfast."

"Good morning, Gram." Michael sighed, planting a kiss on her cheek. "Breakfast smells delicious, as usual." He swung one long leg over the chair and straddled it.

"I'm sorry, Michael, I didn't mean to be short with you." Mabel poured him a mug of coffee. "It's just that I'm so worried about Cori. She hasn't been herself lately. If I didn't know better, I'd say she's suffering from a broken heart."

"You wouldn't be too far wrong," Michael mumbled between bites of pancake. "Where's Poppy this morning?" Michael asked, trying to divert his grandmother's attention.

"He's gone out for his paper, and don't change the subject." Mabel's tone was stern. "Tell me what you meant by 'not too far wrong.' What's going on with your sister?"

"I can't get into it with you, Gram. Cori asked me not to." Michael sighed. "But I will tell you that Cori has made a terrible decision, and she's too stubborn or too scared to admit it."

"A terrible decision? You're not making any sense, Michael."

"I know, and I'm sorry, Gram." Michael finished his breakfast and carried his plate to the sink. "Talk to Cori. Maybe she'll listen to you." He reached for his car keys, which were hanging on a nearby hook. "I'm going to go on to the restaurant, so the two of you can talk in private. Don't let her off the hook, Gram. Somebody needs to talk some sense into that girl." Michael kissed Mabel's forehead and left for work.

Thoughtfully, Mabel watched her grandson leave. "What on earth was that about. . . ." Mabel puttered around in her kitchen—washing the few dishes, preparing a fresh stack of pancakes—trying to wait for Cori to emerge from her room. Mabel had just decided to go up and wake her when she heard Cori's footsteps as she came down the stairs.

"Sleeping in this morning?" Mabel asked as soon as Cori entered the kitchen.

"Yes, Ma'am." She walked over and kissed Mabel's cheek. "I wasn't feeling quite myself this morning, so I thought a few extra minutes sleep would do me good."

"And has it?"

Cori considered her answer. "Maybe a little."

"Well, sit down and have some breakfast." Mabel nodded in the direction of the dinette table. "We've got some things to talk about."

Warily, Cori took her seat. She reached for the coffeepot in the center of the table. "What's up, Gram? Something going on with the restaurant?"

"This has nothing to do with the restaurant, Corinthia Justice, and you know it." Mabel placed her hands on her hips and leaned in close to Cori. "I want to know what's going on with you. You've been moping around here for days, not eating, barely sleeping, and I want to know what's wrong."

"It's nothing, Gram," Cori began, "don't worry about it."

"Don't insult my intelligence by telling me it's nothing, Girl," Mabel shot back. "I talked to your brother this morning. He wouldn't tell me exactly what was wrong, but it was pretty obvious he knew. Now tell me, or so help me I'll go drag it out of Michael!"

Cori was taken aback by the vehemence of her grandmother's words. After a moment, pinned under Mabel's glare, Cori decided she'd better tell all.

"It's about Brad, Gram, and that accident he had a couple weeks ago." Cori took a deep breath and launched into the unabridged version of the events since Brad's accident.

Once Cori finished her story, Mabel sat back in her chair, stunned into silence. The silence stretched between them until Cori felt uneasy. Finally, Mabel was able to express her thoughts.

"How arrogant of you to assume that God spared Brad because you made a deal!" She huffed at Cori. "Why do you think God's mercy is dependent on your actions?"

"Arrogant?" Cori choked on the word. "I never thought of it that way."

"Sweetie, I'm going to say you haven't thought of it at all. You have set yourself up as this noble, self-sacrificing martyr. 'Oh, I want to be with Brad, but God won't let me.' Cori, that's the worst kind of all the kinds of nonsense there are." Mabel paused to allow herself a moment to calm down. "Let me tell you what I think . . . now I'm no shrink, but it sounds to me like the one you're protecting here is you."

"Me?"

"That's right. I'm guessing you are afraid of loving again, afraid of giving your soul to another man." Mabel looked at her granddaughter closely. "Maybe you're even feeling a little like you're betraying Tony and his memory by loving Brad."

Cori sat in bewildered silence, overwhelmed by her grandmother's words. "That's not it, Gram . . ." she started. "It can't be that. Tony died over five years ago. I'm allowed to go on with my life."

Mabel shook her head. "I hear you saying the words, but does your heart believe it? I wonder . . . because if it did, you'd be by that man's side right now. Think about what I've said to you, Cori. I might be an old woman, but I'll bet I know a few more things about life than you do."

The restaurant had not officially opened for the day, so Michael had a little down time to himself. *I hope Gram is able to talk some sense into Cori,* he thought, *because this whole situation is getting more and more ridiculous.* He checked the wall clock. *I wonder how Brad's doing today. I should give him a call at the hospital and let him know I'm thinking about him.*

Michael was just considering the merits of that plan when a knock on one of the front windows attracted his attention. He walked over and parted the curtains to peer out.

"Brad!" Michael hurried over to the door and unlocked it. "Man, you're a sight for sore eyes! I didn't know you'd been released from the hospital."

"Just today," Brad shook Michael's extended hand.

"And you have no idea how happy I am to be outta that place."

Michael held the door open for Brad to enter. "How did you get here? Surely you didn't drive yourself."

"Naw, Vern picked me up from the hospital and I had him drive me right over here. He's waiting outside." Brad looked past Michael into the interior of the restaurant. "I need to see your sister. Is she here?"

Michael shook his head slowly. "Sorry, Man. She didn't come in this morning."

"Well, do you know when to expect her?" Brad felt his frustration growing again.

"I don't, but I'll be sure to tell her you stopped by," Michael offered.

"Fat lotta good that'll do!" Brad's temper boiled over. "I've been leaving messages for her for nearly a week, and she hasn't bothered to respond to a single one!" Brad looked shrewdly at Michael. "So what's going on? And don't tell me you don't know. You're closer to her than anyone in the world."

Michael looked away, hesitating.

"Okay, I'll make it easy for you. Just tell me this—when Cori came to see me at the hospital, she said, 'I don't know what I would have done if you'd died, too.' Too? What does that mean?"

Michael looked Brad square in the eye, sizing him up, deciding if he could be trusted with Cori's pain. After a moment, he made his decision.

"Come have a seat with me." Michael gestured in the direction of the bar. "We need to talk."

Once the men were settled on their bar stools, Michael launched into Cori's story.

"Five years ago, Cori lost her husband and young daughter in a car crash," he said without preamble, "and everything in her life since has been colored by that tragedy. The main reason we moved to Charlotte was to get away from the painful memories in Chicago. And then once we got here, I signed the restaurant up to sponsor a race car.'' Michael hung his head, ashamed now of what seemed a thoughtless move. ''That's why she freaked when you took her to the track that first time. That's why she was so resistant to sponsoring your car in the beginning.'' Michael fixed Brad with a serious stare. ''And that's why she has had such a hard time dealing with your accident. It seemed to her like history was repeating itself.''

Brad sat quietly, mulling over the information Michael had just provided. ''After all she's been through . . . and I race cars for a living. Lord, it's a wonder we got together at all.''

''Try to understand, Brad. I'm sure she wants to be with you, but she's afraid of losing someone else she loves. Maybe that's why she's been so hard to reach lately.'' Michael decided to keep the story of Cori's ''deal'' to himself.

''I think I get it,'' Brad said slowly. 'But quite frankly, I have no idea what to do about it.'' Brad climbed down off the bar stool. ''Thanks, Michael.'' He extended his hand. ''Whatever happens, you've been a good friend, to both of us.''

Michael shook his hand and watched as Brad left the restaurant. *Whatever happens?* Michael's brow furrowed. *I hope I haven't done something I'll live to regret. Again.*

Vern straightened up in the car seat when he saw Brad approaching.

''So, how'd it go? Did you get to talk to her?''

Brad climbed in the passenger seat. ''No, Cori wasn't there, but I did have a heart-to-heart with her brother. He had some interesting information to share with me.''

''Well,'' Vern prompted as he started the car, ''what gives?''

''Remember when we first met Cori, and Michael told us she was a widow? Well, what he didn't tell us is that her husband and child died in a car accident.'' Brad shook his head sadly. "A car accident, of all things! That's why she's been so resistant to the sponsorship. And according to Michael, because of my accident, she's afraid to get too involved with me for fear I'll die and leave her, too."

Vern gave a low whistle. "Wow, that really explains a lot."

Brad nodded his agreement. "But it doesn't explain to me what I need to do. How can I keep her in my life?"

"I don't know, Cowboy. Only you have that answer. You have to decide what you want, and what you're willing to do to get it." Vern shrugged. "Then you'll know what to do."

"You know what, Vern?" Brad grimaced. "For the first time since I've known you, you have been of no help."

Vern grinned good-naturedly. "Hey, that's what friends are for."

When they arrived at Brad's condo, the crew chief offered to come in and help Brad get settled.

"That's okay, Old Man," Brad declined. "I want to have some time alone to do some thinking."

Vern nodded. "You know where to find me if you need me. And Brad, whatever you decide to do, I'll always be in your pit."

Brad hugged his friend. "That's the one thing in my life I can always count on—you in my pit. Thank you for always being there."

Vern huffed, embarrassed by the show of emotion. "I'm goin'. I'll talk to you tomorrow."

Brad closed the door behind his friend and turned to survey his home. *Everything looks much cleaner than I left it,* he decided. *Julie or Mom must have come over and given the place the once-over.* He smiled, grateful for his family's thoughtfulness.

He wandered into the living room and plopped down on his sofa. His eyes immediately drifted to his trophy shelf, which displayed all the proofs of his victories. Usually, his trophy collection lifted his spirits, but today the sight of all those tiny golden cars and marble bases only reminded him of what he had at stake.

What am I going to do? How can I keep Cori in my life? The questions came much more easily than the answers. *Racing is all I've dreamed of my entire life. Can I give it all up? Am I willing to make that big a sacrifice, for a woman?*

Brad heaved himself up off the couch and went to a nearby window. He flung it open, hoping a breath of fresh air would help clear his thoughts.

The unexpected sound of his doorbell broke his concentration. He strode over to the door and pulled it open.

"Lisa," Brad welcomed dryly, "I'm surprised to see you."

"Why, Sugar?" Lisa eased past him into the condo. "You know how special you are to me."

"Special?" Brad's face betrayed his skepticism. "No, I didn't know that." He closed the door behind her.

"Well, I started to come to the hospital and see you, but that's just not my scene . . . you know, that whole hospital smell, and sickness, and all." Lisa ran her fingers through her hair as if ridding herself of an unpleasant film.

Brad found himself chuckling. "I'll see if I can't get the hospital people to do something about all that sickness and all."

"Oh, Brad, don't tease," Lisa said, pouting. "You know what I mean. And besides, there was nothing I could do for you while you were in the hospital. But now that you're back on your feet, I thought I'd come by and help you make a full recovery." Lisa ran her fingernails suggestively along the muscles in his shoulder and down his arm. "If you know what I mean."

So this is it, Brad thought. *Here's Lisa, ready, willing, and able to accept me and my career choice. Offering herself to me unconditionally.* Brad looked down at her lovely face, carefully arranged into her most sexy expression. *It would be so easy,* he mused, *to go back to this life. No strings, no attachments, no promises. Just two consenting adults providing each other with some much needed release.*

Lisa leaned up on her toes, presenting her lips for a kiss.

No, Brad thought. *This isn't enough for me anymore. I've seen what I want . . . who I want. And I can accept no substitutes.*

Gently, he pushed Lisa away. "I'm sorry, Doll. It's not that kind of party anymore. I've met someone."

"Met someone?" Lisa snapped. "What does that have to do with me? I'm not asking you to marry me here, you know."

Brad looked at her incredulously. "It has everything to do with you . . . or more specifically, with me. I need more out of a relationship than this. And I feel very sorry for you if you can't understand that."

Angry and frustrated, Lisa stomped to the door. "You don't know what you're missing, Sugar," she spat. With a quick jerk, she snatched open his door and stalked out. The slam that followed had enough force to rattle the windows.

"Yeah, 'Sugar', I do know what I'm missing." Brad grinned. "And I think I finally know how to stop missing it."

He crossed the room and picked up the phone. After scanning through a nearby address book, he punched out a long distance number—quickly, before he could change his mind.

"Dwayne Marshall, please. Tell him his brother is calling."

Chapter 22

When Cori finally did arrive at Foster's it was late afternoon. After that conversation with her grandmother she had found herself unable to focus on anything—anything but Brad. She hadn't made any decisions. She just knew she needed to talk to him. Once she arrived at the restaurant, she went straight to her office. She called the hospital, only to hear, "Mr. Marshall has been discharged." Excited by that news, Cori hurriedly called his condo. Her face twisted into a disappointed frown when his answering machine picked up. She hung up without leaving a message.

Where are you, Brad? Am I too late?

Her attention was diverted by a knock on the door.

"Come in," she called, distracted.

"I'm glad you didn't ask who it was. I was afraid you wouldn't let me in if you knew it was me." Brad tentatively pushed open the door.

Cori stood up, an expression of shock on her face. "I was just calling you." She looked down at her hand, still placed on the receiver.

"You were?" Now it Brad's turn to be shocked.

"Yes. We need to talk."

He cocked his head sideways. "That's supposed to be my line. That's what I came here to say to you."

She grinned. "Well, see. Now you can cut to the chase. Come on in and have a seat."

Brad shook his head. "No. I'd much rather you come with me. I'd like to take you somewhere a little more private than your office."

"But Brad," she protested, "it's almost time for the dinner rush. You know I need to be here for that."

"Nope, not today," Brad corrected her. "You see, I spoke with your brother on my way to your office and he agreed with me that Foster's will make it without you for one night." Brad crossed the room to take her hands. "I, on the other hand, might not."

Cori felt the tingle that ran through her blood every time they touched. At that moment, she would have agreed to anything. "So where are we going?"

Brad smiled triumphantly. "I'm going to make dinner for you at my place. I know that's pretty bold on my part— inviting a restaurant owner to dinner—but I'm feeling very confident today." He ached to kiss her. *But not here,* he thought. *If I kiss her now, I might not be able to stop.*

Cori accurately interpreted the hungry look that filled Brad's eyes. Acccurately interpreted because she was experiencing a similar hunger. "I do so love a confident man," she murmured. "What time is dinner?"

Brad gently pulled her hands, leading her to the door. "Right now."

Both of them were silent during the short ride to Brad's condo, each planning what to say once they'd arrived. When they entered Brad's home, it was as if some master switch had been flipped, animating them. Cori and Brad started talking at the same time.

"I need to apologize to you—" Cori started.

"There's something I need to tell you," Brad blurted out.

They paused a moment, then burst into laughter. "My momma always says we can all sing together, but we can't all talk together." Brad laughed. "So let's go have a seat and try this again." He led her to the black leather sofa in his living room. "Now, ladies first."

Cori took a deep breath before responding. "I said, I need to apologize to you. I was wrong not to take your calls or go out to the hospital to see you. It's just that—"

"No," Brad interrupted her, "don't say another word. I understand that completely now."

"You do?" Cori looked skeptical.

"I had a long talk with Michael and he told me all about your loss." Brad leaned in close to her on the sofa. "I am so sorry, Cori. Simple words cannot adequately express my sympathy."

Cori looked away, uncomfortable. "It was a long time ago," she mumbled.

"Still, it can't be easy for you. And then I zoom into your life, making a living racing cars." Brad shook his head slowly. "It's a wonder you talked to me at all."

"Oh, Brad," Cori said, turning to him, "there's so much more to you than racing cars. You are a fascinating, exciting man."

"I'm glad you feel that way." Brad smiled. "Because it'll make my transition so much easier."

"Transition? To what?"

Brad gathered her hands in both of his and looked deeply in her eyes. "To life after racing. As of today, I quit." His eyes had a strange, faraway look in them. "I can't ask you to build a life with someone who's in constant danger. I called my brother and asked him to hook me up with a real job. He was all too happy to oblige. I've got an interview first thing Monday morning."

Cori's jaw dropped open. She was simply speechless.

"Cori, I've realized how much I love you and need you in my life. I'm willing to do anything to make that happen."

"You'd do this for me?" she asked in a strangled whisper.

"Cori, I'd move heaven and earth for you."

Cori snatched her hands away and scrambled off the couch, her mind reeling. Brad looked up at her, clearly confused and concerned.

"Not this, Brad. N—Never this," she stuttered. "You can't give up racing. It's your dream. Remember? 'Racing is not something I do, it's something I am.' Don't you remember saying that to me?"

Brad looked away. "That was then." He rose to face her. "I now know that there are more important things in life than NASCAR." He cupped her face in his hand. "Much more important."

Cori's eyes brimmed with tears. "I can't believe you would do that for me."

"I would do anything for you. Anything to keep you in my life." He pressed a gentle kiss on her lips.

Cori shook her head, unexpectedly breaking the contact. "Brad, I love you for wanting to do this, but I can't let you. You would be miserable with some 'real' job. Racing is who you are. It's one of the elements that defines you. You can't give that up. In time, you would come to resent me because of it, and I couldn't stand that."

Brad's hands dropped to his sides. He couldn't deny the truth of her words. "But what do we do now? How can we know if we're meant to be together?"

Cori pondered the question for a moment. "When you were in the hospital that first day, you almost died. It was one of my most frightening moments."

"That's my point, exactly. I can't ask you to go through something like that again."

"Let me finish," Cori said. "When I thought you were dying, I prayed to God to save you. I promised to stay away from you if only God would let you live. And when you did pull through, I took that as a sign that I wasn't meant

to be with you. That's the main reason I have been avoiding
you—I was trying to keep my word."

She waited for the ridicule she was sure was coming.
Nearly everyone she'd shared her 'bargain' with had all
but laughed in her face.

Everybody but Brad. "You prayed for me? You offered
your own happiness in exchange for my life?" He shook
his head in awed wonder. "No one's ever done anything
like that for me before."

Cori attempted to lighten the moment. "Well, sure, but
how many times have you been at death's door?"

"No, Cori. I'm serious. That was an amazing thing you
were willing to do for me."

She repeated his words. "Anything for you, anything for
you."

Brad reached for her and pulled her in the circle of his
arms. She moved willingly, with anxious anticipation. He
lowered his head and tasted her lips. Her lips parted and
willingly gave his tongue the access he so greedily sought.
Their kiss was electric, fueled by an urgency neither of
them had even known existed. Soon the passionate kiss
was not enough. Brad pulled back, his breathing raw and
ragged, and looked into her eyes. He saw a need there
that matched his own. He knew that whatever happened
tomorrow, this night, this here and now, was meant to be.

He scooped her into his arms and carried her down the
hall to his bedroom. She nuzzled against his chest, planting
small kisses along his neck and jawline. In his room he
gently, reverently, laid her on his bed. He lowered his
weight onto the bed, next to her. Cori reached for him
and pulled him to her, locking him in another hungry
kiss.

Brad's body responded immediately to the passion she
aroused in him. His erection pressed painfully against his
jeans. He shifted, trying to find a more comfortable position.

She noticed the movement. She reached for him, pulling

him closer on the bed. Her hands fumbled for the snap
on his jeans, and after a moment she released the waistband
and slid the zipper down.

A low moan escaped Brad's lips as her hand slipped
inside and found his erection. With one hand between
them, Cori used her other hand to guide his face back to
hers. She sucked at his lips with the same intense rhythm
she used to rub her hand along the length of his shaft.

The combined pressure of the sensations was nearly
enough to drive Brad over the edge. He struggled to regain
his control. He tried to pull back, but Cori would have
none of that. Whereas the last time they'd made love she'd
taken a passive role, this time she was very much the
aggressor.

She released her hold on him long enough to help him
ease the jeans over his hips. She then pulled at the buttons
of his shirt until the shirt lay open, exposing his carved,
ebony torso.

In short order, Brad's clothes were in a heap on the
floor. Cori guided him onto his back. She kneeled beside
him, momentarily awestruck by the exquisite beauty of this
man she loved.

Brad lay perfectly still, allowing her to study him at her
leisure, his body proudly leaving no doubt as to his desire
for her.

After an agonizingly long moment, Cori lowered her
head and flicked his erection with her tongue. Brad very
nearly leapt out of his skin. Smiling at his reaction, Cori
bent further to her ministrations. She drew him into her
mouth, savoring the masculine taste of him.

Brad clutched the edges of the bed, trying desperately
not to surrender to the fire that threatened to consume
him. Cori continued to cast her spell over him with her
mouth and tongue until finally Brad was sure he would go
mad.

"Enough," he growled. "Either we get those clothes

off you right now, or I won't be held responsible for my actions!''

Cori needed no further prompting. Reluctantly, she moved away from him and stood to remove her clothing. Slowly, sensuously, she peeled the linen pants off. She stood before him, wearing only her silk blouse and her lingerie. With all the finesse of a master striptease artist, she loosened the buttons and allowed the shirt to fall open.

Brad was mesmerized by her movements. He lay back and watched her, transfixed, his hunger growing exponentially with every passing second.

Soon, she stood before him, naked as the day she was born. Brad found himself breathless at the sight of her. Her smooth, caramel-colored skin had a rich, healthy glow. Her full breasts were crowned with dark circles that were pebbled hard by her desire. His eyes burned a trail down her body, coming to rest on the triangle of chestnut-colored hair that held unimaginable pleasures.

"Come to me, now," Brad commanded.

Cori did as she was bid. He attempted to sit up to meet her, but Cori had other plans. She pushed him back onto the bed and, keeping her eyes locked with his, eased over him until she straddled him. His shaft slid smoothly into her. Their bodies matched so perfectly it was as if each had been made for the other. Both Cori and Brad felt the jolt of pure electric passion that passed between them when their bodies joined.

After a moment, she began to move over him in rhythmic circles that pulled both of them further into the vortex of sensation. He matched her rhythm with one of his own. The reins he'd managed to hold on his passion thus far fell away, and he succumbed to the heat she generated in him. They moved as one body, one heart, closer and closer to the point of no return.

Then, in a blinding, mind-numbing explosion, together they reached the zenith, a point of passion and fulfillment previously unimaginable.

Cori collapsed against his chest, and his arms reached up to encircle her. It was several long minutes before either of them had the strength or inclination to move. Eventually, Cori eased off of him and moved to lie by his side. Brad cradled her against his chest, overcome by a love that defied words.

Slowly, as his senses returned to him, he realized that they still had a problem. *I still can't ask her to be with a race car driver, not after what she's been through already.*

"Cori," Brad said, hesitant, "I don't feel right about expecting you to be with me, knowing how you must feel about cars and speed. I don't want to lose you, but I don't know how I can ask you to stay."

"And I wouldn't dare ask you to give up your dream," she responded. "So where does that leave us?"

"If only there was some way I could guarantee you I'll never get hurt again, some way I could reassure you that I won't leave you alone."

"But you can't. Only God can make guarantees."

Brad thought about it for a moment. Suddenly, he sat bolt upright in bed, as if a lightbulb had gone off over his head.

"I have a thought. You're right, only God can make guarantees, and He also gives us signs of his intentions, right?"

Cori nodded, unsure of where he was going with this.

"What if we leave it up to fate to reassure us? Look, I have been cleared by my doctor to get back into racing. I didn't really think about it, because I wasn't sure I was going back. But now, I believe racing can point the way to our future."

"You're not making any sense," Cori said flatly.

"Bear with me. There is a race this weekend, and I'm going to enter. I feel so confident about my racing abilities that I'm willing to stake our future on them. There are no guarantees in life, but there are signs. When I win this weekend, we can take it as a sign that we are meant to be together."

Cori looked skeptical. "And if you lose? What happens then? Are you so sure you're going to win that you're willing to risk that much?"

"I don't think it's a risk at all, because I'm confident in our future, and confident in my abilities, and confident in the power of destiny." Brad rolled over on his side to face her. "Cori, you believed in destiny and prayer enough to give me up, because you thought you had been given a sign. Why can't you believe in them enough to trust that my winning is a sign that we're meant to be?"

Cori considered his words carefully. "Okay, Mr. Marshall. You believe in this enough for both of us, and I believe in you. This weekend it is."

Chapter 23

Race day preparations had a special significance today. Brad was particularly meticulous as he shaved his head. His protein shake seemed to have more flavor than ever before. The Prince song that reverberated through his house seemed to penetrate his bones until he could feel the beat pulse through his body as well. Today was no ordinary race.

Brad was more charged for this race than he remembered ever being for any other. Even more than when the NASCAR scouts came. Never before had so much been riding on the outcome of one of his races. He'd never promised a win before; he was just superstitious enough to believe that kind of arrogance would jinx him. But today, he felt totally centered and at peace. He knew, he just *knew,* that he'd done the right thing with Cori. And because he believed beyond a shadow of a doubt that she belonged in his life, he also believed a win today was a foregone conclusion. Not because he was arrogant, but because he believed in destiny.

He was packing up to leave for the track when one

particular song caught his attention. He smiled and paused long enough to sing the refrain with unbridled enthusiasm and conviction.

"Tonight we gonna party like it's nineteen ninety-nine!"

Today, it was Cori who was rushing Michael. This morning, she had sprung out of bed, anxious to get to the race. The more she thought about Brad's words, the more sense they made to her. She was willing to accept today's race outcome as a sign for several reasons, not the least of which was that she wanted him back in her life. If he won today, she'd know for certain they were meant to be.

"Hurry up, Mikey. I want a front row seat!"

When Brad arrived at the track, Vern was already there. Brad found him in the garage making last minute adjustments to the engine. This was a new car; the first one had been totaled in the accident. This new car was an identical match to the previous one, with a burgundy paint job and a gold Foster's logo. The number 34 was again emblazoned across the hood. There was only one difference with this car. Brad had asked for a different inscription under the driver's side window instead of the words "The Ebony Warrior": *For God and Cori*.

"Morning, Vern," Brad said cheerfully. "You're at it early today."

Vern came out from under the hood and grabbed a rag to wipe his hands. "Just want to make sure our girl is ready today. They're back, Cowboy."

Brad looked at him blankly.

"NASCAR. They're back. Heard you were getting back in the saddle and decided to give you another chance." Vern grinned broadly. "You might make it to The Show in spite of yourself."

Brad grinned in return. To him, Vern's news was just further evidence that destiny was on his side today. "I'd better go get dressed. I don't want to be late. Brad headed to the locker room with a spring in his step.

When Cori and Michael arrived at the track the stands were beginning to fill up. They found seats near the front of the sponsors' section. Cori could feel the excitement in the air. She hadn't been to a race in well over two months, and she didn't realize until now how much she'd missed the energy of the crowds. Before she settled in her seat, Cori sent up a silent prayer: *Thy will be done.*

Brad emerged from the locker room with his helmet under his arm and surveyed the track before him. He closed his eyes and began his visualization exercises. In his mind's eye he could see the track's turns and straightaways. He could see his car in a burgundy streak zooming around the oval. Suddenly, a different vision appeared before him. All he could see was a cloud of smoke. When the smoke cleared he saw the wreckage of several cars sprawled across the track ahead of him. Then he saw his car, slamming into the pile.

Brad's eyes snapped open. He took several deep breaths, trying to shake the terrifying vision. *No fear . . . no fear.* He mentally chanted the mantra that had gotten him through uneasy times before. But this time, the words had no effect.

Still shaken by the memory of his accident, Brad scanned the stands. Then he saw her. Cori stood as their eyes met. A current of love passed between them until both of them felt revived and renewed by its force. A slow, sultry smile spread across Brad's face. He nodded at her. Smiling also, Cori returned the acknowledgment.

For God and Cori—the words flashed in his mind, soothing him as his previous mantra could not. After a moment, Brad broke the connection between them and headed for his car. Brad climbed in the car and began strapping himself in. He went through the motions with ritualistic efficiency. He concentrated on keeping his mind blank. It was important not to think about the last race he'd participated in. This was the first race since. . . .

Brad shook his head. *That was a fluke,* he reminded himself. *This is destiny.*

"Gentlemen, start your engines!"

Show time, Brad thought.

"You ready, Cowboy?" Vern's voice buzzed in his ear.

"Born ready, Vern . . . born ready."

The cars started the pace lap. Brad was squarely in the middle of the pack—middle row, outside lane. As the cars picked up speed, Brad did his customary weave from side to side to test the feel of the tires and suspension.

"The car feels great, Vern. You are the king."

" 'Bout time you figured that one out," Vern chuckled into the radio.

The pace car moved off the track. The race had begun.

In the stands, Cori was on her feet, determined not to miss a moment. Suddenly, as she watched the burgundy car circle the track, a wave of anxiety washed over her. Images of Brad's crash clouded her view. Her hands curled into fists at her side as she mentally battled to clear the vision from her mind. *All my energies need to be here and now,* she thought. *This is all that matters.*

Slowly, the blurry images faded. Cori gratefully focused on the race at hand.

The number thirty-four Foster's Chevrolet had advanced a few places and was now running in eighth place. Brad pulled in close to the car immediately ahead of him, looking for an opportunity to pass. The two cars jockeyed back and forth, Brad moving in and then easing off. At the turn, Brad went up high and outside. He punched the accelerator, and the car roared in response. He inched past two cars. When he came out of the turn and moved down to the inside lane on the straightaway, the Foster's Chevrolet was in sixth place.

The radio crackled to life. "Nice move, Cowboy. You're looking good."

In the stands, Cori whooped her approval. Each spot closer to the lead was a spot closer to the future—their future.

It was time for Brad's pit stop. When he screeched to a halt in front of his spot, the crew swarmed around, servicing the car. Within seconds, their work was completed, and Brad thundered back toward the track. Just as Brad was preparing to reenter the race, the number fifteen car passing the Pit Road exit hit a patch of oil and spun out suddenly. The spin happened so quickly there was no time for the cars following to react. Two other cars plowed into the spinning number fifteen. The force of the impact spread the three cars across the track. The approaching field scattered, going both high and low on the track trying to avoid the damaged cars.

It was into this melee that Brad reentered the race. Roaring at full throttle from Pit Road, Brad had only split seconds to react. The accident seemed to appear from out of nowhere—too quickly for Vern to issue a warning, too quickly for any calculated or strategic response.

Brad's instincts took over. He jerked the wheel, first hard right—swerving around one wrecked car—then hard left, weaving around another. He never eased off the accelerator, instead pushed the car even faster.

The crowd was still, transfixed by the unfolding drama. Before anyone at the track had time to breathe, Brad was clear of the debris. The stands erupted into a hail of cheers. Brad's instinctive driving had created a moment the fans were not likely to ever forget.

"Outstanding!" Vern's exuberant voice seemed to jump through the helmet headset. "Boy, I thought you were toast for sure!"

Brad grinned. "Faith, Vern. You must have faith."

Cori watched the whole incident through her fingers. It was several long moments before the reality penetrated:

He made it! He's safe! Cori's hands flew away from her eyes and she waved them wildly in the air.

Standing next to her, Michael could only shake his head in wonder. "How did he do that?" he muttered. "That was amazing."

Cori looked over at her brother, a beatific smile lighting her face. "Amazing? I'd say 'Divine'."

A few rows away from Cori and Michael, a small group of men in baseball caps and NASCAR shirts also cheered wildly. One of the men made a notation on the clipboard he was carrying: Number thirty-four. B. Marshall—superb reaction time."

The caution flag was out on the track. The race was temporarily suspended as the cleanup crews cleared the track. During the caution laps there is no jockeying for position; the drivers must maintain their spots until the race restarts. Brad used the relative calm of the caution laps to catch his breath. That near miss had rattled him a little more than he was willing to admit. He took several deep breaths to regain his composure, and rolled his head around to release the tension in his neck muscles. Soon, he was able to stop the instant replay of that near miss which was running in his brain. By the time the track was cleared and the officials were ready to restart the race, Brad had recaptured his focus. *For God and Cori. . . .*

The green flag came out, signaling the restart of racing. From his sixth place spot, Brad prepared to charge ahead. He floored the accelerator and passed the cars in positions five and four as if they were parked along the side of the track. There were twenty laps to go in the race. From here on out, it was more strategy than speed that would win. Now in fourth place, Brad found a groove along the inside lane and stuck to it. He advanced and retreated, unable to find a safe passing spot. The driver in the third position, of car number twenty-one, kept one eye glued to the rear-view mirror, watching and responding to Brad's every move.

Brad's mouth set in a determined line. *So it's that kind of party, huh?* He backed off a bit, putting a car length between their cars. Lulled by Brad's apparent retreat, the driver of car twenty-one returned his attention to trying to catch up with the cars in front of him. Brad followed a safe distance for a few more laps. Then, once he sensed car twenty-one had completely forgotten about him, Brad made his move. As they approached turn three, Brad jammed the accelerator to the floor. The car's engine roared in response; Brad took the inside track, moving to the bottom half of the track. Before car twenty-one even knew he was there, Brad cut in front of him. Brad waved a jaunty salute in the rear window. The driver of car twenty-one slapped his steering wheel in frustration.

Ten laps to go found Brad in third place. Abruptly, as if it had been struck by lightning, the engine blew in the second place car. The car limped off the track, clearing the way for Brad to make his bid for the lead.

Brad decided it would be easier to go through than around. He advanced on the leading car until their bumpers were almost touching.

"You're too damn close," Vern yelled into the radio. "Back off!"

"Aw, c'mon Vern. I'm just doing a little kissin', that's all." Brad brushed against the leader.

"This is not the demolition derby, Cowboy!"

Brad ignored Vern's comment and pressed further to his strategy. The lead car inched further away, anxious to avoid any contact. Brad fell in directly behind the leader. He used the pull of the draft created by the lead car to help him along. By riding in the draft, Brad was able to hold some of his engine's power in reserve.

Then the white flag came out, signalling the last lap. Brad gripped the steering wheel with steely determination. He began to put additional pressure on the accelerator pedal. But the lead driver, aware of the drafting strategy, anticipated Brad's move. He moved his car to the center of the track, prepared to bank high or come in low to block Brad's passage.

Instantly, Brad made a decision. The inside lane would be the easier pass, but it was also the most obvious. Brad pulled the car toward the inside lane. When the lead car moved to block him, Brad punched the accelerator and quickly switched to the outside. The engine's reserve power kicked in, and Brad prepared to take the lead. But the number one car was too fast, the finish line too close. The opposing driver managed to hold Brad off just long enough. The nose of the Foster's Restaurant Chevrolet took second place by just milliseconds.

Pandemonium broke out all around the track. In the stands, the crowd was on its feet, stomping and cheering the thrilling victory. In the pits, Vern and the crew were stomping and cursing in frustration. It had been so close! The NASCAR scouts dropped their notes, caught up in the excitement generated by the race. And in the sponsors' section, Cori hung her head. *What do I do now?*

Inside his car, Brad pounded his steering wheel in bitter disappointment. He'd been so sure that this race was his. It was supposed to be his destiny! Slowly, he pulled off the track and headed to his pit. As soon as the car was in place, the crew rushed in. Brad climbed out of the car and threw his helmet to the ground. Vern was one of the first to reach his side.

"You never cease to amaze me, Son." The older man looked at Brad with open admiration. "That was some of the prettiest drivin' I've seen you do yet." Vern reached out and fingered the inscription under the driver's window. "But I guess you had some inspiration."

"I was supposed to win, Vern. This race above all races, I was supposed to win!" Brad's disappointment and frustration welled up in his throat. "This was supposed to be my destiny."

Vern patted Brad on the shoulder. "Sometimes, Cowboy, destiny has a way of working itself out."

"What is that supposed to mean? Vern, this race was for Cori and NASCAR, and I just blew it."

"I'm willing to bet things aren't all that bad," Vern offered.

"Brad ... Brad Marshall!" The call came from Jack Carol, the owner of the racetrack. He elbowed his way through the pit crew, pulling along a trio of men in baseball caps. "Brad, I've got some people here who want to speak with you." Jack stood aside and motioned for the men to come forward.

"Mr. Marshall," the man in front said, "we're here from one of the NASCAR teams, and we'd like to talk to you about your future."

Brad smiled. *Maybe destiny does have a way of working itself out.* The moment he'd worked for his entire professional life had arrived. But he realized it wasn't enough. Not by a long shot.

"Thank you," he said shortly, "but there's someone else I need to talk to about my future first. Please excuse me." He brushed past the startled scouts and scanned the crowd. *Where is she?*

"Mikey! Why aren't we moving?" Cori was flattened against her brother's back by the crush of the crowd.

"It's just too crowded!" Michael yelled. "I can't get through!"

We'll see about that! Cori pushed past Michael and began clearing a swath through the throng. She was bound and determined to get to Brad. Now.

Brad noticed an unusual movement in the crowd off to the left of Pit Road. As he watched, Cori emerged with Michael close on her heels, having elbowed and shoved her way through. He headed to meet her, oblivious to the NASCAR scouts who were waiting for him. Right on the edge of the area designated for Pit Road, Cori and Brad met.

"I'm sorry." He hung his head. "I didn't win. I made a deal with you, and I didn't keep up my end of it. I don't know what to say."

Cori reached for his face and lifted his chin until their eyes met. "Brad, if I have learned nothing else these last few weeks, I've learned that everything happens for a reason. Maybe you didn't win so I would learn to trust my heart, and not my superstitions."

Brad felt hope building in his chest. "What are you saying?"

"I'm saying that win or no win, you and I are meant to be together. Or should I say, we are destined."

It seemed as if Brad's entire body was warmed by the smile that beamed from his face. He opened his arms; she walked into them with no hesitation. Their hug was intense, electric, and personal, despite the fact that they stood in the center of a crowd. Then they kissed, a kiss full of passion and promise and faith.

"Now do you believe in my love for you?" he whispered against her lips.

"Never doubted it for a second." She smiled.

"Cori Justice, will you marry me?"

"I can't think of anything I want more."

They kissed again. This time the crowd around them "oooh-ed", caught up in the magic of Brad and Cori's love.

When the kiss finally ended, Brad wrapped his arm around Cori's shoulders and turned back to face his team.

"Hey, Vern," he yelled across the crowd, "she said yes!"

"Guess this means your racing days are over, huh?" Vern yelled in response.

Brad looked questioningly at Cori. She leaned up on her toes and kissed him deeply.

"Not a chance, Vern," Cori shouted. "Not a chance!"

Dear Arabesque readers:

Look for the May, 1998 release ROSES ARE RED by Arabesque newcomer, Sonia Seerani. In this romance, Kendra Davenport runs her father's newspaper, the largest black paper in England. When she is confronted by handsome American Shay Brentwood, the son of her father's most bitter enemy, about embezzlement, she is outraged. When the man tells her she has a few days to find the money or lose her newspaper, she's desperate.

Shay has a hard time disliking his father's enemy's daughter. She's beautiful and smart, and the kiss he stole from her haunts his every waking moment.

Shay soon finds a way to regain his money and the heart of Kendra—if only Kendra will agree.

Following is a preview of ROSES ARE RED.
Take a peek . . . and enjoy.

ROSES ARE RED

Sonia Seerani

Chapter One

"Girl," the old man raged furiously, his brown eyes blazing with his displeasure at seeing the young woman standing before him. "Get your pretty legs out of my house."

The chandelier in the mansion hallway glittered mercilessly above his head, and Kendra Davenport felt its diamond glares of yellow light bathe her stunned, oval face. She stared in disbelief at the man's cold, mahogany profile, aware that the jazz music and laughter she could hear from within the house had stopped abruptly, replaced by the echo of approaching footsteps. The people who materialized, dressed in patterned African clothes and more contemporary styles, sporting elaborate hairstyles and expensive gemstones, began to form themselves in a circle of comradery, eyes intent on lending support to their host.

"I'm not here to cause any trouble," Kendra pleaded shakily, allowing her mouth to form a faint smile in an attempt to appease him.

Benjamin Brentwood, a man grazing sixty-three, was obviously enraged to see her. His majestic frame and giant,

Jamaican-American baritone were enough to dim the thundering outside his Wimbledon estate in London and cause his twelve speculating guests to congregate in the hallway and look on in curiosity. Everything about his expression registered a measure of alarm inside Kendra, and she wondered why on earth she'd ever made the impulsive decision to come there.

But she knew why: one of his two sons had trumped up false embezzlement charges against her innocent sister, and she'd thought that by confronting the Brentwoods head on she could persuade them to leave her family alone. But Benjamin Brentwood seemed intent on reminding himself of the deep-seated hatred he had for her father— particularly for the newspaper her father had single-handedly molded into the largest African-Caribbean press in England. She now realized, with some foreboding, that she was not going to make any headway, and that perhaps the best recourse for her now would be to leave.

"I'm sorry I bothered you," she declared helplessly, retreating a step back out onto the porch. "I only wanted—"

"Always wanting something," Benjamin pointedly interrupted, ignoring Kendra's plea to be heard as he transferred a smoldering Cuban cigar from one hand to the other. "Well, take this message to your papa. Tell him that I'll never forget what he stole from me, and I intend to make him pay."

Kendra looked at him, a little puzzled. Surely he couldn't mean the newspaper her father had presided over for more than thirty years, of which she was now editor-in-chief. That had been dutifully paid for, despite Benjamin Brentwood feeling outdone, and Kendra quickly took it upon herself to remind her enemy of that point. "My father worked hard and paid dearly for the *Nubian Chronicle*," she told him heatedly. "He would never cheat anyone."

"Your papa is a thief," Benjamin admonished loudly, the icy blast in his voice made more horrific as it eclipsed a current of lightning which chose to strike at that precise moment. "Now get off my land before—"

"Pops?" A soft, mellow, American voice halted Benjamin in midstream, and instantly turned everyone's attention toward the direction from which it came. The figure which slowly emerged from the shadowy interior of a room adjacent to the hallway was that of a man in his mid-thirties whose expression showed particular concern with the commotion that had disturbed him. "What's going on?" he demanded with impatience.

"Son, we have been honored with the presence of a Davenport," Benjamin announced with sardonic irony. "What do you think of her bringing her bony behind all the way over to my yard?"

The newcomer stepped forward into the lighted doorway and took a good look at what had interrupted his father's traditional domino party. With persistent slowness his gaze moved across Kendra's slim bodice, taking in her slightly wet, auburn, relaxed hair, damp, pale blue, linen suit, and startling, ebony complexion which was an asset to her wide, mink-colored, almond shaped eyes.

Never in her twenty-eight years had Kendra felt subjected to such flagrant masculine appraisal. For several seemingly interminable seconds, no one moved as the coolly brooding glance from startlingly dusky brown eyes raked her slender figure and delicate features. She was immediately conscious of every line of his taut, muscular body, from his shoulders beneath the open-necked, white shirt to a slim waist and lean, athletic build beneath the dark trousers he was wearing.

Yet, as his gaze intensified Kendra did not feel unnerved by the newscomer, for his was a kindly face, and he offered her a casual smile when he spoke. "I think she has amazing courage for a sista so skinny," he uttered finally, advancing yet another step so that Kendra was made instantly aware of his towering frame, which suddenly seemed to diminish her five-foot-eight inches. "I'm Shay Brentwood," he introduced with a lazy grin. "You must be Arlisa's sister. Kendra, right?"

Kendra clutched her car key as she looked into his warm, embracing face and felt at last that there was hope she might actually be heard. "Yes, I am," she answered coolly, surprised that he knew her by name.

"I guess your sister's holed up somewhere?" he asked curiously. "Not in the British state penitentiary, I hope."

Kendra's eyebrows furrowed. Benjamin's son was not going to be of any help to her. His question about her younger sister signified his involvement in trying to get her falsely convicted. Shay Brentwood was the culprit she was looking for. He was the cause of her family's recent anxieties and anguished ordeal in keeping Arlisa protected against the accusations leveled against her. And he was the one who almost got Arlisa fired. It could hardly be true of someone with such a nice face, she thought treacherously, with such friendly eyes that looked as though they could be trusted.

"My sister is not in prison, where you'd obviously intended to put her." She bristled knowingly. "Arlisa's safe at home with my father."

"Is she?" Shay's dismissive casual tone caused Kendra instant alarm. The arrogant mouth twisted. "Are you both all right?"

"No, we are not," Kendra declared angrily. "That's why I'm here. Life may be fun and games to you and your lying, conniving, deceiving family, but for me, my sister, and my father, it's important. It's about honesty, decency, and respect." She drew in a steadying breath before surveying all the enraged faces set on her. "There's enough famine and disease in the world without people like you making things worse."

"But see ya," a jowly West Indian female screamed from the small, congregated crowd who were all making sounds of discontent and showing general uneasiness. "What an unruly child."

"Your momma never teach you manners?" another woman bristled.

"Ben, no bother with the girl," a Saint Lucian man derided smoothly. "I want to play my domino hand. Come, let's finish the game."

Benjamin Brentwood's heavy eyebrows knitted furiously. "You better go now, Girl," he ordered sternly.

"Don't worry, I'm leaving," Kendra snapped, stepping off the porch and out into the rain. The torrid downpour washed her hair and soaked her skin and clothes as she rushed over to her white convertible. Throwing herself into the driver's seat with the sound of rain drumming on the roof of the car, Kendra wondered through the unholy torrent what on earth could motivate such people to be so truly disreputable. Igniting the engine, she couldn't resist glancing backward in her rearview mirror to look at the group, who seemed like alien beings from another universe. But she was surprised to see only Shay Brentwood, standing in the lighted doorway.

He had a guarded look in his eyes which gave Kendra a shiver that seemed to reach every nerve in her body. He was watching her, his caramel profile aimed intently in her direction, as if he'd become suddenly intrigued. To her chagrin, she found herself recalling his compelling features: a hard-hitting, square face with no softening features, his nose broad but straight as a blade, his mouth harsh and yet sensually formed, and his short hair—sleek, black as a raven, with tiny curls that seemed as silky and soft as a baby's.

Power seemed to emanate from him as he stood there, magnified by an illumination of lightning which suddenly flashed above his granite image. His demeanor revealed him to be a man who'd taken charge of his own destiny, whose finger was at the pulse of self-empowerment and achievement. What a shame that the feud between their families had shaped his destiny into an endless chase down the same narrow alleyway of deceit and revenge it had his father, she thought angrily, determinedly flooring the accelerator.

The screech of rubber tires pierced the night air like a giant scream as she reversed the Golf Cabriolet and backed to the spot where Shay Brentwood stood. Flicking the switch to lower the windows, Kendra kept the engine purring as she bent her head forward and yelled, "If I had a shred of evidence, you'd be the one heading for the high jump. As it happens, I only have my well-founded suspicions and a few tips on good authority."

"From the eligible Selwyn Owens, M.P., no doubt," Shay answered with a curling twist of his lips. "Well, you'd better tell the Minister of Parliament to back off before he gets more than his feelings hurt."

"He told me that you'd threatened him," Kendra admitted with a level of disgust. "Afraid that he might pull a number of skeletons from your family's closet? My, I await with baited breath."

"Then I hope the worthy Selwyn Owens lives up to your expectations," Shay roared above a crack of thunder, his dark eyebrows raised in mock sincerity, though he told himself that he was up against a remarkable woman. "It would be terrible if your hopes were to be crushed."

"I'm sure he will expertly manage to disturb your comfortable little life," Kendra retorted.

"You disturb me," Shay answered. His eyes made no secret of it as they roamed across her delicate features with an intensity that almost took Kendra's breath away. The brief scrutiny made her feel ridiculously shaky, for even in her heightened state of anger Kendra found herself having to admit that Shay Brentwood was irresistibly attractive. Without another word, she automatically switched the window shut and pressed her foot down on the accelerator, keeping it there until the car sped down the estate's long driveway toward the main road. She did not look back. She dared not look back. In truth, Kendra realized with self-loathing, she had enjoyed the way Shay Brentwood looked at her. Kendra slammed the door of her bedroom and rushed over to her wardrobe. Selecting a grey suit, she quickly went to where her fresh underwear was neatly folded in a drawer and took her pick before slipping out of her wet clothes and seating herself at the dressing table. For a few seconds, as she began to tissue the rain from her wet face, a feeling of panic hit her. She should never have gone to see Benjamin Brentwood. His temper had frayed at just the mere sight of her, and—though she had matched his temperament measure for measure—if her instincts were correct she might just have lit a long fuse destined for a terrible explosion.

Shay Brentwood would most likely detonate it, she thought, consciously forcing herself to take a steadying breath as she reached for her pink towel. That arrogant man would have to be stopped before he caused her family further harm, she decided sternly. She was about to contemplate a strategy for how she could best proceed when her bedroom door shot open and her younger sister by three years hurried in.

Kendra straightened in her chair and wrapped the pink towel around her damp hair, her thick, dark lashes disguising her recent ordeal as Arlisa suspiciously closed the door. "Sissy," Kendra remarked, calling her younger sister by her childhood name. "I haven't time to talk to you right now." Swiftly removing her shoes before deftly unclasping her watch and onyx necklace, she added, "I'm meeting Selwyn, and I'm already late."

She frowned, unsure now whether she actually wanted to attend the dinner they'd been invited to at Lord Conrad Finsbury's London home in Belgravia. Kendra felt out of character mixing words with political types, most of whom had received an old-school-tie education. They did nothing but talk shop, mainly party politics and election promises, omitting the finer details of serving their constituencies. She was aware that Selwyn, whose father was a Guyana-born war veteran determined his son should be a public school boy, was raised to believe that such socializing was a means to advancing himself, and so she sighed and said, "I forgot to ask Selwyn whether the dinner party tonight is formal or informal. There's nothing worse than being over or underdressed, and you know Selwyn—such a stickler for protocol."

"Kendra, you have to help me," Arlisa said, panicky, the tremors of anxiety and frustration etched in her voice. "I need to talk to you. I've been waiting for ages for you to get back."

Kendra quickly scrutinized her sister. She'd never seen Arlisa look so shell-shocked. Her usual glowing, tawny complexion was cane pale with anxiety, and her chiseled, rounded cheekbones were wet with tears that had spilled over from her huge, fawn brown eyes. Kendra wondered what was wrong. Knowing of the colorful lifestyle her sister led, she quickly hazarded a guess. "Don't tell me you're pregnant?"

"No, it's nothing like that," Arlisa cried, slumping her tall, slim body onto Kendra's bed. "You're going to hate me for this," she began miserably, "but I didn't know what else to do."

Something slimy and snake-like seemed to twist through Kendra's innards as she rose out of her chair and joined her sister on the bed. Facing Arlisa, epecting to hear something disturbing, she queried, "What is it?"

"The money." Arlisa chewed at her lower lip. "I took it."

Kendra's eyes widened. "What?"

"I had some debts to pay," Arlisa explained with regret. "The easiest way was to take money from the Black Press Charity Fund."

"Oh, God," Kendra murmured, reminding herself of the terrible confrontation she'd just had with the Brentwoods, and more precisely what she'd accused them of. "But—but I thought you said the BPCF committee had cleared you of embezzlement," she muttered weakly, unsure of whether she could bear to hear the answer.

"They did. I replaced the money with funds I borrowed from the Association of Black Journalists," Arlisa confessed tearfully, the relief of disclosing her secret evident on her face. "As treasurer I have access to both accounts, but if I don't replace that money by Friday, then I'm in deep, deep trouble."

"I don't believe this." Kendra sighed heavily, her voice pathetically weak, her mind wheeling on how her misguided father had used his influence to place Arlisa into such a position of importance. Not only was she taken aback by her sister's deceit, but she was shaken with the awful realization that she owed Shay Brentwood and his father an apology. Slowly removing the towel from her hair in disbelief, she faced her sister, anger beginning to mount in her gut. "Why didn't you tell me this before?"

"I thought I could replace the money," Arlisa stammered, nervously fingering her long mane of braided hair and not daring to look at Kendra. "How was I to know that Joel Brentwood and his wife saw me at the bank and overheard the clerk tell me that I had exhausted the funds?"

"So, Joel Brentwood saw you," Kendra concluded, tightlipped. Mindful of the fact that she might've accused the wrong brother, she consoled herself with the thought that she was still correct in her assumption that a Brentwood was guilty all the same. "And let me guess. It was he who went to the BPCF committee and tipped them off. How clumsy can you get, Arlisa?"

"That's not the worst of it," Arlisa continued, panicked and thoroughly shaken. "His brother, Shay Brentwood, is one of the members of the Association of Black Journalists. Remember? I told you he'd joined? Anyway, Cedric Carter is in hospital mending his broken leg, so Shay Brentwood was asked if he could be responsible for countersigning all checks for withdrawals at the bank. He agreed, and now

he's due to examine and balance the books on Friday."
Arlisa's eyes were stone grey with remorse. "If he ever
finds out that I forged his signature to put a hole in the
Association's account, then—"

"We could be scandalized," Kendra concluded in shock.
"My God, Arlisa. The *Nubian Chronicle* would be linked to
the scandal, on the strength of your being the proprietor's
daughter." Kendra felt mortified, numbed, and terribly
sick. She closed her eyes for a fleeting moment, unable to
digest everything because it seemed so horribly untrue and
unreal. Rubbing her forehead with agitation, she eyed her
sister coldly with a quick solution. "I'll give you the money
to credit the account. How much was it?"

"One hundred and fifty thousand dollars. U.S. dollars."
Kendra rose abruptly from the bed, her eyes bulging
wide, her voice a pale whisper. "What?"

"I know how it looks," Arlisa began shamefully by way
of an answer, "but you see—"

"That's how much you took?" Kendra thundered, her
face murderous like that of a raging bull having just seen
the color red. "This is going to kill Daddy," she breathed,
shaking her head in denial. "Why did you do it? What on
earth were you thinking of? Have you any idea where I've
just been?" She heaved a sickly breath in recollection.
"The Brentwoods were not happy to see me, Sissy, but I
risked going there to protect you. And guess what? I
accused *them* of committing your now obvious indiscre-
tions. Heaven knows what I have just done."

"Kendra, I'm sorry," Arlisa cried with renewed tears,
ejecting a hiccup for good measure in the hope of reducing
her sister's anger. She knew how ruthless Kendra could
be. Many of the *Chronicle*'s executives often had slight panic
attacks as soon as she buzzed them on the intercom, and
after every morning conference journalists left sharing
glances of relief and clutching vital editorial statistics to
their chests as if their lives depended on them. Secretaries

sidled out of Kendra's way when they saw her coming, to avoid confrontation.

If Kendra was anything, she was excellent at solving problems, at getting the task done, however difficult. Arlisa'd seen Kendra in action, witnessed firsthand her sister's demonic working pace, so she naturally felt Kendra would have a solution to their problem. "What are we going to do?"

"We?" Kendra yelled, shaking a stern finger. *"We* are not going to do anything." Adopting a deathly tone, she said, "Whatever it is that *you* have bought that *you* cannot pay for can go right back to the point of purchase first thing tomorrow, if I have to drag you there with it myself."

"It's not a purchase . . ." Arlisa cried, ". . . and please don't shout. Daddy might hear us."

"Right now, I don't care if our father has to hear the sins of his youngest daughter at full volume," Kendra raged in return.

"I paid off a gambling debt," Arlisa screeched.

Kendra's voice instantly dropped two octaves. "What do you mean, a gambling debt?"

"I owed money to the Rolling Dice Casino in Monte Carlo."

"Wait a minute," Kendra said incredulously. "Are you telling me that all those trips to the south of France were to gamble away a hundred fifty thousand dollars?" When Arlisa remained mute, Kendra yelled, "You're mad. That's what you are. Mad. I could ring your bloody . . . ." Kendra took her seat on the bed again and attempted with supreme effort to calm herself.

Rationally, she knew the situation was grave. Memories came flooding back into her mind of a man who'd stood beneath a torrent of lightning, determination to destroy her and her family set in his sparkling, dusky eyes. The thought made Kendra conscious of a sudden tension in her limbs, a feeling of irrational panic threatening to choke her. She had to think. Think fast.

Swallowing hard on the tightness of her throat, she faced Arlisa's tear-washed face, intent on exploring all their options. "Can any of your sugar daddies bail you out?"

"I've split up with Jarvis," Arlisa admitted sheepishly, "and Brad's in the Bahamas shooting a video. His camp just won't put me through."

Kendra's brows furrowed briefly. "What about Todd?'

"Dear Todd." Arlisa bit her lip. "He's still contesting the family will for his inheritance of that Jamaican estate in Montego Bay."

Kendra couldn't resist aiming a jibe. "And to think you dropped Jerome, that fine, rich, upstanding Nigerian barrister, for Todd. One of these days, your past is going to catch up with you."

"I can get him back," Arlisa declared, executing another hiccup.

"You may need to, at that," Kendra added in truth. "He'll probably waive the standard retainer when he represents you in a court of law."

Arlisa winced just as there was a knock at the bedroom door. "Girls, are you in there?" their father beckoned.

"Yes, Daddy. What is it?" Kendra asked, breathing shakily as an involuntary shiver ran through her.

"Selwyn is here for you."

"For me?" Kendra asked, recalling that she and Selwyn were to meet in the lobby at the Grosvenor Hotel on Buckingham Palace Road before taking the short ride to Lord Finsbury's house. "I'll be right down, Daddy."

"Well, no keep him waiting," her father answered. "He's in the den."

"He's here with the police." Arlisa panicked, twisting her hands in anxiety.

"Don't be silly," Kendra whispered, curious as to why Selwyn had come there. "He must have changed our plans for tonight. I haven't time to change into anything. Hand me my bed coat. And for heaven's sake, Sissy, calm down."

Donning the flimsy, pink chiffon garment over her damp

underwear and casting a warning glance at her sister, Kendra re-wrapped her hair with the pink towel and made her way downstairs.

Taking a deep breath on reaching a pair of whitewashed doors which sealed the sun den, she stoically repressed a shiver before making her entrance. Surveying the room and its abundant plant life interior, she couldn't see Selwyn's lithe, tall body anywhere. Feeling confused, she was about to consider whether to call her father when a rush of heat and cold at all the same time traveled quickly along her veins.

Shay Brentwood stood next to the room's wide glass windows, studying her with penetrating intensity as she stood facing him; the glittering sweep of his dusky eyes charted the translucence of her ebony brown limbs beneath the thinness of chiffon lace.

"You!" She swallowed convulsively on a high note.

"You might as least look pleased to see me," Shay returned evenly. "I'm the answer to your prayers."

Chapter Two

'What are you doing here?' Kendra barked, unable to believe that Shay Brentwood, her enemy, stood within the confines of her father's house.

Unnerved, she wondered whether she had imagined the note of satisfaction in his voice, and found herself curious to know whether that same satisfaction was etched across his face. At that moment, she couldn't quite tell.

Shay had taken a step toward her, and in so doing was momentarily lost against the nebulous dim of the houseplants around him. But as his face came into focus, Kendra couldn't prevent her tiny, indrawn breath. She had thought Shay attractive before, but he was devastingly so now, having changed into blue Karl Kani jeans, overshirt, Timberland boots and a Koschino jacket.

Feeling underdressed, she hastily pulled the pink colored ties of her pink bed coat closer together, a movement quickly detected by Shay which instantly brought a grin to her enemy's craggy face. "I think it's time we talked," he told her with a smirk that left Kendra feeling ridiculously uncomfortable.

"How did you get past my father?" she countered crisply. "I can only imagine that you lied and told him you were Selwyn."

"I told your pop I wanted to see you," Shay answered coolly, his heavy feet slowly obliterating the distance between them until his very closeness made Kendra intensely aware of him and the musky tang of his expensive aftershave. "Ain't my business who he thought I was."

Kendra pulled a grimace to disguise the sudden, delicious rush of turbulence she was feeling, and swore an oath that she would, as soon as possible, introduce her father to Selwyn Owens—if only to prevent Shay from ever coming there again. "What do you want?"

Shay allowed his mouth to quirk faintly. "I thought after you came to my house, accusing my family and insulting my father's guests, that I'd come over here to get your personal apology."

"What?"

"And talk about my proposition for the *Nubian Chronicle*," Shay concluded evenly.

Kendra tapped one bare foot profusely. "So you're here to pledge a personal offer for my father's newspaper," she surmised, annoyed. "Your father isn't wasting any time, is he?"

"This is a matter between you and me," Shay told her firmly, slipping out of his Koschino jacket. His gaze lazily traveled the length of her body before making a rapport with her eyes. "And I prefer to concentrate on the matter in hand than . . . let's say . . . more alluring prospects."

Kendra almost stumbled a step backward in surprise when he began to drape his jacket around her shoulders, a motion she instantly blocked by shedding the warmth and comfort of it. "Tell your father we're not interested," she said obstinately. "And since I have a dinner engagement, I'd like you to—"

"Good business practice should permit you to listen to what I have to say," Shay interrupted bluntly. "So before you go for drinks with Mr. M.P., I think you ought to know that I'm also here about your sister.''

Kendra glared at him, profound shock rendering her immobile.

"She's still hiding?" Shay chortled knowingly. "I can't say I blame her. A one hundred and fifty thousand dollar problem is a hard rap to take."

Kendra felt her entire body quiver with an overwhelming adrenaline rush. She hardly knew how to react. The realization swiftly sprang to mind that this man had come there to win his father's war. "What do you really want?" The question was out in a strangled whisper before she could stop herself.

"So you know?" Shay sounded a little puzzled. "The way you were acting, I assumed—"

"I just found out," Kendra admitted forlornly. "I should not have held you responsible, but your brother Joel has a lot to answer for."

"What does *he* have to do with your sister's problem?" Shay's brows rose with annoyance.

"He didn't have to report her to the BPCF committee," Kendra snapped. "Arlisa did replace the money."

"It's not my brother's fault that your sister is unfit for treasurer status," Shay answered in return. "She could have financially crippled the BPCF, and was stupid enough to risk the solvency of the BJA to try to rectify one set of depleted funds. And forging my signature, not to mention that of Mrs. Adina, the company secretary, is a criminal offense."

Kendra's body quaked. Her stomach tightened with nervous tension, even panic, as she was mindful of the fact that she had no choice but to listen to what Shay Brentwood had to say. It made her tremble. His family wanted the *Nubian Chronicle,* and her sister's indiscretion was just what the Brentwoods needed to get the paper back.

Memories suddenly wheeled through her head of how hard her father had worked to build the foundation of such a great newspaper. She remembered him sweating over the books on bright, summer weekends, rearranging the house furniture to hide the threadbare carpet. And when she had first started officially working for the paper at twenty-two, after graduating in journalism six years before, her father was still getting slammed door rejections following weeks of preparation to bring in huge budget advertising, the source of income for any newspaper.

It was all for a dream; not only of wealth and leisure, not even of security, but something to acquire and bequeath to his family, to his race. That was all her father ever wanted. And he'd achieved it, too, through sacrifice, dedication, and the will to survive. He'd also done it without Benjamin Brentwood.

She'd heard the puzzling story. Benjamin Brentwood and her father were once partners. The *Nubian Chronicle* was founded in Jamaica by the two, but Benjamin moved to New York and got married, leaving her father with a bank loan tied to the newspaper. Her father was forced to pay off the loan, and then he emigrated to London, where he and her mother were married before he revamped the paper into what was now Europe's leading and most influential Afro-Caribbean broadsheet.

Then Benjamin Brentwood, like a seafaring buccaneer, decided he wanted his share of the *Chronicle* back. Tirelessly he reminded her father, through a barrage of lawyers, that he had never legally signed over his rights. The shock at receiving stipulations in legal typeface had simply added to her father's grief, coming days after her mother's death. Kendra saw Benjamin Brentwood as a person only inter-ested in extending his power to gratify an insatiable ego. He had already built an African-American cable empire in New York. He had only one objective—to be the biggest. To be the best.

She'd never talked to her father about him, but the family rumors were enough to put her on guard. That night Benjamin Brentwood had made it clear to her that he wanted the *Chronicle* back. She couldn't understand why he had waited so long to launch his bid for it, but knew she'd inadvertently given him the privilege of telling her personally. And now one of his sons was right there in her very home, purporting to know of her sister's grave shortcomings.

Passing her tongue over her dry lips, she blinked hard, trying to force her whirling mind into focus. "Let's get this over with," she said harshly. "Exactly why are you here?"

"I thought I'd come over and offer my help."

Kendra's eyes narrowed suspiciously. "In return for what?"

"Well, that's up to you." Shay's voice deepened as his eyes roamed across Kendra's thinly concealed body. She was not to know that her damp underwear had caused her pink bed coat to cling seductively to her trembling limbs, allowing her feminine curves to magnify her womanhood. Nor would Kendra have cared. For at that precise moment, her mind had settled on something far beyond how she was dressed, or the desirous emotions Shay Brentwood was already evoking in her. She knew exactly why he had come there, and she also knew that she had to keep a level head if her father were to retain ownership of his newspaper.

"What did you have in mind?" she queried, undaunted yet nervous at the very prospect of their ensuing conversation.

One of Shay's heavy eyebrows shot up. "I thought something that would appeal to your sense of fair play," he answered easily.

Kendra tipped her chin in silent rebellion, disguising her internal instability with a glacial smile. "I need a drink," she said.

"Then I'll join you," Shay responded.

She marched on her bare feet toward a split-level archway which led directly into a pastel coordinated lounge where a large, blazing, open fire welcomed them into the room's warm interior. Heading straight for the wine cabinet, her mind filled with unpalatable thoughts of how she could protect her father's newspaper even as her ferocious enemy followed in hot pursuit, she asked, "What would you like?"

"Actually, nothing for me. I'm driving," Shay answered. "But you go right ahead."

Kendra fabricated a smile and turned to find her fingers trembling as she clasped a bottle of liquor. She willed herself to suppress the motion long enough to pour a small measure into a glass, but as she brought the glass to her lips she was suddenly struck by a spastic shaking and the glass jittered against her teeth as she emptied it.

Placing it back on the cabinet, she braced her hands against its wooden frame to steady her nerves, then returned her gaze to Shay, who had seated himself in one of the soft, floral chairs by the fire. "This is a nice room," he said with a warmth underlying his tone which Kendra hadn't detected before. It didn't make her feel any better, only more suspicious.

"Let's get to the point," she jabbed.

"Is your temper always so combustible?" Shay inquired in a relaxed voice.

"Only when there's an adversary within the confines of my sanctum sanctorum intent on blowing smoke in my direction," Kendra chimed rudely.

Shay chuckled. It was a warm, soft chuckle, almost tranquil, and for a fleeting moment Kendra was reminded that his startling, dusky brown eyes reflected a sweet gaze of genuine warmth she so seldom saw in the countenance of a man. Only fate could play such a cruel hand by allowing that same devastatingly handsome man to be a foe at her heel.

"You can relax," Shay declared openly. "This morning, I replaced the money your sister took out of the BJA account. She can now avoid the stain of another investigation."

Kendra's eyebrows rose in disbelief. She swallowed hard on the tightness of her throat, the superficial fear vanishing, only to be replaced by a far more tangible awareness of the man sitting opposite her, whose motive she had yet to hear. "Why?" she asked finally, anxiousness causing her to lean against the cabinet for blessed support.

Her skin felt almost ice cold, even though the room was warm. She was not unnaturally cold because she had on little clothing, but because the *Nubian Chronicle* was most definitely at stake. Her fears were confirmed. "I thought I'd take your pop's newspaper as payback," came Shay's crude reply. "I think he'll hear it better coming from you."

"No!" Kendra screamed, then placed her hand against her mouth. Lowering her voice, she pleaded, "Please don't." Panicked, she walked over to him and stared into those same dusky brown eyes she'd found so attractive. "You can't do this to my father, not so soon after what—" Tears sprang to her eyes as she heaved an unsteady breath. "I know you must've heard about my mother—you seem to know everything else. She died last year. Everyone knows how withdrawn my father became afterward. That's why I was forced to take over the newspaper. I now suspect that Arlisa's gambling is just part of the instability she's suffering."

"Yeah, your sister is sure mxing with some . . . interesting people." Shay nodded. "Sista sure knows how to party."

"She's just a little outgoing," Kendra derided sternly.

"Especially with the opposite sex?" Shay chuckled derisively.

"You're not paying any attention to what I'm saying, are you?" Kendra bristled coldly. "You've come here like a burglar in the night to steal something that isn't even yours."

"Steal!" Shay exclaimed, his eyes suddenly losing their familiar warmth. "My father worked his tail off for that paper. All hell would've frozen over before he sold out his rights. Your father—"

"My father was left with the debt that your father ran away from," Kendra screamed. "What is Benjamin Brentwood, anyway? A man or a mouse?"

"Are you insulting my father?" Shay stormed, raising himself out of his seat to his full six-foot-three inches. "He believed in what he was doing."

"Really?" Kendra goaded. "He's waited all this time for an opportunity to roll all over my father and you're here, right now, waiting to run home to Daddy to tell him how my sister's stupidity has given you the key to the *Chronicle*'s lock. Well, not while I'm still in the house. You're sadly mistaken if you think some big time media deal is going down here. So if this is your idea of appealing to my sense of fair play, then there's the door. Put yourself on the other side of it."

Shay frowned as he glared at Kendra, some sixth sense alerting him to how deeply wounded she was. His mind was stamped with the impression of intense feminine sexuality, a powerhouse of a woman who was larger than life, voluptuously curved and all female, yet, highly accomplished with polished acumen and a mind as sharp as a saboteur's knife. She didn't seem the sort who would miss a trick, but he could challenge her. He'd heard that she thrived on risks, not unlike Arlisa.

"You know," he began, unsure as to why he wanted to win this woman's trust, "when I was a kid and I saw something I wanted, I always doubled my efforts to get it. But I never cheated, and I never played dirty. So I'm going to give you seven days to raise the money."

"What?" Kendra whispered, almost unable to believe her ears.

"On one condition."

"What's that?" She panicked.

"You kiss me."

Kendra laughed. "I've met enough frogs in my time," she bit through clenched teeth, "but never one so bloated with self-importance, and particularly one who is attempting to humiliate me." She paused long enough to analyze her antagonism, for Kendra knew she was jolted by the sheer magnetism Shay's words projected. It had almost seemed that the earth had shaken under her feet to think that she could so easily seize the opportunity and kiss him. The thought of what it would be like had certainly crossed her mind. On leaving his mansion, all she had recalled was a mouth that flagrantly invited ravishment and sensual indulgence, a vision she had stoically repressed out of a sense of loyalty to Selwyn.

Fueled with that same faithful indignation, she chimed, "As Arlisa is the one who owes you the money, I suggest you take your proposition to her."

"I don't want Arlisa." Shay's voice was husky and deep. "I want you."

An involuntary tremor passed through Kendra as he stared down at her. To her surprise, she felt her heart give an erratic thud as his eyes held hers and deepened with an intensity that held her captive. She wanted to shake him for his arrogance and for the financial hold he had over her, but as his warm breath fanned against her cheek she was only conscious of a new kind of awareness which caused the discordant thudding of her pulse. "You can't have me," she said, determined. "And I'm not going to give you any leeway to humiliate me. I'll find a way to pay you back your money, with interest."

"Until then," Shay said, his voice deep, velvety, and unmistakably American. "I'll take my first installment now." Before Kendra could even begin to comprehend his meaning, Shay reached out and jerked her into his arms, his lips capturing hers within seconds of locating them. Kendra instantly tried to push him away, but her body felt weak, as though it had become possessed by some great sensual influence.

The sensation was exquisite. The kiss was deeply persuasive, making Kendra's head swim with the realization that it would take no effort at all to become a serious collaborator to this man's proposition. He was terribly good at what he was doing; his lips pulsing tantalizing little caresses over the tissues of her mouth in slow, coaxing, tempting motions. In the turmoil of her mind, she sensed that Shay was fully aware of her, for his hands had begun to mold themselves around her waist, slowly familiarizing their way across her back as though they would at any moment delve beyond the thin, pink fabric of her bed coat.

She felt the warmth of his body reach out to her like an invisible bond, its hold so frighteningly intense that she felt almost powerless to break free. To her chagrin, her own response was as needful as his possessive invasion. Any space between them was crushed out of existence as their bodies instinctively made their own exploratory discoveries, making small shifts and adjustments to push their addictive revelation further.

And it wasn't just one kiss, although where one ended and the other began was not easy to define. Rather, it was one long, sweet, raw, lazy, insatiable manifestation, generating heady nuances of sensation which began to intensify the moment Kendra felt the soft, testing tip of Shay's tongue delve briefly against her parted lips. It was a sobering shock to feel such a fiery emotion so quickly, and in her desperation she pulled her mouth away, reminding herself sternly how dangerous it would be to try to reciprocate any of this man's feelings.

"Don't get stuck on the idea that I'm some wide-eyed young bait," she gasped, her limbs still quaking with emotion from what they'd just shared, her mind acutely guilty and embarrassed by the experience. "Your money will be back to you within seven days,"

Shay's voice was rough-edged as he reached to the chair where he'd been seated for his jacket. "I hope I don't have to count on that," he answered raggedly, his hand brushing against her shoulder. Brief as it was, the contact was sufficient to trigger a whole wealth of signals Kendra was working desperately hard to suppress.

When Shay left, she went over to the wine cabinet and poured herself an extra large liquer, applying that to her eager lips with the same motion she had earlier. Her anxiety had returned, and she was suddenly struck with the depressing thought of having to find a hundred fifty thousand dollars.

She paced the floor, taking the bottle with her only to place it on the coffee table in her progress. She was afraid to sit down, afraid that if she relaxed too quickly she would scream. But, as the alcohol began its sedating effect she realized that what she was suffering from wasn't so much the pressure of keeping hold of her father's newspaper, but the fact that she wanted to experience again the way Shay Brentwood had kissed her.

ABOUT THE AUTHOR

Crystal Wilson Harris is an Assistant Professor of Developmental English at Sinclair Community College in her hometown of Dayton, Ohio. She holds a bachelor's degree from Howard University in Washington, D.C., and a master's degree from the University of Dayton.

When not writing or teaching, Crystal enjoys spending time with her family and serving her community through her church and her sorority, Alpha Kappa Alpha Sorority, Inc. Her other interests include jazz and cyberspace, and she has a closet affinity for all things Star Trek® (Next Generation, of course).

Crystal has been writing romance novels for several years, and reading them for even longer. Crystal loves to hear from other romance novel fans. Write to her at P.O. Box 17544, Dayton, Ohio 45417-0544.

BOOK YOUR PLACE ON OUR WEBSITE AND MAKE THE ARABESQUE ROMANCE CONNECTION!

We've created a customized website just for our very special Arabesque readers, where you can get the inside scoop on everything that's going on with Arabesque romance novels.

When you come online, you'll have the exciting opportunity to:

- View covers of upcoming books
- Read sample chapters
- Learn about our future publishing schedule (listed by publication month *and author*)
- Find out when your favorite authors will be visiting a city near you
- Search for and order backlist books from our online catalog
- Check out author bios and background information
- Send e-mail to your favorite authors
- Meet the Kensington staff online
- Join us in weekly chats with authors, readers and other guests
- Get writing guidelines
- AND MUCH MORE!

**Visit our website at
http://www.arabesquebooks.com**

ROMANCES ABOUT AFRICAN-AMERICANS!
YOU'LL FALL IN LOVE
WITH ARABESQUE BOOKS FROM PINNACLE

SERENADE   (0024, $4.99)
by Sandra Kitt

Alexandra Morrow was too young and naive when she first fell
in love with musician, Parker Harrison—and vowed never to be
so vulnerable again. Now Parker is back and although she tries
to resist him, he strolls back into her life as smoothly as the jazz
rhapsodies for which he is known. Though not the dreamy innocent she was before, Alexndra finds her defenses quickly crum-
bling and her mind, body and soul slowly opening up to her one
and only love, who shows her that dreams do come true.

FOREVER YOURS   (0025, $4.50)
by Francis Ray

Victoria Chandler must find a husband quickly or her grandparents will call in the loans that support her chain of lingerie bou-
tiques. She arranges a mock marriage to tall, dark and handsome
ranch owner Kane Taggart. The marriage will only last one year,
and her business will be secure, and Kane will be able to walk
away with no strings attached. The only problem is that Kane
has other plans for Victoria. He'll cast a spell that will make her
his forever after.

A SWEET REFRAIN   (0041, $4.99)
by Margie Walker

Fifteen years before, jazz musician Nathaniel Padell walked out
on Jenine to seek fame and fortune in New York City. But now
the handsome widower is back with a baby girl in tow. Jenine is
still irresistibly attracted to Nat and enchanted by his daughter.
Yet even as love is rekindled, an unexpected danger threatens
Nat's child. Now, Jenine must fight for Nat before someone stops
the music forever!

*Available wherever paperbacks are sold, or order direct from the
Publisher. Send cover price plus 50¢ per copy for mailing and
handling to Kensington Publishing Corp., Consumer Orders,
or call (toll free) 888-345-BOOK, to place your order using
Mastercard or Visa. Residents of New York and Tennessee
must include sales tax. DO NOT SEND CASH.*